Queen Mecca

NYC Mecca Series Book 4

By: Leia Stone and Jaymin Eve

To the Kings and Queens who rule our hearts.

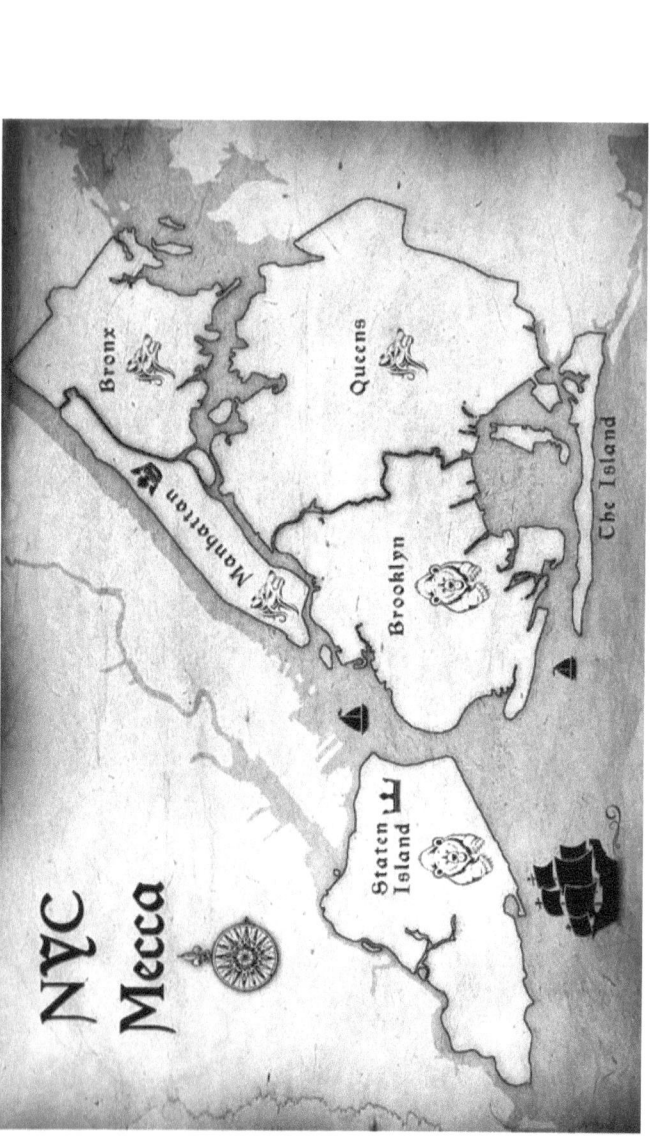

Chapter One

*Mirror, mirror on the wall. Who is the fae-est of
them all?*

A PAIR OF startling turquoise eyes stared back at
me, eyes that should have been familiar
considering I had been seeing them in my
reflection for twenty years. Except they weren't.
They had changed.

I had changed.

"You look even more beautiful, Ari. Don't let
this throw you." Violet sat cross-legged on my
right, Blaine on my left, the three of our knees
touching, just like when we were kids, as we all
stared into the huge and ornate mirror hanging
in the foyer of Kade's mansion.

The fae side of me unlocked when I was in the Otherworld. I had known that I was affected by this — senses much sharper, powers increased — but I hadn't really had the time to focus on the physical change, to truly see myself as I was now.

"I just ... I don't look like me," I finally murmured, leaning forward, observing the way my eyes were now shot through with gilded sparks. Around my iris was a thin circle of gold, and the green almost looked shimmery, if that was possible. The shape was also a little different, larger and more catlike.

On top of the altered eyes, there were my new fae ears, slightly pointed at the tip — not as much as a full highborn fae, but enough that if you were looking closely you would notice. My hair was still white-blond and long, waves giving it a slightly unruly look when it was let loose, but just like my eyes, it seemed more shimmery now. Same with my skin — still a golden color, but that gold was brighter. Shiny.

I'd thought my darker coloring, including eyebrows and lashes, was courtesy of my Polynesian father's ancestry. But that father was completely made up, a lie. My true biological father was the evil fae prince of the Winter Court, a man whom had unfortunately passed on quite a few physical traits. And hopefully, no psychological ones.

had been a huge sense of urgency. Bear and wolf shifters from all around the East Coast had converged on the five boroughs, no one allowed to leave until the threat came to pass, or we were all safe. The weaker members, children, pregnant shifters, and elderly were being hidden away in the human world, in California, far from the mecca and boroughs. It had been a very hard decision for us to make, but we knew the fae wanted our mecca, so we hoped they would focus their attack on the boroughs and leave the outer world alone. Kade and I were staking a lot of lives on that, so I was praying we were right. The second wave of people, the young queen heirs, nonessential staff, and not-combat-ready shifters, were leaving for California tomorrow.

Speaking of children. "Excuse me, Your Highness..." The soft voice interrupted my heavy thoughts, and I turned to find Jane, one of the bear shifters who helped keep an eye on Winnie. I gave her a smile. Jane ran a nervous hand through her long strands of honey-brown hair. No matter how much time she spent in my presence, she remained nervous. But I liked her, for the soft way she spoke to the children, the caring little hugs she gave them when they were hurt. She was one of my sister's favorite companions. Winnie seemed to love bears much

Blaine stood, reached down and pulled me up and away from the mirror. Blaine and Violet had remained behind with me on Staten Island, on queen protection duty. Not that I really needed them anymore. I was powerful now. Extremely powerful. But it was a relief to have my two childhood best friends with me today. They had been with me through most of my big changes in life. So this felt right.

"Getting closer to the mirror won't change your new look, Princess," Blaine said.

I had to swallow hard as I tilted my head back to see his face. His eyes were generally a light green, darkening when he was angry. Thankfully, they were their normal calm color, which actually helped me push down some of my panic. "And Violet is right, you're even more beautiful. Plus, as a double bonus, you now have the sort of power the rest of us could only dream of. You're going to be the one to bring us together. To save us from the dark fae."

No pressure there. The tightness in my chest increased to the point I could barely breathe, but a few calming meditative thoughts and I managed to relax myself again.

It had been two weeks since Dalia fell through the portal on the Island and died in my arms. Two weeks since she had declared that the Winter Court was coming for us all. At first, there more than wolves; she had really found her place here in Kade's home.

Violet and Blaine moved on either side of me as the three of us stepped forward. The young bear shifter continued in a rush: "Your cub is demanding to speak with you. She's refusing to leave."

Winnie, my baby sister, or truthfully more like my daughter, was supposed to be leaving now in the last of the first wave, heading to stay in the home of a Californian alpha wolf that I trusted.

"Thank you, I'll go find her now," I said, striding past Jane and toward the back door of Kade's house. Even though I was queen again, the ceremony having taken place last week, I had refused to return permanently to live in the Manhattan royal estate. Too many bad memories there. Too much history. I remained with Kade, my bonded mate, on Staten Island. Once this war was over, we would figure out a compromise with ruling together.

Stepping through the back door, I crossed the porch and went down the stairs. My sister would be in the garden. She basically lived out there. A love of nature was something she shared with Kade. I had spent many hours in the last two weeks watching those two play, and garden, and bond. It was pretty much the most perfect thing I had ever seen, and I would not let the Tuatha take it away from me. Now that I had a taste, I was hooked.

"How many shifters did you send to protect the children?" Blaine asked me as we started to cross through Kade's stunning landscaped yard. "Are you sure they will be safe?"

We were all extra-protective of Winnie — all the children really. It was so hard letting them go, not being there in person to ensure they were safe.

"I sent a dozen of my best fighters. Kade also sent a dozen of his. On top of that, there are a few hundred elders and pregnant women. I'm also sending Seamus and Jesabele, since we have Nikoli and Violet. The children will be well cared for, but nothing is definite."

It was a hard decision to send away two of our magic born. There weren't many in the pack, and I would no doubt need all the firepower I could get. But if we perished in this war, I needed to know someone with magic remained behind to protect the rest of our people. I would not let shifters fall to extinction.

"I wish there was another option, but there are no neutral or safe places for them here. The winter fae will come to the mecca, we know that. They will try and destroy us all."

Not to mention they would no doubt try to use the children to take me down, like the winter queen had in the Otherworld.

Violet's voice was hard: "Why do you think they haven't attacked yet? I mean, it's been almost two weeks. What the hell is that Winter bitch up to?"

She had been tortured and almost killed in the Otherworld, and it had changed her. Unlike my changes, hers were all internal. She was harder now, more ruthless. And with a bloodthirsty need to cut the fae down. She wanted the Winter Court annihilated and Queen Isalinda's head on a stick. Considering I was part winter fae, I didn't know how I felt about that, but I did know that I would not hesitate to stop any and all fae who tried to attack my people. The winter queen's head on a stick ... completely acceptable ... but the people ... I would not take out an entire court just because they were ruled by evil.

"I have no idea, but whatever it is, I'm sure it's not good," I replied.

"Maybe it's the timing," Blaine interrupted. "We know time moves different between Earth and the Otherworld. So possibly, they are still on their way, it's just going to take longer for them to send the army across."

This was all true, but something in my gut told me there was more to it. I was worried. "I wish there was a way to speak with Prince Caspien. Violet, are you still working with the flowers?" I asked, veering off the garden path to follow a child's shriek. Winnie was in the "pirate's grove." I should have known.

Violet nodded. "Yes, but I'm not receiving a reply. I've started working on that water spell. I think I've nearly got it perfected."

I nodded, pushing my impatience down. After Dalia fell through the portal, I had tried to contact the fae, to no avail. I wanted to offer my condolences for the loss of Dalia, and also get specifics on this war. We had to assume they were either busy fighting themselves or had lost the flower we'd given them so long ago. Violet thought she could make some type of water two-way mirror, but it was a complicated spell, so I was trying not to push her.

"Have you had any more trouble with the council?" Violet asked, changing the subject, her voice flat. She had hated the wolf council as much as I did. I don't think any of us were sad to see them go.

"Nope, they have all up and disappeared." I had no time to bother with tracking them down. Nor did I want to. Traitors had better stay away unless they wanted to lose their lives. "At least it looks like they didn't get back to the royal estate before fleeing. All of the spell books and Red

Queen's possessions are intact and well guarded."

I would have to search through the Red Queen's things again when I got a chance. For more clues. "I'm heading over there this afternoon," Violet added, doing that thing where she seemed to read my thoughts. "You should join me."

"Sounds like a plan."

Our conversation came to a halt when a tiny firecracker of a shifter burst out of bushes to my left, ambushing us, holding a long, thick piece of wood in her hands.

"Stop or ye shall walk the plank," she growled, letting the wolf spirit inside of her free. "This be my treasure trove!"

The three of us immediately surrendered, arms up in the air, faces screwed up in exaggerated fear. Winnie's red fox familiar, Rhett, was circling us slowly, trying to keep his bushy tail from wagging.

"You wanted to see me, Pirate Winnie?" I said, trying not to grin.

She growled again. "That be Captain Pirate Winnie to you barnacles."

I couldn't stop the smile then, or the laughter that burst out of me. "I think you've been spending too much time with Chase, Captain Pirate Winnie."

Kade thought of Chase like a nephew, he was the son of his cousin and he'd known him since birth. Chase was a little older than Winnie, and very smart. He was teaching my sister a world of new words.

She dropped her weapon then, her tiny face crumbling. "I miss Chase," she wailed. "Why did he have to go?"

I took two steps to her side, dropping to my knees and wrapping my arms tightly around her. "Winnie, sweetheart … I know a lot of stuff is happening that you don't understand. And I'm sorry that everything is a mess again. We're being attacked by some very bad people, so the children have to go away. To be safe. If you miss Chase so much, how come you don't want to go be with him?"

She burrowed closer to me, tucking her little head into my neck as Rhett lay his face on her lap. "I would miss you more, so I had to make a hard decision."

My heart hurt then, like someone had just wrapped their hand around it and squeezed tightly.

"I don't want you to go either," I murmured close to her, a few tears trailing down my cheeks. Queens weren't supposed to cry, to show weakness, but I had decided to do things differently in my reign. I would not hide my emotions, I would not keep myself from my people. The rules were changing, and I was glad. "But I also can't stand the thought of you being hurt. I need to know you're safe, because if anything happened to you, Win. If you got hurt..." My voice broke. "I can't let anything happen to you."

I pulled back to see her face, and so she could see mine. "Do you understand? I don't want you to go. I would do anything to make sure we never have to be apart again, but these bad people ... they hurt kids. They would hurt you. So will you please reconsider staying with Chase, just for a few weeks?"

I was trying to make it seem like a question, but I would force her if I had to. I was praying it would all be over within the month, but without knowing the time of the fae attack, I was just guessing. She was quiet, staring at me, watery eyes locked on my face. Finally, she leaned forward and kissed my cheek. "I trust you to keep me safe. I will do as you ask and go to California."

The tears in her eyes spilled over, which prompted fresh rivulets to track down my own cheeks. I wanted to sob, but I knew that would upset her more, so I just hugged her as tightly as I could.

I felt his presence moments before strong arms wrapped around both Winnie and I. Kade's warmth encased us. He pressed a kiss to the top of my head, and I felt him do the same to Winnie.

"It will be okay." His low growly voice was the most comforting thing in the world to me now. "The fae picked the wrong packs to mess with. We'll take them down and then all go on a vacation."

His declaration had Winnie's little head poking up. She struggled back from our hug to see the bear king better. "Hawaii?" she practically shrieked, her tears drying up.

Kade laughed, the rich sound echoing across the garden. Ever since Winnie saw a brochure for Hawaii with pineapples, hula dancing, and the whole relaxed beachy vibe, she'd been begging to go. As he pulled back and I could see clearer, I noticed that Violet and Blaine were no longer close by. They had moved about fifty yards away and were talking to Gerald and Bianca, the Boston alpha. All four of them were part of the new combined bear-wolf council.

"Hawaii is a definite." Kade brought my attention back to him and Winnie. "Wherever my girls want to go, then we will go."

His girls. Two very simple words, but they meant so much. Not just to me, but Winnie also. Neither of us had parents anymore, all we had were each other. We were a family now. A true family like so many others I used to watch with envy.

"Yay! You're the best, K. I love you," Winnie was still shrieking as she turned to me. "I'm ready to go now."

The heavy pressure in my chest increased then, and I found myself locking eyes with Kade.

I don't want her to go, I sobbed through our bond, keeping the grief internal. *What if we never see her again?*

Her safety has to come first, Ari. I don't want to send her away either. I want our family together in the same den. But until we deal with the fae...

He was right. We both knew it. But that didn't make the decision any easier. It didn't help the ache in my heart, which seemed to be increasing dramatically.

All I knew was that the fae had messed with our lives for too long. I was done. If they didn't come to Earth soon, I was going to take my army to the Otherworld and take them out first.

That was a promise.

I stood and wiped my eyes, giving Winnie one last hug before she ran off to play pirates. "Can you watch her for me for a minute?" I asked Kade. "I'll be right back."

He brushed a hand across my cheek, before pressing his lips to my forehead. I closed my eyes briefly at the pure perfection of him, opening them again as he pulled back.

"We'll be right here waiting for you," he said, and he took off after a screaming Winnie.

Traipsing through the backyard to the mansion, I stepped inside to find my soon-to-be mother-in-law Annette in the living room, sitting in a chair at the window, holding her tea and looking out into the garden at Kade and Winnie.

She turned to me. "Hello, daughter." She'd already accepted me as family and it was one more thing to bring tears to my eyes.

"I need a favor," I told her. I knew she was more than capable of staying behind and fighting this war with us, but I had heaviness in my heart for the future of my kind and she could ease my burden if she agreed.

"Anything," she replied, straightening and setting her tea down.

I smiled weakly. She was too good to me. What did I do to deserve such love?

"I'm sending the queen heirs off to California to remain safe and continue their studies. I know we haven't decided how the future monarchs will be chosen..."

There was a world of possibilities now. Would it still be a male bear who accepted the crown from Kade, and a female wolf heir who fought

her way through the Summit? Or maybe a vote from the people?

"And I know we have decades to decide, but I want to protect the heirs and teach them the ways of the bear so that in the future it will always be us working together."

I finished my speech in a ramble and Annette nodded. "You want me to go with them to California and teach your heirs how we do things? To protect them and help in the event that..." She left it open but we both knew what words would come next.

I nodded. "Yes, in the event I die, I want the next queen heir to be a friend of the bears." I knew it was impossible to not fall in love with Annette, and that my fellow heirs would respect and bond with her, allowing for any future ruler to be as closely aligned with my way of ruling as possible. "Will you?"

She grinned. "Of course. I'd be honored."

She stood and wrapped me up in one of her trademark bear hugs. As we embraced, a huge weight lifted off my shoulders. If this war came to pass — and I suspected there was no way now to avoid it — and I didn't make it out, then Winnie would be okay, my people would be okay, and the new wolf leader would have a soft spot in her heart for the bears.

That afternoon, after Winnie and Annette were safely on their way to California, Violet found me in the kitchen of our Staten Island home. I was just about to leave to take a vortex to Manhattan.

"I did it!" she shrieked, coming in from the garden.

"Did what?" I asked as Violet tugged at my arm, dragging me out to the back yard before I could say anything more.

I saw Blaine and Monica standing at the water's edge. They were on guard duty today while Kade and Victor were preparing our land in Upstate New York for the final run with all the shifters today. I wanted one last run as a wolf with my people before I had to fight like hell to keep our home safe.

Jen had gone to transport Winnie, making sure she made it safely, and then would return to me. That left my inner circle of dominants — that was once six — down to two. At least for today.

I was truly mystified as to what Violet was talking about until we got closer to the water's edge. Then it dawned on me why they would all be crowding around here.

"The summer fae?" I asked her, peeking over into the water, and sure enough, in the reflection I saw a wooden grove and those bright bursts of flowers that were distinctly Summer Court. It was as if she had opened a mini portal to the Otherworld.

"I've connected with one of the water fountains in the summer castle's courtyard," Violet told me. "It took a while to get anyone's attention, but finally a guard came over. He's run to get the prince."

I sat up straighter and smoothed my hair. I'd been waiting for this moment since Dalia fell into my lap two weeks ago. Movement in the back of the fountain caught my eye, and I recognized the stunning fae jogging toward us.

Violet leaned into me. "I'm not sure how long the magic will last, and you might have to scream to be heard over the bubbling water fountain on their side."

I nodded as Prince Caspien stepped fully into view. He was breathing faster than normal but hardly winded. "Queen Arianna, I've been meaning to make contact but we've had our hands full and there was no chance for me to leave our lands. I'm so glad Violet found a way."

I nodded. "We don't have much time, but I wanted to offer my deepest condolences for the loss of Dalia. She was a treasure, and I will never forget her help in getting Violet back."

The prince bowed his head solemnly. "Thank you. We have had no time to grieve, but she was an honored warrior and will be deeply missed."

He shook off his sadness and then got to business. "The winter fae attacked us in the night, sent assassins to try to take out our highest commanders. We killed all but one. That one we questioned thoroughly. He admitted under magical duress that the Winter Court wants to eliminate the Summer Court completely from this land, and they also want to commandeer the Earth-side mecca." His eloquent manner of speaking was a little more rushed than usual.

My gut churned with anxiety. "We've had nothing happen here for weeks. What's the wait? When should we expect this attack?" The image wavered then, almost disappearing, but Violet thrust her hands forward and it held.

The prince's drawn features came into clear focus again. "We're holding them at the edge of the winter woods, but if they really wanted to, they could overthrow us. We think they're waiting as a part of their strategy. Aligning wi—" The image flickered again, before blanking out. This time Violet couldn't hold it.

My eyes bugged out, mouth open. "Violet!"

She looked pained, throwing spells and powders at the image as the water swirled in a funnel. Finally, she sat back. "It's gone."

"Can you make another one?" I urged. I needed to know what he was going to say.

Aligning with whom? Fall Court? Or something more sinister. The Dark Fae Lord?

Violet stared at the water, resigned. "Ari, that was fae magic. It took me weeks to teach myself and I had to try to match up time, which is different in our two worlds." I knew she was internally punishing herself. She wasn't used to failing at magic.

I sighed and straightened. "It's okay." I patted her shoulder, careful to touch only the cloth and not her skin. "I got enough. We have time before they attack. Now let's get to Manhattan and learn everything we can about the fae." Those recently unsealed fae books were waiting for us, information that had been hidden away by the former council. There had to be something within those pages which could help us.

Blaine and Monica fell into step with me; they would be on guard duty for the rest of the day. There was a convoy of SUVs at my disposal here, just as there had been in Manhattan. A bear drove us to the Staten Island vortex disc and waited for us to enter past the guards in that secure building.

As I had the last few times, I waited for some sign of the Red Queen — her voice in the mecca energy, a vision of her, anything to let me know she was still there, still trapped in the swirling purple world. Since I had learned she was my birth mother, I found myself thinking of her more often.

So far there had been nothing.

And even though she had not been much of a mother … who was I kidding? She had been no mother at all, but she had protected me against the Winter Court. Against my father. It was worth something.

"Your Majesty…"

The mecca guards dropped to their knees as I appeared on the disc in Manhattan. There were three wolves and three bears. We were forcing all of them to work together. It was the only way to push aside previous prejudices and accept the new alliance. In truth, it had gone much smoother than I ever would have expected. It seemed the shifters had wanted change long before I was crowned. It's just that no one had listened. It certainly helped that Kade and I were bonded mates and engaged. I was now queen of the bears as well as the wolves.

There were still a few resisters, which was to be expected. But they were slowly getting weeded out — many leaving on their own. The greatest resistance had been from some of my oldest wolves. And honoring my promise to be a fair and just queen, I allowed them to live in segregation in the Bronx borough. They still recognized me as their ruler and would

ultimately follow my command, but had asked to not be forced to mingle in their daily lives with the bears.

I could respect their choice and so I granted it. Bronx was the only borough without much of a bear presence, so it was the logical choice. As long as they did as I asked, I would not fault them for being resistant to change. I also expected that eventually they would come around. They just needed some time.

Kade's people seemed much more open; only a few had fled from our rule. There had even been a dozen or so bear-wolf bonded pairings to emerge after we started to mingle the two worlds together. Shifters could no longer deny the proof that bear and wolf belonged together.

Violet, Blaine, and Monica followed me out of the vortex building and onto the sidewalk.

"I'll meet you all at the mansion," Violet said. "I want to get a head start."

I just nodded, and she popped out of existence, her favorite way to travel. I enjoyed the short walk to the royal estate, having missed my borough. It did feel like home being here, but also like things had changed. I wasn't really sure where I fit anymore.

Guards bowed as I walked into the royal grounds; doors were held open for me, shifters lowering themselves as I passed. I hadn't ever really enjoyed the subservient nature our rulers demanded from their people, but I could only try to change one thing at a time.

Monica and Blaine stayed right behind me, one of either side, and I saw the way their keen eyes took in the room. It gave me comfort to have them at my side.

The moment I stepped into the room filled with magic books, Violet jumped on me. "I think I found something."

I chuckled. "Well, that was fast. You've only been here for like ten minutes."

She didn't smile or join me in laughter, she just gave me that serious look she wore most of the time now. Those hard eyes. "I had an idea of where to start looking, and luckily it provided some important information."

Crossing the room, I peered over Violet's shoulder, looking down at the book she held.

"You can read this now, right?" she asked.

I nodded, leaning even closer. "Yep, this is the language of my people. Apparently."

Blaine gave a snort from behind us. Yeah, it was another one of my changes — I could now read the fae language.

Scanning the page, my stomach dropped. I read aloud: "Forged in revenge, of evil and bone, the Dark Fae Lord rose to be one of the first fae demons." *Great.* As if I didn't have enough to worry about with the winter queen, aka evil-grandmother, who was hell-bent on ruling the Earth-side mecca, now I had to worry about an honest-to-God demon. The summer king had mentioned him of course, but information was limited.

"Okay..." I started pacing. "I want to know everything about this fae demon. Where does he live? What does he eat? How the hell do I kill him?"

Kade was going to flip when he heard about this.

"That's not all," Violet piped in. "I did a little scrying spell to see if this Dark Fae Lord was even alive."

I swung around to face her, my eyes wide as I opened and closed my mouth. Finally I said, "Can you *please* try and be a little less reckless? I need you alive and safe after the Otherworld experience. At least let me know when you're playing with magic and demons." I'd known for years that Violet was probably going to be the death of me one day. There was no other person I worried about as much as her. Even more so now, after she'd been taken.

"So what did you see?" I didn't really want to know. No way was it good.

Her lips creased into a tight line. "I saw a dark shrouded figure, which I assume was the Dark

Fae Lord. It was impossible to make out any defining features, but he was speaking with someone who was very clear. And familiar."

My stomach dropped. "The winter queen."

Violet nodded.

"Shit!" I bit out, frustration in my voice.

Blaine and Monica, who were taking point on either side of the main door, keeping guard, both spun around, weapons in their hands. Yeah, I might have overreacted a little, but the last thing I needed to hear was that Samson, the summer king, was right, and those two psycho evil fae had teamed up.

"Could that be the delay?" Blaine said, dropping his sword back into its sheath. "She's cementing this alliance with the demons, and then both of their armies will come at us full force."

I'd had that thought already, and it looked like we had to accept that inevitability. No one spoke; there really wasn't anything that could be said. In that moment, we were all caught in a tangled web of fear.

Finn's energy entered the room a moment before he did. I reached along the bond I had with my familiar, allowing his vast strength to brush against me. Finn and Nix had been out patrolling Central Park and the waterways, as the pair did every day.

Finn stepped to my side and brushed his soft white fur against my leg. *Demons or not, we can win this. We just need more knowledge.*

I nodded, letting my body relax. Finn was right. Knowledge was power, and I intended to find out all that I could about this Dark Fae Lord.

"Violet, Blaine, Monica, Finn," I called out, "we're having a sleepover. We're not leaving this room until I have identified and read every book that pertains to the demon fae." I paused. "Well, except for the run we have tomorrow morning. But other than that, we are on study duty. You're going to cram like you've never crammed before."

Blaine's random crooked grin washed away some of my stress. It reminded me of when he was a little boy, always up to some mischief.

"What are you smiling about?" I fake huffed, acting affronted. Truthfully, it brought me true joy to see him looking like his old self. Things had been strained between us since Kade — since Blaine told me he'd expected that one day we would be together romantically. I never wanted to lose him, I needed him in my life, but Kade was like part of my soul. A part I could not and would not live without.

I thanked the gods that Blaine and I had found a way to be just friends again. Even better, it was finally starting to feel like he had accepted that there would be nothing romantic between us.

His grin turned into a full smile. "Remember when we all had a sleepover for Monica's thirteenth birthday?"

Now it was Monica's turn to bust up laughing, but I didn't find it so funny. I remembered that sleepover very clearly.

"Yes, Blaine, I definitely remember. You fell asleep with your stupid mouth open and your gum got in my hair. I looked like a jacked-up Barbie doll for months after we cut it out."

I'd had heir duties and photos that month too. Suffice to say, the Red Queen had had more than a few nasty comments to make about my new hairstyle.

It *was* pretty funny looking back though.

Blaine and Monica were shaking with barely contained laughter, until finally the sides of my mouth quirked.

"I nearly killed you," I told him.

He nodded. "That you did, Princess. And I gave up chewing gum on that day."

I chuckled. "Well, for old time's sake, one final sleepover?"

Violet nodded; she had even been smiling, which I loved to see. "It's a deal. I'll invite Nikoli. He can help with the magical end of things." I wondered if she knew how her voice softened —

her face too — when she spoke about the bear magic born.

"Really, tell me more about Nikoli?" Blaine teased. Clearly he had picked up on it too.

Violet gave a devilish grin. "Well, he's a pretty good kisser."

Whoa! Kisses ... she wouldn't, right? I mean, not without telling me — I was her best friend. Blaine seemed shocked too, his eyes widening as he blinked in her direction. Monica leaned in a little closer. She might have been a serious sort of warrior chick, but she loved gossip. Jen and her always had the juiciest information about the other shifters.

Violet gave a shrug. "It just happened. At first I was looking for a distraction, and Nikoli is a very nice distraction. But then it felt like something more. Plus, the guy went all the way across the Otherworld to rescue me. He deserved a little something."

"Do you have problems kissing another magic born?" I asked. "Do your powers collide or something?" I'd always been curious about that.

She'd always said touching me was harder than most people; I had so much mecca in my energy. Even before I became queen it was like that. Probably my undiscovered fae side causing problems. Still, I expected another magic born would be even worse.

She shook her head, arms crossing over her body as the grin disappeared. "Actually, it was perfect. Our energies meshed, which is a rare occurrence between magic born. It was definitely ... unexpected."

My mind was racing. My best friend rarely got into relationships. No one understood what it was like to be a magic born, to not be able to touch without getting overwhelmed. So this was huge. Violet dropping her guard to kiss Nikoli ... triple extra huge.

Blaine leaned in close to her. "Hey, baby, I traveled across the Otherworld to rescue you as well." He puckered his lips.

Violet snorted, some of her old humor returning. "You wish. Besides, you already have a girlfriend." The second the words left her mouth she seemed uncomfortable. "Or ... I mean you will."

Blaine dropped his sleazy act and went very still. "Explain. Now."

Yeah, what did she mean?

Violet chewed at her bottom lip. "It's just one of my future-sight things, that's all. I saw something, but I'm not supposed to tell you about it. It can mess up the timeline — I shouldn't have mentioned it at all."

She spun around and began rifling through a box of books; Blaine was staring wide-eyed at her back. The moment he recovered from her shocking statement, he strode closer.

"You have to tell me who it is." His voice was low, controlled, but I could hear the wolf in there threatening to break free.

Violet looked over her shoulder, giving him an "Oh, do I?" look, before turning back around.

"Violet..." I prodded. I needed to know too, mostly to make sure she was good enough for my best friend.

She turned to face us both. "Look, the future is an ever-changing thing. If I tell Blaine who it is, it might mess up the timeline. Like, what if he goes after her now, before he's meant to, and it doesn't work because of that? Or if I say who it is and he always wonders if his feelings are real, or if I influenced them? It needs to happen naturally in order to last. Just trust me."

I dropped my hand on his forearm, giving it a squeeze. "Sorry, buddy. That actually makes a lot of sense."

Blaine opened his mouth, no doubt to argue the point, so I laughed and pushed him back toward his books. "Let's get to work. It's going to be a long night. I'll have Calista order in pizza."

My advisor and her chosen mate Baladar had been house-sitting the Manhattan royal estate while I was living on Staten Island. I was so grateful to have someone I trusted here.

I always had a lot to be grateful for.

Here's hoping the fae didn't steal it all away before any of us had a chance to truly live our new lives.

Chapter Two

One, two, three, four. Oh look, a hidden door.

THE NEXT FEW hours passed in a blur of books and food. Calista kept us well supplied with sustenance, and Baladar put his wisdom and magical skills to use. He seemed to be able to sense where the most important books were, ones pertinent to the information we needed. He was also really good at translating obscure pieces of information. Some of the language was old and complex, and some of it very riddle-like in its prose — like reading a ton of Shakespeare, but the Tuatha version of the great bard.

So far we had a pile of about twenty books, half a dozen on the Winter Court, two on the Fall Court, and another half dozen pertaining to the Summer Court. Lastly, there were another few that might have a possible mention of the Dark Fae Lord. Everything about him was very obscure: guesswork, myths.

We weren't giving up, though. There had to be something here that would give us an edge against the fae. We just hadn't found it yet.

It was after midnight when I received word that Winnie was safely in California, which knocked relief and sorrow into me at the same time. Finn was close by, curled up at my side, resting his head across my thigh. I absentmindedly patted his fur to calm myself.

"This queen business is not easy." I said, speaking to no one in particular. "Some days I wonder if I'm doing everything wrong. Sending the young away feels like the right decision, but it also doesn't. How can I protect them when they are thousands of miles from me?"

Baladar lifted his head from where it was buried in a pile of aged parchments. "The rarity of a leader who stops to wonder if they are making the right decision ... I'm not sure I ever heard the Red Queen express an iota of doubt. Most leaders believe they are crowned through divine intervention — by genetic right. And therefore they are always correct in their decisions, because what they want is by default always the right decision."

"A true leader should be confident," I interrupted. "We have to make split-second decisions. We cannot waver."

Those wise, kind, and thankfully no longer blind eyes met my own. "There is a difference between confidence and arrogance. Never stop questioning yourself, Arianna. It is the very thing which makes you a worthy queen."

A soft chuckle escaped me, and Finn's tongue emerged as he too looked happier. "Thanks for everything you've done, Baladar."

"It has been an honor, Your Majesty."

My chuckle turned into hard laughter now. "Please, don't start with protocol now. I much prefer that you call me Ari. All of my friends will refer to me by my name now, even if we are out in public."

Protocol could kiss my pampered butt. I was done with the ways of old.

Blaine and Monica just shook their heads at me, before going back to their shelves. *Probably going to take more than a few reminders to break years of training*, Finn reminded me.

I sighed. *Yeah, I know, but I have to start somewhere.*

Speaking of, it was time for me to move to another pile. Jumping to my feet, I was just heading into the far back corner when Violet popped out of nowhere, scaring the crap out of me.

"Stop doing that!" I practically yelled, one hand on my chest, as if I could slow my heart down by holding it.

"Still got it," she trilled, buffing her nails on her chest. "I was just going to tell you that I'm almost finished in that corner."

My eyes trailed across the small space. "So what's left?"

"The Red Queen's chambers are still full," Calista reminded me, crossing the room with a pile of books in her arms. "You've found clues in her things before. Maybe she had some of the more important stuff squirreled away."

I let out a huff, dusting my hands across my pants. "Yep, you're right. It would be much easier if she'd just appear in the vortex or something. Then I could ask her."

I still didn't trust my biological mother; she'd almost always been a shifter out for her own gain. Something I didn't think had changed. But ... I wished she would make contact. It seemed her soul would be trapped in the mecca forever, just as she wanted it, which might be useful if I needed to speak with her again. That is, if I could figure out how to reach her ...

"Maybe you need to touch the mecca stone again?" Blaine said from across the room, mirroring my own thoughts. "Force the connection."

I shook my head, turning to leave the room. "I'll leave that as a last resort. I don't want to make it easy for the fae to cross to Earth by opening a portal straight here. I'm also worried that attracting their attention might speed up their attack, and we need all the time we can get."

Everyone nodded, worry spilling across their faces. I was basically out the door by then, Finn by my side. "See you all soon. I'll just be in the Red Queen's room."

No one followed; Finn and I were pretty lethal on our own, and everyone was busy with their searching. But I knew Monica and Blaine would be along soon. My dominants didn't leave me unprotected for long, not even in my own home. I crossed through halls and up a few flights of stairs, waving to members of my royal household. They hadn't seen much of me since my re-coronation, but everyone knew it was a time of war. They expected the queen to be busy.

Most of the Red Queen's possessions were still in her private wing, I hadn't had time to move all of them, and thankfully neither had Selene. The moment I crossed over the threshold I sensed the Red Queen's energy. It was like everything in here was laced with it — or maybe she was actually here, whatever part of her could be here from her prison in the mecca world. It would be great if her spirit could guide me toward something of interest.

"Ari..." The rumble of my name had me spinning from the open doorway and running straight into Kade's arms. He lifted me with ease; my legs wrapped around him as I pressed myself as close to him as I could get.

"I missed you," he murmured close to my ear, before his lips pressed gently to the sensitive spot high on my neck.

Tilting my head back to give him slightly better access, I said, in a breathy voice, "I missed you too, and it's only been a couple of hours." This bonded mates thing was a serious connection. I was getting better at ignoring the ache his absence caused in my soul, but when we were back together it became so clear how much I'd been struggling without him.

He captured my mouth, a moan slipping out between my lips as he crushed me closer. I lost myself for a minute; everything around me disappeared. *Still here*, Finn said, sounding amused and a little disturbed.

With a chuckle we pulled apart, and I was set gently on my feet. Kade laced his fingers with mine, and we turned back to the open doorway, and beyond it the pile of boxes. "Violet said you were tackling the Red Queen's room. I'm glad I got here before you had to do that alone."

I stilled, tilting my head back to meet his gaze. "You think I'm going to find something bad?"

He shook his head. "Not bad, but maybe ... upsetting. More secrets. She was clearly the queen of those as well as the wolves."

Truth.

Kade gently pulled me in the direction of the queen's private quarters. "Nix spotted a harpy above Brooklyn," he said casually. Far too casually for that sort of information. I froze and jerked him to a stop.

"What?"

With a heavy exhalation, some of his casual ease was replaced with worry. "I'm not all that surprised. It makes sense that they would have some spies. Be preparing for their attack. We need to be extra careful is all. Nix took that particular one down, but instinct tells me there will probably be more over the coming weeks."

My mind was racing. "Do you think the harpy knew about us sending the kids to California?" If there was even the slightest chance Winnie, or any of the little ones, were in danger, I would pull them right back.

Kade shook his head. "I doubt it. Nix has been patrolling the skies for days. She's still out there right now with Jota and Kian. At this stage, that was the only one."

Kade's brother was working with Gerald, both of them leading our armies.

"They'll send something else next time, won't they? Something in the water? Or maybe under the ground? They have so many different beings at their disposal. We're going to have to be extra vigilant." I tried to keep my voice calm, but it was a near impossible task.

We were sitting ducks, waiting for the fae to decide when to attack. It didn't feel right to me. Just waiting.

Kade's warrior bear face was in place, his voice a low growl. "Kian is taking care of it. We both spoke to the patrols and royal guards. They're aware of these spies, and that an attack could come from any angle."

A shiver caressed my body, forcing me closer to the heat of my mate. "And with that happy reminder of our impending war, let's see if we can find something to tip the scales in our direction."

As we crossed the sitting room and reached the door to the queen's private bedroom, a heavy tension settled in my neck, which I tried to loosen by tipping my head to either side. A harpy ... here in New York City. Not only was that scary, it was also bold and careless. These winter fae

cared nothing about humans learning of our world, or the chaos it would cause if our secrets were revealed.

My hand stilled over the ornate golden knob, which I was just turning to open the door to the next room. "Kade, you don't think they would ... hurt the humans as a way to get to us?"

Usually humans were off limits; we did not involve them in supernatural affairs. But the Tuatha played by their own rules.

A low thrum of energy caressed my skin, lifting the fine hairs on my arms. Kade's power was whipping around as a dark energy descended across him. "If the winter queen exposed our kind to the humans, it would change everything. We would be hunted by the humans as well, and the humans would be caught up in a battle they had no chance of winning. We cannot let that happen."

Our bond meant he could read my panicked thoughts, but before I could freak out too much, Finn nudged my leg. He had grown tired of waiting for us. *Worry not on what has yet to pass. Humans are not on the faes' radar at this time. They will focus on the threat of the shifters first.*

Kade and I both heard him; I was starting to get very good at separating and mingling their presences in my mind. My familiar's wise words didn't completely put me at ease, but they definitely helped bring my focus back to the task at hand.

I nodded once, decisively. "Yes, we won't worry about that today. Let's get this search done."

I opened the door, letting it swing silently inwards. As everything came into sight, an unexpected wave of grief washed over me. The queen's bed was neatly made, covers tucked tight under the mattress. Her favorite pen and writing pad were sprawled carelessly on the nightstand. There weren't many other personal effects in here, no photos or keepsakes that screamed sentimental.

Who was this woman? Here in her private room, when she didn't have to be the cold Red Queen ... who was she really? The only thing I truly knew about her was that she was my mother. My blood. My throat tightened as a whirlwind of emotions slammed into me. Would my life have been different if she hadn't smuggled me away, if she hadn't kept our relationship secret? Would my father have killed her and me all those years ago, changing the course of history forever?

Kade and Finn waited patiently as I processed it all. My life had been a lie. My mother, the one I believed I shared with Winnie, had been a lie. But at least I had some answers now — I understood

better why she had been so ... distant with me —
extra hard on me. I loved her, but some part of
me, deep down, knew she had never acted like
my real mother.

"You okay?" Kade's voice was low, husky. He
would be feeling every one of my emotions
through our bond, all the broken pieces inside of
me that I was trying to rearrange into some sort
of a whole. I sensed he was even siphoning some
of the pain away, taking some of the burden.

I nodded and stepped farther into the room. I
was okay. I had to be. There was no other choice.
"Let's start with the bedside tables."

Kade gave me a look but didn't say any more.
He knew I would talk about it when I was ready.
For now, I needed to stay busy. Finn brushed
against me in his comforting way, then the three
of us got to work.

I took the bedside to the left, Kade walked to
the right, and Finn shuffled under the large,
heavy-dark-timber, antique, four-post frame of
her bed. Sitting on the edge of the bed, I opened
the drawer. My first surprise inside was the
novel sitting atop a white blanket. It wasn't the
fact that there was a book in there — the Red
Queen loved to read — but the bare-chested,
muscled man on the front suggested this was a
straight-up romance novel, which I did *not* think
would be to the former leader's taste. Just

another one of her little secrets. Thankfully, this one was more amusing than anything else.

I flipped through it to make sure nothing fell out, before setting it aside. Then I gently lifted out the small blanket and my heart pinched. It was a baby blanket. Crocheted white with a yellow trim. Since I was her only child, that meant ... this was mine. She had kept it?

Something deep inside of me fissured; an ache settled in close to my chest as I clutched the dusty piece of cloth. Squeezing my eyes closed as tightly as I could, I forced myself to set it aside, knowing that all of my regrets were for nothing. The past could not be changed. I had to let my pain go or it could consume me. Underneath the blanket was a card. It looked like a hand-painted watercolor, on thick, expensive cardboard, an array of flowers on the front. I flipped it open to find a perfect cursive script inside.

Queen Rosalina,

The nights are long and cold without you. Never have I felt such unbridled love and adoration for any woman as I do for you. Your power and beauty are unmatched and I long to spend the rest of my life with you. I wish in another world, in another time, that we could openly be together. Until then, our love will have to remain my most treasured secret.

All my heart,

Prince Luca.

Anger coursed through me as I chucked the letter back in the drawer. The winter prince had played the Red Queen like a fiddle. He never cared for her, or maybe he did once, but it was not enough. He killed her. That bastard had to die.

"Ari, sweetheart, you need to come over here and see this." Kade's voice brought me out of my rage, and I looked up to see him standing in front of a large painting of a lake. The piece was clearly ancient; the thick, gilded frame was starting to peel and darken in places.

"What is it?" I stood and crossed to him. Finn was close behind, having finished his inspection under the bed.

Just as I reached Kade's side, a heavy energy settled over me, pressing down into my center. I swallowed hard, fighting the urge to rub my hands up and down my bare arms. It felt ... evil and ugly, crawling like electricity across my skin.

"What is that?" I asked.

Kade's brows were furrowed. "I don't know, but it feels dark. Very dark."

I reached out to touch the painting and his hand caught mine mid-air. "No. Let's get Violet and Nikoli first."

Reluctantly I withdrew my hand. He was right, the darkness here was not of any normal magic variety. It would be foolish to take the risk.

Somehow I'd just have to find my patience. Wherever it was buried.

Twenty minutes later, Violet and Nikoli stood at our sides. My best friend was rubbing her temples as she stared up at the painting.

"You okay, Vi?" I reached out to gently touch her arm, but stopped myself when I realized what I was doing.

She nodded, giving me a wan smile. "It's making me nauseous is all."

Nikoli took her hand, gently linking their fingers together. Apparently she had no problem with him touching her, because she didn't pull away.

Kade's magic born stepped back a few feet, pulling Violet with him. "I have an idea," he said to her. "We should invoke the power of three."

Violet looked much better now that she was away from the energy, and at his suggestion an almost full grin lifted her cheeks. The pair stared at each other for a few extra-long seconds, until finally Kade asked, with some humor in his tone, "What's the power of three?"

With some effort, Nikoli finally pulled his eyes from my friend and turned to his king. "It's a

spell which requires three magic born. A triangle of power, focused on a single point. Together we should have enough energy to pierce through the darkness, and hopefully learn what is being hidden there. Either the painting is a powerful dark artifact, or it is hiding a powerful dark artifact. Either way, with this level of dark power, I would not want any of us to touch it until we learn a little more about what we're dealing with."

Violet grinned. "We need Baladar. The power of three is any three magic born combining their energy, which considering our limited numbers, is actually harder to achieve than one would think."

"You rang?" Baladar popped his head into the room.

I jumped, cursing. Freaking magic born.

Violet looked more animated than I had seen her in a long time. "We need to do a power of three spell."

Baladar's face lit up too. Apparently this spell was a big deal. "Oh, fun. I haven't done one of those in ages."

As he stepped closer to us, his attention was drawn to the painting, and I saw what looked like a dark shadow flicker in his gaze. The lightning color which broke up his icy blue eyes shimmered, reacting to the energy. "I see."

He examined the piece for a long time, stepping closer and closer until he was only about a foot away. He ran his hand a few inches off the painting. Eventually, he turned and returned to where we were all waiting.

"I'm glad you called me before tackling this. The painting is not emitting the darkness, it comes from an object hidden behind it. It's beyond my knowledge of the dark arts, and trust me, I have a lot of information squirreled away about that branch of magic." He looked more than a little perturbed by this.

Shaking that off, Baladar rolled up his sleeves and started barking orders. "Violet, fetch some twenty-four karat gold powder. Nikoli, get the salt."

They both nodded and did their freaky magic born thing, disappearing in an instant. Baladar knelt before Finn, who was at my side. "Sweet Finn, might I trouble you for a few drops of your majestic blood?"

My eyes widened, but Finn just calmly tipped his head to show his assent.

Are you sure? I asked my other half.

He needs it, was Finn's reply.

Baladar produced a small dagger from within his cloak. Finn extended his right paw and Baladar whispered a few words before cleanly slicing a small incision and taking only a few drops of my familiar's blood, catching it in a tube. Finn didn't even flinch, which was no surprise to me. He was one of the toughest beings I had ever met.

"Boo!" Violet yelled just over my right shoulder, and I jumped, clutching my chest.

With a laugh and a wink, she stepped past me.

"You need therapy," I told her.

Violet nodded. "I absolutely do."

Nikoli popped in then and suddenly the laughter dried up. Baladar was all business as he instructed Kade, Finn, and me to move back and sit on the bed, away from their immediate spell area. Kade wrapped an arm around my shoulders, and the three of us perched on the edge of the bed. It felt weird; this was where the Red Queen slept, and although her body was gone, her spirit wasn't. She'd hate us even being in her private quarters. On her bed would be even worse.

I focused then as the spell began. "Violet, present your offering," Baladar instructed.

Violet nodded, placing a small jar of powered gold on the floor in front of the painting. It had no lid and was only half full. Next, Nikoli spread his salt in a circle around the three of them and then placed the remainder inside Violet's jar of powdered gold. Then Baladar sprinkled Finn's blood around the circle of salt, letting the last drops land on the salt and gold inside of the jar. A sudden and strong energy came over the room, which had my pulse racing erratically as the mecca inside of me started to thrash about.

The three of them quickly held hands, forming a triangle as they began to chant. "The power of three, the power of three, the power of three. Do not harm thee. Do not hide from me. The power of three, the power of three, the power of three. Reveal to me! Reveal thyself to thee!" At the last they shouted in unison, and with a pop the painting flew off the wall and crashed to the floor in front of the circle they had created.

Nikoli, Baladar, and Violet still held hands, but they were now all looking at the small safe that had been hidden in the wall. When the painting had flown off, the safe door had also popped open. *Holy mother.*

I was up and walking towards it before I even realized what I was doing.

"Arianna!" Kade growled, at the same time Baladar said, "It's okay to approach it now."

Of course Kade didn't take his word for it. He was also up off the bed, stepping in front of me before I could reach the safe.

"I'll look inside first." His tone was hard. He was not taking no for an answer.

That was my overprotective bear. Always putting himself before me.

I stayed right behind him as he side-stepped the magic born and their circle, closing in on the safe. "The dark securities are mostly dispelled," Baladar reassured us. "But whatever is inside that safe is also dark, so proceed with caution." Not the best reassurances, but we'd take it. We didn't have much choice.

I peered around Kade to see that the hole was small. Not much could fit inside. "What can you see?" I murmured, feeling for some reason like I needed to whisper.

He didn't answer immediately, leaning closer. "It's ... a book."

A book? I wasn't sure exactly what I had been expecting, something a little crazy maybe, like some sort of crystal, a severed finger from a fae. Basically anything, which would explain the crazy darkness that felt like it was still lingering about.

But a book...

"Don't underestimate books," Kade said, tuning into my thoughts. "Words are more powerful than almost anything else in the worlds. We have no idea what sort of information this book could contain."

Violet hovered at my right shoulder. "It could be a special spell book. Maybe it is one of those lost from the original witches. Or the fae. One which deals in magic long forgotten."

That piqued my interest. "Maybe it's magic that can take down the Winter Court?" I breathed my hope out loud. "We need to open it."

Chapter Three

Yin and Yang. Dark and light.

BEFORE KADE COULD stop me, I dipped under his arm, popped up in front of him, and snatched the small book up. The sound of him cursing was lost as energy slammed into me and my knees buckled. I dropped down, my eyes locked on the black tome clutched between my hands.

"Ari!" Kade and Violet both yelled my name.

With a lot of effort, I lifted my head and said, "I'm okay, it just took me by surprise." Large hands fitted under my arms and lifted me back to my semi-steady feet. "This energy is weird," I said breathlessly. "Like familiar ... but also like nothing I've ever felt before."

I noticed Baladar had remained in his spot across the room, his expression creased in concerned lines. He was peering at the book, but didn't seem to want to get closer.

"Do you know something about this?" I asked, narrowing my eyes on him.

He sighed. "Tell me about the symbol on the front cover."

I wasn't even surprised that he knew there was a symbol on the cover, despite the fact he had not stepped foot near me or the book. I let my eyes run across it, but didn't move my hands to trace it as I would normally. This was mostly because my hands were molded around the sides of the book, seemingly held there by my fae and mecca energy — which was smashing inside of me like crazy.

The symbol was etched into the cover, which was not made of any material I had ever seen before. It was thick and smooth, like leather, but with a consistency that felt hard like a metal. It was definitely organic ... an animal skin maybe. It actually kind of reminded me of the ercho that tried to kill me in Central Park.

Baladar let out an impatient sound, so I quickly focused on the symbol. "It's carved into the cover, and it looks like an inverted tree, gnarled and dead, roots sticking up from the top, and the branches burrowing into the ground. There is a stone in the center, the heart of the tree."

The ancient magic born staggered forward. His face was frozen, mouth open, eyes wide. I found myself mimicking his panicked pose, part of me wanting to thrust the book away, but still being unable to remove my hands.

He spoke, barely above a whisper: "Is the stone black?"

I nodded, and in a flash he surged forward, his body shrinking into a half-crouched position. He began chanting and waving his arms wildly in the air. I looked to Violet, who was watching him with a look that was part shock and part intrigue. I knew, though, that just like me, she had no idea what he was doing.

As I turned back to Baladar, he thrust his hands at me and Kade, and suddenly a gale force wind slammed into us, knocking us both back into the wall, and in that moment the darkness that had been leaking from the book was gone.

As I straightened myself off the wall, low growls were rocking my chest. My wolf didn't like being thrown around like that. And judging by Kade's scowl, he wasn't much happier about it. Baladar spoke quickly, throwing in a bow for extra measure. "Forgive me, Your Highnesses, I had to act quickly."

Ignoring the magic born for a moment, Kade turned to me. His face was still etched with dark lines of anger, but this faded slightly as his thumb traced across my cheek. "Are you okay?"

"I'm fine," I said. Which was mostly the truth. The right side of Kade's body had slammed into mine; my shoulder and elbow were aching, but that would heal soon enough.

Kade draped an arm around me, his fingers softly stroking my shoulder. He could feel my pain and he wasn't happy about it. Together we faced Baladar.

"What did you do to the book? How dangerous is it?" I asked, knowing he would have only acted that way if we were dealing with something serious.

The book felt lighter in my hands now, as if Baladar had chased away the darkness completely.

He stepped closer now and peered down, shaking his head. "What you hold in your hand is the origin of dark magic ... the birth of evil ... the opposite of all that is good in this world. If the mecca is Yin, then this is the Yang. The great balance requires both dark and light. Welcome to the dark."

I opened my fingers and let the book crash to the floor.

Kade growled lightly, his arm tightening for a brief squeeze, before he started rubbing my arm again. "You said it was okay to approach."

Baladar bent and picked the book up, careful not to touch the crystal. "I never expected this could be inside the wall. How the Red Queen got her hands on something like this is far beyond me. But it's harmless now, as long as nothing reawakens it."

A wave of tingles worked down my spine, goosebumps crossing my skin. "Reawakens it? It's alive?" No wonder the material felt like skin of some kind. Violet had better run me one of those salt good-juju baths later, because I was feeling energetically icky.

Baladar didn't answer me. I was pretty sure he wasn't even listening to me. His eyes were locked on the book, and no doubt the wheels were turning in his head. That incredible intelligent brain would be running through all of the possibilities.

"This explains a lot about the changes in the Red Queen," he blurted, as though he couldn't keep the thoughts contained any longer. "She would have had no idea what this was. Nor Sabina or the council. No one is old enough. But she would have felt its power. That's why she stupidly kept it close. It must have infected her ... sleeping so close to the darkness, night after night."

My breathing slowed. I had heard rumors that the Red Queen hadn't always been so ... cold. She had always been strong and merciless in war, but there apparently was a time in the beginning of her reign when she was kinder ... more genial. Calista and I discussed it a few times, both of us blaming her multiple miscarriages and wars for her hard, cold exterior — the burden of being queen had hardened her. But maybe it was this.

Kade let me go, stepping closer to the book. "What's inside?"

Baladar shook his head. "No one left alive has that knowledge, but history tells us that this book should *never* be opened. The information inside would turn the purest of magic borns into the devil himself. Besides, it's not what's on the inside that matters, it's what's on the outside."

Violet stepped forward. "The crystal," she whispered, hovering her hand over it. Nikoli was watching silently from afar. His eyes were not on the book though, but on Violet.

Baladar nodded. "There is one story, told only by word of mouth, that has been passed down to me from my ancestors. To be quite honest, I didn't completely believe it. As a young magic born I thought it was more metaphorical, and as an adult I never saw any evidence to prove it, but ... not now. This confirms it."

Violet, who had her eyes still locked on the dark stone, lifted her head to Baladar. I didn't like the spark of excitement I could see in her

light eyes. She was intrigued. Which wasn't a problem in itself, but darkness was not something she needed to be close to again.

Baladar set the book down on the edge of the bed and motioned for us to join him in the living room of the queen's quarters. It was like he didn't want to tell the story in front of the book. We all followed him out, taking seats on the sofas. Finn curled up at my feet.

Baladar was the only one standing. "In the beginning of time, the four great gods created the Earth. They argued over which races they should create, who should have what powers, and what would govern them all. In the end, they created the humans, witches, and fae. After this, they each took a piece of their soul and infused it into the Earth as a power source for their creations. This became the mecca."

Kade said what we all were thinking: "This is not the story we are told of creation."

Baladar gave him a sad smile. "Creation stories get changed as the next generation sees fit. Everyone wants to put their spin on it. This is one which was lost over time, and it was one I have never believed." When no one said any more, he added, "Shall I continue?"

Kade nodded, and through our bond I could sense that like me, he wasn't shocked by this revelation. We had been lied to about wolves and bears being bonded mates and meant to rule together, so it wasn't a crazy jump to expect we'd been lied to about other things as well. Still ... the mecca was a piece of the gods' souls ... that terrified and excited me. No wonder the power felt limitless.

I leaned forward as he started speaking again, not wanting to miss one word.

"One of the gods was obsessed with fairness. He argued that there must always be balance in this newly-created world ... that nothing should be too good or too evil. In the end, the gods agreed and the mecca crystals were fashioned. They would give extra powers to the rulers so that justice could be served when needed." Baladar put up a finger. "Then the God who was a little obsessed with fairness decided that the mecca crystals weren't neutral in power. He argued that they felt a little too light in energy, which meant there would be an imbalance. The other gods disagreed with him, and as an act of control, or revenge, the God of fairness decided to create a dark mecca crystal. He split it in two, wrote an accompanying book, and hid each crystal book pair in each world, believing it would balance out the purple stones."

I shuddered again. I had almost touched that black crystal on the book. What would have happened if Baladar didn't neutralize it?

Violet stood and crossed her arms. "That's not balance. That's manipulative and psychotic." I was glad to see some of her desire for darkness waning from her face. She now looked queasy.

Baladar shrugged. "Hence why I always thought it was more metaphorical. 'Keep the balance.' But gods aren't known for being rational. They do as they see fit and they move on."

"So that thing on top of the book is the dark crystal created by that god?" I wanted to confirm that this was the only one we needed to worry about.

Kade stood. "Let's destroy it."

Baladar stepped forward, both hands held in front of him. "That is not the crystal. It is a tiny sliver of it. The original piece was broken in two, and they are out in the world, no doubt making someone very, very powerful and evil."

I sucked in my breath. "The Dark Fae Lord."

Baladar nodded. "It is rumored he has one piece and that the Earth-side one is missing."

Violet growled. "How big are these pieces?"

Baladar lowered his arms, hands clenched tightly at his side. I'd never seen the powerful magic born so out of sorts. "I've told you all I know. The God of fairness left the dark crystals, and the accompanying books, and then disappeared."

"I still think we should destroy the book." Kade's hand was on the hilt of the sword he always carried.

Violet put her hands out. "Easy there. If we can connect with the small shard on the book, we might be able to do a spell and find the stone."

Nikoli nodded, finally jumping into the conversation. "It would take a few days but it could be done."

Baladar watched the two young magic born, his posture and drawn features screaming out his weariness. "To do that, you would have to reawaken the book and the darkness inside."

I shared my thoughts: "Assuming the Dark Fae Lord has one of these dark mecca stones, and we use this book to find the other one, is there something we can do with it? Can we interrupt the power the stone is feeding him? Disable his armies?"

I locked eyes with Baladar, struggling to read his expression. "I don't know," he finally said. "Let's see if we can even activate a spell to trace the stone. Then we can work out how to neutralize them."

We sat there as a group, letting his words weigh into our minds. It was a risk, but it could turn this war in our favor. If we could dismantle the Fae Lord and his power, we had a chance.

Ultimately, the decision rested with Kade and me. We were the rulers. The thoughts of erchos, harpies, and other unthinkable creatures flooding into Manhattan had my decision made. Through our bond, my mate's thoughts were tumultuous, torn about what to do. But he seemed happy to go along with whatever I decided.

"Do the spell. Find the stone," I said with force.

Baladar nodded. "Just be aware that any or all of us could be corrupted by the dark mecca. It's a huge risk."

I already knew that, and I hated that my family was in this position, but...

"What choice do we have?"

Part of me was hoping someone would come up with another option, but no one spoke. It might not be the right decision, but we had to try. Especially, if it would help our people get the upper hand in this impending war.

If only I could just ignore the sinking feeling in my stomach that made me think we might be messing with something that could destroy us all, even more so than the fae.

We spent the rest of the night searching through the queen's stuff, but after the dark mecca crystal discovery, everything else was mundane and boring. The Red Queen apparently had a secret love of romance novels, and crocheting. Which definitely brought a smile to my face. But I would have preferred something more we could use in this fight.

By the time we all called it a night — technically it was early morning — we had gathered quite a bit of new information to study, which at least felt like a step in the right direction.

I watched as Baladar wrapped the dark book in a thick, spelled material he had worked on for most of the night. "I'll keep this book with me," he said. "I've placed securities on it which I have mimicked off the safe. Minus all of the darkness."

"Are you sure you will be okay with it?" I had to ask. The last thing we needed was a crazy, evil, powerful magic born on the loose.

He threw me a withering look. "I'll be fine. My spell will keep it contained for a long time. Plus, even if it did awaken again, it would take years to fully corrupt *me*."

That shouldn't be a problem. I was pretty sure we only had days, or maybe a few weeks, until the fae attacked.

"How long will it take for you guys to set this spell up, to track the dark crystal?" This question I directed to the three-magic born in the room.

Violet and Nikoli exchanged a glance, both turning to Baladar, who let out a bark of

laughter. "This wasn't my idea, young ones." As their faces fell, he let out a deep breath. "But I also won't leave you to try and navigate this dark book alone. I will need a day to cleanse an area, set up special spells of protection, and to let light into my soul. We will all need to do this. Otherwise, the darkness could claim us."

Violet blanched, her already white skin turning an almost sickly gray shade. I hurried to her side, grabbing her as she swayed. "What's wrong?" I gripped her arm tighter, ignoring the swirls of energy zapping us both.

She recovered with a few rapid shakes of her head, her eyes focused on me as she gently pulled her arm free. "Letting light into my soul means I have to face the darkness in there. If I cannot be cleansed of it, I cannot be part of this spell."

She might have pulled herself together, but I could see by the shimmer of emotions on her face that she was terrified.

"I don't think I can face the darkness," she whispered.

Oh, Violet. What happened in the Winter Court? What did you sacrifice so that you could keep my fae essence safe?

From the dreams she'd shared with me, I had a reasonable idea of what she had gone through. I saw some of the marks on her, felt the pain in her soul. But I had no doubt she hid much from me. Which I hated. I'd been waiting for her to come to me, to tell me everything, which would be cleansing for her, but so far she'd remained mute. I didn't want to push her, but something had to change soon. It was slowly killing her.

Before I could think of how to console my best friend, Nikoli was there placing both hands on either side of her face, capturing her full attention. "You can face anything. You are far stronger than even you know. The Tuatha did not break you, Violet, they reformed you into something unbreakable, like steel tempered over fire." His voice lowered, I could barely hear the last few words. "We will do it together."

My friend's entire energy changed then; she relaxed and almost fell into him. The anguish that had been sliding across her body like a second skin was dissipating. She leaned into Nikoli as if he was her only strength. This was much more than a fling. This was serious. I was torn between overwhelming joy for them both and that continued worry that I wasn't doing enough— that this war was distracting me to the point where I neglected the ones I loved. Ultimately, I was trying to save them, but there were smaller battles each was waging, battles I could not be there for.

At least she wasn't alone, she had Nikoli, and she would tell me everything when she was ready.

Kade slipped his hand into mine. "Let's all get some sleep. We can deal with the rest in the morning." His voice was gruff, and at the mere mention of sleep I felt like a hundred-pound weight had settled into my body. We had been weeks, months even, without decent rest. It was catching up to us, but we would soldier on.

"Take whatever guest rooms you like," I told them, assuming no one wanted to travel all the way back to Staten Island tonight.

Nikoli, who was still holding Violet's hand, chuckled. "Never thought I would be sleeping in the Red Queen's house."

Violet just grinned and then walked down the hall, Nikoli following behind her like a lost puppy.

"Don't forget the run in the morning," I called after them. "It's mandatory. Last run, bonding exercise, you know the drill."

I got some waves and mumbled agreements, and then they were gone.

With a yawn, I let out a muffled goodnight to everyone else, stumbling into the hall with Kade. The others branched off to different areas, and I led my mate down the long corridor to my wing of the mansion. As we approached my door, two of my guards stood outside.

"Good evening, Your Majesty. We did a sweep. It's safe."

I raised an eyebrow. "How did you know I was sleeping here tonight?"

"Calista," Michael said. He was a short and stocky shifter with dirty-blond hair. One I didn't know very well, but Blaine had vouched for him.

Blaine and Calista were worth their weight in gold. It might seem like a queen ruled her people alone, especially in the dictatorship style rule of the shifters, but that couldn't be further from the truth. It took a village of people to lead properly.

After entering, Finn curled up on the couch, and we made our way to my room. We both kicked off our shoes and slipped out of our clothes. Kade sat in his boxers on his side of the bed, appearing lost in thought. I knew my bear, he was bothered by that dark stone. By what we had discovered.

I inched along the duvet until I rested close to his back, then I rose up to my knees and dropped my hands onto his shoulders. It took all of my strength as I started working out the kinks; his muscles were hard, the tension he carried making it even more so.

He let out a low groan, tilting his head around to flash a sexy grin at me. My body, despite its exhaustion, perked up at that look on his face.

His face, which was far, far too gorgeous, was distracting. I forgot everything in my head when he looked at me like that.

I paused my massage, leaning in to kiss him gently. He let out a rumble of bear-like annoyance when I pulled back, and I resumed kneading his hard muscles, letting my hands trail around the front of his pecs and along his hard, chiseled abs.

As my hands trailed lower, Kade growled again, and then in a single move that should have been impossible, lifted me up and over his shoulder, dropping me down into his lap. By instinct, I wrapped my legs around him, molding our bodies together as my inner wolf growled with pleasure.

His molten copper eyes raked over my black bra as he said, "How tired are you?"

I grinned. "I'm wide awake actually."

Chapter Four

Spell breaker.

IT FELT LIKE moments after going to sleep I was awoken by a light knocking on my door.

"Go away," I mumbled. I needed ten more hours of sleep and another sexy session with Kade before I was ready to face the mess of a world we had going on.

"Arianna, the Summer Court is here. They're in the dining hall." Calista's stern but hushed statement had both Kade and I bolting upright.

"Be right there!" I leapt out of bed and flew to my closet.

Kade, who was calmer than me, pulled on his clothes from yesterday and went to use my toothbrush. "We need to bring some of your stuff here," I said, following him, one leg in my pants

while I hopped around to get the other in. "Looks like we're going to have to spread our time more evenly between the two royal estates."

Kade finished up at the sink, turning to me, leaning himself back on the marble countertop. Immediately the room felt smaller, and I wanted to drag him back to bed. He just did casual confidence in such a way that it was sexy without trying.

Needing a distraction, I quickly said, "I only spoke to Prince Caspien yesterday. Do you think something has changed in the Otherworld that fast? Is the war finally here?"

Kade ran a hand through his hair, somewhat taming its natural curl. "I hope not, we're not ready."

We weren't. If the fae flooded through a portal today, we would be defeated — I knew that. Especially in light of this recently discovered dark mecca stone situation. We had been unknowingly up against something like that the entire time, and it was kind of scary how easily that could have destroyed us all. Learning the origins of that dark stone meant the Dark Fae Lord was even more powerful than I had previously thought. Possibly undefeatable.

"Well then, hopefully they have good news." I forced a smile, before brushing my teeth, and both of us left the bathroom.

Finn and Nix were waiting for us outside, Kade's familiar perched on the wolf's back. "Jota is still in the sky. They are taking breaks," Kade explained as we hurried toward the dining hall.

Slowing for a second, I turned to the familiars and brushed my hands along one of Nix's massive wings, which she had pressed against her body. "Thank you, we appreciate you working so hard to keep us safe." I added my other hand to Finn. "Both of you." They had been relentless in their patrolling, never faltering on their duties once.

It's nothing, Ari. This is what family does.

Finn's words filled me with warmth.

Thanks for being my family, I told him.

He let out a low howl, nuzzling into me, and I kind of thought Nix looked pleased as well. Hard to tell on her bird face.

I remembered the Summer Court then, and we again hurried toward the dining hall, prepared for anything. As we opened the doors, I was surprised to see not only Prince Caspien, but also Rowan, a Summer Court magic born. They were seated at the table, having tea with Violet and Nikoli. At our arrival, Prince Caspien stood and gave a small bow.

"Greetings, Your Highnesses."

I took a second to look him over closely. The prince was very handsome, one of the most perfect specimens of man I had ever seen, actually. For my personal tastes he was too refined and pretty, but there was no denying his beauty. There was a glow about him that was very enticing, drawing you in to his warmth.

He had changed since the last time I'd seen him in person. I'd noticed it a little in the magic water door yesterday, but today it was very clear. He looked healthier, strong, his skin flush and sparkling with a golden tan that was deep and rich in color. The restoration of mecca had done him well.

"Greetings, Prince Caspien. I'm so sorry for the wait. We had a late night researching." I nodded my head as Kade shook the prince's hand.

Prince Caspien waved a hand toward me. "It's fine. We have not waited long. I have come with a gift from my father, a thank-you for restoring the mecca, and for your continued alliance with our court. I also bring more news of developments in the Winter War, since we were cut off last we spoke."

The Winter War must be what they were calling it. I was excited and nervous about his news — not to mention that we had some of our own developments to share on that front too.

I turned my attention to Rowan, who had also stood. Kade and I both greeted her with a hug. She had saved us in the Otherworld and healed

Violet. For that she had our eternal gratitude and friendship. After our greetings were over, we all sat at the table again, and Prince Caspien waved a hand toward Rowan. She gave him a simple nod back before producing a small jar of purple powder.

"Your gift has two parts," she said, handing me the jar. "Part one is mecca power."

Violet gasped from her place at the table, and when I looked at her, her eyes were locked on the purple powder. Swallowing down the lump in my throat, I reached for the mecca powder with an awed reverence. It was priceless.

The moment it touched my hand I was zapped with energy, which felt akin to the stone we had here. Akin but not the same, a smaller scale, but somehow still as potent. "Thank your father greatly for this," I said, as magic continued dancing along my skin.

Violet had been trying to figure out how they ground up the stone, but so far nothing she'd tried had worked. After seeing this powder in action in the Winter Court, I knew how incredible it was. I was hoping that having some of our own would at least give us a shot against the winter queen.

Prince Caspien looked pleased, his eyes sparkling as he leaned forward. "The second part of our gift is Rowan."

I reeled back, some of my joy fading away. "What?"

Magic born were highly valuable, but they were people and not gifts to be given. The prince seemed to recognize my unease with that wording he used and gave me an understanding smile. "Only for two weeks. She was the one who offered actually. She'd like to train you. She feels it's time you learned to harness your fae magic. Then we may have a shot at beating the winter queen. You're the secret weapon in this fight. You hold magic from the Winter Court and your Red Queen's line, and therefore have a lot of power to wield. A lot of unexplored gifts."

My eyes locked with the fae magic born and understanding flashed between us. I nodded a few times, leaning across the table. "Do you think I can actually learn anything in time? I barely have control over my mecca powers, and I've trained for that my entire life. The fae side is a whole other kettle of power." It was constantly smashing around inside of me like a crazy beast. It didn't scare me anymore, and I had used it in a battle situation, but I still didn't feel in control of it.

"I wouldn't be here if I didn't think I could help you." Rowan's soft voice somehow cut through the room and drew all attention. "I am well trained in our ways. I have studied mecca power and fae magic for many years. And I was once a prisoner of the Winter Court, so I know their ways well. I can help you tap into your powers and hone them as a weapon."

I had not known she had been a prisoner of that court. Although Dalia did say that Rowan knew the ways to sneak in and out ... I'd always wondered how. Now I knew.

Violet spoke up then. "As someone else who was held prisoner there and learned a few things, I would also like to help with the training." She turned toward Rowan. "I know your knowledge would be far beyond anything of mine, but I would like to learn as well as help, if you would accept me."

Rowan smiled warmly. "Of course, Violet. I would be honored."

Prince Caspien smiled. "Well then, it's settled. Now I must share some news and then be on my way. We have a lot going on back home, and as you know, I can't be away from my land too long without it negatively affecting my people."

I nodded. "Of course. I understand."

Caspien looked uncomfortable for a moment. "What I got cut off from telling you yesterday is that we received word that Isalinda has gone deep into the Dark Fae Lord's territory, while her son prepares their army."

My pulse immediately kicked into gear, adrenalin rushing through me. Just the mental image of the queen and the darkness together had me on alert. It was what we had all feared.

It was time to let Prince Caspien know what we knew as well. "Last night we found something, a book the late queen had. After consulting with our oldest magic born, I'm told it's the book of the origin of dark fae magic. It's connected to one of the dark crystals. We assume the Dark Fae Lord has the other one of these dark crystals, and that's where he gets his power. My magic born are looking into how to find the other one, and how to destroy them both."

The prince was very still, listening to my every word with care. After an extended pause, he said, "It's our worst fear. The dark stones are legend in the Otherworld, and my father has believed for a long time that this is where the Fae Lord draws his power. But we never confirmed it."

I swallowed hard, rubbing suddenly clammy hands across my pants. "I'm also afraid of what this means. Even if we find the other dark crystal, it will be almost impossible to wield without one of us falling to the darkness."

What looked like shooting stars sparked across the fae's eyes, and for a moment he looked so otherworldly that I couldn't imagine that we both shared even a shred of the same DNA. When he spoke again, it was weighty, the words drifting out in a melody of sorts.

"Light and dark are just two sides of the same coin. Without one, you could not experience the other. The mecca has these properties. It can be used for good and evil as you have seen, depending on the user. But these dark stones, they are pure evil. That being said, I believe that if you harness the light, you can banish any darkness."

I wasn't sure anyone was breathing as we all hung on his powerful words. I felt the weight of them settle inside of me like a promise — a journey I would go on.

Caspien stood, sweeping his hands out in a broad gesture of thanks. "Thank you for your time today, for sharing this news with me, for allying with us in this war. If you can use Rowan, feel free to include her in anything that has to do with the dark book project."

"Of course. She's welcome in our home, and we will hopefully be able to get word to you if we learn anything new."

He seemed lost in thought for a brief pause, staring off at the painting on the wall. Finally he met my eyes. "I think it would be a good idea — if you could spare some warriors — for our people to train together — in the Summer Court.

My warriors could teach your shifters what to expect from the Winter Court, and how to kill fae. And you could teach us about this city, about the energy of Earth, the humans even."

Kade shifted forward in his seat, long arms extending across the table. I felt his approval through the bond, and sensed the others around the table also approved. It was a good idea. But who would I send? It would have to be someone I trusted, who was a top warrior, who had a lot of knowledge of our world. Blaine ideally would be the best choice; he had been to the Otherworld, he knew what to expect, and he was a top fighter and strategist.

Part of me immediately refused to put my best friend into harm's way like that, but I knew he would not appreciate me holding him back from this. I needed to think on it, discuss it with him. Kade could also send one of his bears so that each side had a representative, and they could bring their knowledge back to train with us here on the Earth side.

Realizing I needed to say something to Caspien, I smiled. "That's a great idea. We will need a day or so to organize our people, but consider it done."

He gave us a small bow. "Send your warriors through when they are ready. Rowan and Violet can create a portal. Also, Rowan has a special mirror. You can watch over our progress through that."

Kade and I both walked with the prince as he left the room. "Tell your father thank you for the gifts."

Caspien nodded. "I will. Good luck." And then he was gone through the double doors, presumably off to the fae lands.

As I turned from the door, I found Rowan and Violet behind me. "I'm so glad you're here," I told the magic born again. "And ... I just wanted to tell you how sorry I am about Dalia. I know you two were friends. Her loss is a great one. The world needs more fae like her."

Rowan's delicate features crumbled for a brief second, before she recovered. "Thank you, I truly miss her. But she went out like a warrior. She will be honored by the gods."

I nodded my agreement.

Clearing my throat, I changed the subject. "We have a run this morning, with all of the wolves and bear shifters. One last run together, so training might have—"

She interrupted me. "I will prepare some training exercises for you. You do what you need, and we can meet when you return."

I gave her one last hug, and then directed one of the guards to show her to her room. She would be in a suite close to mine, one of the more luxurious.

Calista wandered over. She had been in the kitchens no doubt, judging from the slightly pink hue to her cheeks. It was always hot and steamy in there. "Okay, so the buses will be out front in approximately twenty minutes." She swiped across her tablet a few times, checking everything over. "They've already picked up shifters from most of the points, and it looks like almost everyone is coming along for this last shift."

My wolf stirred in my chest. She was a lot quieter since my fae magic had unlocked. It seemed to soothe her in a way the mecca never had, but knowing we were so close to shifting had her shaking that coat off and baring her teeth.

"Let's grab some breakfast first, and then we're good to go," I said. I could see from the grins of the others in the room that my wolf wasn't the only one who was excited.

First run for bears and wolves together. Here was hoping this didn't end in disaster.

There were dozens of buses in a line as we left the city behind. Normally the queen would not ride with the other shifters like this, but Kade and I believed that by mingling with the shifters we would show them the bond between us. They needed to see our mateship.

We were heading to a shifter-owned property in Upstate New York. It was over a hundred acres, which was not a huge distance for us to run, but it would do for today. This was more about letting our beasts out one last time before the buses were cut off, and the second and final wave left for California. It would take about three hours to get there normally, but with a little Violet and Nikoli help, we cut that time in half.

I spent most of the trip dozing against Kade. He had me wrapped up tight in his arms, and even though we didn't talk, it was a very comfortable sort of silence. We were content.

When the buses finally arrived, we all exited. Throngs of shifters had already arrived before us; the buses had been running all morning. The energy was high and with mixed emotions, excitement for the run and trepidation for the oncoming war. I walked over to Kade and his war counselor, Gerald.

"You're asking me to cower!" Gerald was saying.

Kade looked tired. We'd been in this war mode for weeks now, and it was taking its toll. "I'm asking you, my most trusted counsel and friend, to go to California and train Nathanial in the event Kian and I perish. He is the last of our

bloodline and will need wise and strict council if he is to become king."

Kade and I had spoken and agreed that both of us dying in this war was a possibility. We needed to take action to set up for the future of the monarchy.

Gerald gritted his teeth. "I should be on the front lines with you."

Kade placed a hand on Gerald's shoulder. "There is no one else I trust with this task. Kian is stubborn, he strongly believes that during war time, his place is with our people. As long as there is no immediate threat to the children, he's only going to be there long enough to settle his son in. I can't command him to stay. So it has to be you that teaches the young our ways."

Gerald sighed, resigned, and nodded. I then stepped forward, making my presence known.

"Ready for this run?" I asked excitedly. Finn stood a few feet away from me, scanning the crowd of shifters.

Kade looked out into the mix of wolf and bear shifters as well, almost looking emotional. "It's a historic day. Bear and wolf running together."

I slipped my hand in his.

"Hopefully this is the first of many times we do."

And with that, Kade called for everyone to begin their shifting. We all stripped where we were. I might be queen, but nudity was nothing to shifters who so often had to call on their animal. My shift was seamless, my new energy giving me a speed to change I had never had before. And practically no pain.

Finn actually wagged his tail for a second, overcome with excitement.

It's been too long since we ran together, I told my familiar, padding over to his side. I was a lot smaller than him. Usually he was the largest in the pack, but with so many bears around he was average size.

Much too long. I'll bet I'm still faster though. He gave me a wolfish grin and I playfully nipped at his neck.

The sound of cracking bones and tearing flesh filled the clearing, and once bear-Kade was beside me, a hulking mass of brown fur, I tipped my head back and howled. Kade roared next to me, the ground shaking with the vibrations. Howls and roars rang out and I took off running, hoping to secretly catch Finn off guard. No such luck. Finn and Kade were right on my heels, as were the rest of our people.

I had been secretly worried that this experiment would fail, that seeing the huge difference between a bear and a wolf would really scare our people. But if anything, the fact that we ran, hunted, and were free in the same animalistic way only brought us all closer.

That day we ran as one, and it further cemented my hope that one day we could all be living happily ever after.

By the time we arrived back at the mansion, I was more relaxed than I had felt in a long time. Freeing our beasts was something we needed to do pretty regularly. I could go a very long time between shifts, but there was always this tension inside which wouldn't abate until I shifted.

"I'm going to go find Rowan," I said to Kade.

"No need," she trilled, stepping into the front foyer, where I stood with a multitude of other shifters. "I've been waiting for your return. Are you ready to train now?"

I nodded, shaking my arms out. "More than ready. I just need to grab some lunch. Want to meet in the basement? We have mats and everything set up in there."

Rowan shook her head. "No, we can't be indoors for this. Do you have a garden? Somewhere we can see the sky? Somewhere with flowers, and plants, and life? Nature is essential to all fae magic."

I caught Kade's eye, and I knew both of us were thinking the same thing. My mate's family was very connected to the mecca, Kade more so than any before him. This probably meant he was connected more to his fae side, which explained why he loved his gardens so much. I loved them too, especially when I found the time to wander through the flowers, but it wasn't the same for me.

Somehow Rowan read my mind. "You're winter fae. They draw power from nature in different ways. Less blooming gardens — which is a Summer Court thing — and more snowflakes, icy lakes, flurries of wind and ice..."

I nodded a few times. "That actually makes a lot of sense. I love winter. I used to just lie in the snow and let it coat me head to toe. Drove my mother insane." My pretend mother that is. I tilted my head to take in Kade. "You're descended from summer fae, aren't you?"

He wrapped an arm around me, pressing his lips into my temple. He smelled of sunshine and life, of spice and man ... yes, he was definitely summer fae.

He pulled away slightly and said, "I have never felt more at home than when we stepped into the Summer Court lands. I believe I am either summer or spring descended." His voice got very growly as he answered my unspoken fear. "And I believe it matters nothing that you're winter fae. We're bonded mates. The division of their lands is as destructive as the division of our boroughs were."

I breathed deeply, silently thanking the fates for him. "I agree. I would choose no other. I want no other."

Rowan was smiling again. She gestured to Violet, who was hovering close by, and the pair started toward to stairs. "Violet can show me the garden. I'll meet you there."

Violet gave me a wink as she swiveled her head to look back at us. "I'll start spelling the garden so that the humans don't see anything weird."

"Perfect," I called after them both, and they were off like two long lost friends, chatting side by side. It was good to have Rowan here. She might be exactly what Violet needed to accelerate her healing. I was glad she'd come.

Kade's arms fully swept around me then, distracting me. With one arm he lifted me higher so our faces were close together, and then used the other hand to tenderly stroke my cheek. "While you train, I'll work with Baladar and Nikoli on the secret project. We'll call for Violet if we need her."

Right, the dark book. There was so much going on I didn't know what to deal with first. It was nice having a partner to share the responsibilities with.

"Be careful," I felt the need to add. "I'm worried about that book, and the … the possibility that the darkness could consume us."

Here was hoping we were strong enough to withstand it.

"I think the magic born are more susceptible to being drawn under its influence. They were born to wield magic. If I help, I can keep an eye on them. Make sure they're okay," he said seriously.

Kade. Always the protector. Wrapped in his arms, I was trying to decide if it was worth separating myself from him. I mean, how badly did I really need to learn my fae powers? His chuckle startled me, his huge chest rumbling around me.

Then he kissed me, his lips capturing mine. When he kissed me it was never enough, I always wanted more.

"Later," he promised, pulling away.

Nikoli appeared in the doorway then, bagel in hand. Somehow he knew Kade was ready to go now, and with one final wave they disappeared through the double doors, off to wherever Baladar was. The ancient magic born had not accompanied us on the run. He said he preferred to wolf it alone, but in truth, I wasn't even sure he ever shifted anymore. He was powerful enough to contain the wolf.

I entered the dining room, and was pleased to see the normal buffet of food set up. We fed a lot of shifters in the mansion; there was almost always food in here. I quickly piled food on my plate. If I was about to expend a ton of energy, I needed to be fueled up. Almost silent footsteps caught my attention, but I didn't have to turn to know it was Finn.

He settled in at my side, and I fed him bits and pieces of my food. We enjoyed the moment, just the two of us. It was rare that we were alone anymore. And sure enough, more footsteps soon echoed down the corridor, and Calista dropped down in the seat across from me.

"How are you holding up?" she asked, not wasting time on small talk. "Baladar is working on the book, but I'm worried about messing with that dark crystal."

I sighed, dropping my roll. "I'm worried about it too, but I can't see another way. We need to understand the power we're up against. And maybe we need to figure out how to use the darkness to fight back."

"What if it consumes you?"

"I don't know. I'm afraid it could destroy us all, but burying our heads in the sand won't change the truth. And the truth is that the winter queen has allied herself with the Dark Fae Lord. And they have a dark weapon." I hesitated before adding, "I'm not sure I can win this one. I'm not sure I'm strong enough."

I had always been able to tell Calista what was on my mind. She was my sounding board, my voice of reason. I did not have to be a queen, or an heir, or anyone special with her, I could just be myself, show my fears. I had very few people in the world I could do that with. Kade, Violet, Finn, and Calista were pretty much it. Even for Blaine I put on a brave face.

Calista placed her delicate hand on top of mine and she smiled. "I have watched you grow up, Arianna. You were strong and fearless, despite having no real support in your family. I have never seen you fail at something you really set your mind to, and I know you won't fail your people. I have no doubt that you will defeat the winter queen and the Dark Fae Lord, and whoever else tries to harm your people."

Her words were a soothing balm to my bleeding soul, to my stressed brain, but I still didn't think she understood what we were up against. "Cal, you weren't there. You didn't see her magic. And now she probably has a dark crystal at her disposal."

"It doesn't matter. I see you. I see how loyal you are to your people. I saw the mecca test the day you were born. I've never seen the magic react that way. You won't let anyone harm us. I know it."

Finn pressed to my side, agreeing with her through our bond. I sat a little straighter then, despite the weight of my responsibilities trying to crush me. They were definitely right about one thing. I would fight and kill, and take whatever hits I had to in order to keep my people safe. I would not fall. I would not falter. And if I died in this war, I would know I did everything I could for my people. No queen could give more than that, and I had to accept that fact.

Calista reached across the table and grabbed a bagel off my plate, before patting me on the arm. My smile was genuine then; she had lifted my mood enough so I could finally finish my food. We ate in a comfortable silence, and when she left, Finn went with her, back to patrolling.

I left to find Rowan and Violet. It was time to fully embrace all sides of me. I was going to learn to be part fae. May the gods be with me.

Rowan and Violet were on the rooftop garden. It was late afternoon, the sun just starting to lower in the sky. As I emerged from the elevator, my eyes were immediately drawn upwards, to the glint of a very pale purple, the faintly glittering surface of the solid bubble of magic above our heads, no doubt hiding our doings from our New York neighbors.

"I'm ready," I offered, striding forward without hesitation. To be honest, I had no idea what to expect. I was born with the mecca magic pulsing through my veins. As a queen heir it was inherently part of me. It was familiar, and I knew somewhat how to control it. This fae magic was new, unbridled, and at times it scared me. Maybe if it hadn't been stripped from me at birth, hidden away, it would not be that way. It was like I was a baby all over again, trying to learn how to walk. Only this time I didn't have legs, I had weird stilts attached to my legs — foreign objects — and I felt uncoordinated and off-balance.

Rowan approached me, her arms relaxed at her sides. "Okay, so you're born of the Winter Court, which means, as I said before, that your affinity will be in water, ice, wind. But you're also part shifter, and a queen tied to the Earth-side mecca and her people ... so, I'm going to have to do a bit of experimenting."

Great. Experimenting. My favorite thing. Violet's eyes were shining, so were her teeth as she smirked at me. She was no doubt enjoying my unease. I didn't deal particularly well with being bad at things.

Rowan placed her hands out in front of her. "Okay, Violet, shields up."

Violet's smile dropped in an instant and she straightened, putting up a shield to protect herself.

Rowan focused her attention on me then. "Start by letting the magic free inside of you. I can feel that you have it locked down. You need to let it move about … mingle within your center."

I was standing with my feet slightly apart, braced for whatever was about to come for me. I relaxed my stance slightly, needing my muscles to unlock so I could free the magic. Rowan was right about me having most of my energy locked down. There was too much to have it free all the time. I'd probably start randomly zapping people around me.

There was a slight resistance as I loosened the bonds, like part of me was still not comfortable enough with the energy to let it bounce about inside of me, but there was only one way to get more comfortable with it. Right?

My knees buckled slightly as the first wave of magic smashed through the small cracks I had created. It filled my body, filtering through every part of me. Rowan must have felt the energy, because she too looked like she was bracing herself.

"Place your hands out like mine. Let the magic flow out and see where it wants to go, what it wants to do."

I brought my palms up, feeling the tingle already within them. "Just like that? Let it come out and play?"

Rowan nodded, her expression hardening even more as her hands went in front of her in a half fight position. Worried, I stepped back a few paces, not wanting to hurt her. Then I took a deep breath and searched through all my energy for that buzzing wire inside of me that was the fae magic. It was there, entwined with the mecca, and I called to it, letting some of the magic seep from my palms. The energy that emerged was the dark midnight sparkle of color I had seen in the Otherworld.

"Good!" Rowan coaxed me. "Now where does it want to go? Walk around to the flowers, the fountain."

Even though it felt like an odd request, I did as she asked, walking as the magic trailed from my fingers. It brushed over the flowers without leaving a mark, same with the fountain. It took me about thirty seconds to realize exactly what it was doing — floating upwards, into the sky.

Rowan was staring curiously at the magic as it floated higher and higher. "Okay, well, it's giving

you a direction. Now it's time to give it a push. Make it do something."

This was not the kind of training I had envisioned, but I didn't hesitate. Confident that no humans would see, and that both Rowan and Violet were shielded from getting hurt, I lashed out with all of the energy inside. Instead of allowing a small trickle, I released my hold and let it flow free.

The magic soared up to the protective bubble and with a pop it shattered it. *Holy ... crap.* With all of my strength, I yanked the magic back toward me. It was certainly a lot harder to pull it back than to let it go free, but eventually I contained it again in my center. Spinning around, I realized that Rowan and Violet had been thrown backwards when the shield shattered.

"Vi! Rowan!" I ran to their sides, trying to assess if they were hurt. Neither of them were even looking at me. They were staring at each other, wide-eyed.

"What? Oh God. Speak," I told them, my words a frantic jumble. What had I just done?

Rowan's eyes met mine and she shook her head. "You can break magic." Her voice was light with notes of disbelief in each word. "The bonds of the mecca energy."

I wasn't sure what she meant by that.

Violet jumped to her feet, hurrying closer to me. "You're like a magic born, only a thousand times stronger. No one should have been able to break that ward, or to lower our protective shields. Not without training. You just took those down like they were made of paper."

"I ... I didn't mean to..." How could I use this to protect my people?

Rowan was circling me now. "If you can repeat this, it means that any spell the winter queen does, you can undo. Whatever she throws at us, you can shatter it before it hits. Possibly also shatter their shields."

A memory of Isalinda turning Kade into a frozen sculpture ran across my mind. Knowing I would be able to undo that was a huge relief. "That might explain why I could break through her ice magic after I touched the fae side of my energy."

Rowan was nodding enthusiastically, the most excited I had ever seen her.

This was a good thing. It was the first positive news we had received in a while. "Okay ... how do we test it? Make sure I can do it every time?"

Violet grinned, letting out a little peal of laughter. "We fling a crapload of spells at you and see if you can break them all."

Chapter Five

Deer me. When darkness calls, don't answer.

THAT NIGHT I crawled into bed, utterly spent. Violet and Rowan had spent the rest of the day testing my spell-breaking abilities, and despite a few mishaps I managed to shatter every single spell they sent my way. Eventually though, I was starving, exhausted, and my energy was too drained for any more. Rowan had promised we'd pick up again tomorrow morning.

Kade wasn't back yet, but Finn was. He crawled up on the bed next to me, like we used to, snuggling his warmth into my side. *I'm so glad you're here*, I murmured, tiredness catching up with me. *I'm turning into one of those shifters who can't sleep alone anymore.*

Finn's deep chuckle was nice, allowing more of the dark clouds of sleep to pull me under. *You've never liked to sleep on your own, but you do like to have your own space in the bed.*

So true. I used to enjoy sleeping on my stomach, spreading right out so all my limbs were nicely stretched. Now Kade tended to wrap me up, and even though I had thought I would hate that … I didn't. Being molded to him was much better than free space.

I have not heard of a spell breaker in many years. Finn had been following my progress today, same as I followed his through the streets of New York. *A strong magic born, or witch, can use a counter spell to break other spells, but that is not what you are doing. You don't have to be stronger, more powerful, able to think up a spell to counter another, you are simply breaking the mecca energy, breaking the bonds … almost like you're controlling the mecca. It's incredible.*

I was silent for a bit, staring up at the dark roof, before I let out a deep breath of weariness. *I will take any advantage I can get at this stage, but I'm not sure I'm comfortable with all the gifts I am receiving. Feels almost like too much.*

Finn nuzzled me again. *Don't question what is. You are unique in this world. Unique beings are often blessed with powers no other has.*

I smiled, drifting off to the soothing and familiar rumble of Finn's chest. The comfort of sleep was exactly what I needed. Darkness took me, and for a while I had no concept of time or space as I drifted, until a tendril of energy caught my attention. It was shadowy, but somehow also sparkling, like moonlight washing across a midnight sky. Its beauty was stunning, the pull it had on me complete, and I didn't hesitate to reach for it.

The moment I touched it, my fae side responded. Although depleted from all my spell work and training, there was enough left within me to rise up and intertwine with the dark tendril. A jerk around my energy caused a flicker of unease to sprout, and I was just wondering if I'd made a mistake when I was swept through time and space.

This was reminiscent of my dream-walking with Violet, except it was heavier, murkier, and I felt completely out of control. Suddenly my bare feet slammed down hard onto an icy, frozen-over lake. I could *feel* the cold and I found myself asking the question … was this actually a dream?

I spun in a full circle, trying to take in my surroundings. I had no idea how these dream worlds could feel so real. It was almost like a physical part of myself was standing there, able to interact with this place. It was quite dark, an eerie kind of twilight. I stood in the middle of a frozen lake, unable to see much outside of the small space I occupied; the air held an icy chill that was causing sharp pains and a numbing sensation to all exposed skin. It was the sort of weather that would kill a human in minutes if they didn't have adequate protection. As a shifter, I would have a little longer.

But not much.

I couldn't shake the feeling of familiarity. Not the lake. I knew I hadn't been here, but this world's energy. It felt like ... *the Otherworld*. A strong and bitter version, like the energy had gone a little sour in the time since I was here last.

I focused on the few dying trees I could make out along the lake's edge, and I was about to start walking toward them when I heard a deep rumble of laughter behind me. I had no weapons, not even a pair of boots as I was dressed in my pajamas. I was definitely at a disadvantage.

Turning slowly, I came face to face with a tall fae. I recoiled as waves of inky power swirled in arcs around him, shrouding his face and body so I could not see him clearly. I knew who he was, though. There was no other being it could be. *The Dark Fae Lord.* Something inside of me, deep in my soul, could feel the true evil energy this fae wielded. It was strong and elemental like the

mecca, but also ... not. Like the energy of this land, it felt bitter and sour.

He took another step toward me and some of the fogginess of his features disappeared. As his face came into sight, I was surprised by how handsome he was. I wasn't sure what I expected, but definitely not the broad shoulders and shoulder-length blond hair he was sporting. His features were sharp and defined, dark eyes shrewdly watching me.

The only thing, outside of the darkness he wore like a cloak — that indicated he was not a regular fae — was a set of deer antlers coming from each side of his head. The tips of them looked like they had been dipped in a black oily substance, which matched the fae's eyes. No white showed at all, just pure and eerie blackness. In his hand was a long staff; at its tip sat a black, multi-faceted crystal, which I could now see powered that swirling dark energy that surrounded him. Well, it looked like the dark fae definitely had one of the crystals. Shit.

"What do you want?"

I cut right to it. Because I was pretty sure my feet would end up frostbitten if I stood here much longer. I would have to shift to my wolf soon and run if he didn't let me go.

"Arianna..." He drawled my name in a low, seductive purr. It immediately set every nerve in my body on edge, and I fought against my dual instincts to attack or run. The fae opened his arms wide and walked closer to me, looking my body up and down with a gaze that would have gotten him an ass kicking if Kade had been here. No way would the bear have been able to control his temper.

The Dark Fae Lord showed no signs of stopping. He was getting far too close for comfort, so I reached for my energy. Thankfully it responded, even though we were in a dream world.

I hoped it was a dream world anyway.

Pushing my power toward him, I said, "Stop right there."

My voice held no fear. I was not the sort of queen to cower before a dark fae. That was not how I would lead or protect my people. I had a unique opportunity to observe our unknown enemy. I needed to find out all I could.

Heeding my orders, he actually stopped, even though the mecca I'd pushed at him splashed across his chest, breaking apart as if I had thrown a harmless egg at him. *Great. I was screwed.*

He grinned, showcasing the dimples in his cheeks. Which might have been cute if it wasn't for the freaky black eyes. "Mecca magic won't work on me."

"What do you want?" I asked again, preparing this time to shift into my wolf form. She was fast, and I was going to have to get away quickly.

The Dark Fae Lord gave me a half smile. "Oh, I thought that was obvious, Ari. I want you. I want to rule Earth with you by my side."

Stage five creeper. How did he know my nickname? "Don't call me that. I'm already mated, and he does not like to share."

He gazed into the seemingly endless black crystal on his staff and frowned. "Oh, Kade? I'm afraid I've seen his future and it ends in death. Might be easier if you start to distance yourself from him now. Together we can rule the world ... we can command the dark magic."

His mention of Kade's death sent ice water through my already frozen veins. My wolf howled within me and I wanted to join in. But I couldn't let this fae see how rattled I was. "Talk about my mate again and you'll be the dead one." This time I let my fae magic swirl to the surface, mixing with the mecca.

"Yes!" he shouted, nearly making me jump. "That's it. That's the magic I need. Your fae essence is so unique, it can harness the dark magic, just like mine."

No goddamn way! I wouldn't believe that. I was nothing like him ... *was I?* So what if I felt some sort of connection to this icy land, to that book we found in the Red Queen's room. That was just because of my connection to the mecca and being half fae.

"What are you?" I asked him. "How can you wield the dark magic?"

He looked toward the crystal again. He was spending a lot of time staring at the stone, a slightly obsessed look on his face. "It matters not who I am. All that matters is the being I have become. I am strong now. Powerful. I was born of the Fall Court, and they rejected me because I was small and weak. So I sought out true power. I made myself formidable."

Sounded like he'd stumbled across the dark stone and was easily corrupted. His weakness had made him an outcast in his fae court, so he decided to create his own world.

But how could he just stumble on the stone? "I assume the dark crystal was … drawn to you, because you're special, right?"

Got to appeal to their ego. It was essential.

His eyes were on it again. "Oh, yes. I was in the royal library. The book was hidden within another book, and I found it. It was all fate. The book called to me, and I used it to find the stone."

So Baladar was right. There were two books. Which meant we definitely should be able to use our book to find the stone.

"You don't have to follow this path," I told him, trying to appeal to the innocent he used to be. The world had hurt him, and he had fought back. "There are other ways to gain power. Why are you allying with the winter queen anyway?"

His smirk died, and I was faced with a torrent of dark anger. "She is giving me the Fall Court and the Earth side of the mecca. I will use the Earth power to control and bend the Fall Court to my will, teach them their place. The same way they did with me."

This was all about revenge for him. He wanted to rule over his old court, and the winter queen was the only one able to grant him that.

"I won't help you destroy two worlds." My voice was firm. I took another step back on my frozen feet. "This is not the right path. The darkness has corrupted you."

He grinned; it didn't reach his eyes. "It calls to you, *Ari*. Deny it all you want, you're convincing no one, not even yourself." He tapped his staff. "I've actually seen it. I know what I'm talking about."

I forced my expression not to change, even though my insides were twisting at the thought that he could use the stone to view me. I wondered if we could do the same with the book, or the mecca stone if we found it.

"The winter queen has promised the Earth side of the mecca to her son..."

I was stalling, trying to give myself time to build up a mass of my fae magic. It was swirling just beneath the surface of my skin.

He shook his head, acting like he was almost disappointed in me. "Your stupid father will believe anything she says. No. I have been assured that in exchange for helping win this war, I will be given dominion over whatever I want. And I want Earth and Fall. I have waited a long time for this."

This fae was ... broken. I could feel the cracks littering his soul from a life of abuse and ridicule. Cracks which were now pure darkness and could never be reversed. My heart ached for him, but I also knew I couldn't let the sympathy I felt toward him cloud my judgment. Because I knew that now he had seen my fae magic. Now that he thought we could control the darkness together, he would never stop coming for me.

I was going to have to kill him. Eventually. Straightening, I let my magic swell even more, preparing to blast out at him, when he said,

"I promise none of your people will be hurt if you side with me willingly."

I paused in my attack, just briefly, as I let the horror of that promise penetrate my brain. An offer to save all of my people? To keep this war

from ever starting? It was like I was back in the Summit all over again, having to choose duty to my people over my love for Kade. I had done the right thing at first, and it only ended in everyone being miserable. Then I chose with my heart, and I got my people and my mate.

My decision was clear.

"Go to hell," I told him. At the same time, I released the gathered magic inside of me, flinging it right at his staff. He let out a snarl, his smirk drying up. The moment my midnight-colored magic touched the crystal, I was falling, and then with a slam I woke up.

Surging up from the softness of my bed, I let out a yelp upon seeing Baladar and Kade standing at the foot of my bed. Finn was whining at my feet and I realized I was shivering, teeth chattering. Reaching down, I felt my feet and recoiled. What the hell? They were freezing.

"Ari?" Kade seemed at a loss for words.

I pulled the blanket up as he dropped down beside me and ran his arms up and down my shoulders, warming me. I snuggled closer to him, thankful that bear shifters always ran at a temperature akin to the desert in summer.

It was Baladar who found his voice first. "Where did you go?"

I shook my head, still trying to wrap my mind around it. "Some dream land with the fae lord."

My answer startled Kade and Baladar; both of them looked alarmed. "You weren't dreaming, Ari. You were gone," Kade said gruffly.

"I ... uh ... what?" I didn't understand. "I went to sleep here with Finn. I thought it was just like those dreams with Violet in the Otherworld." If I actually went somewhere in my physical body, then it did at least explain my frozen feet.

Finn ceased his grumbling, calming down now that I was back. *One minute you were at my side, and then next there was a burst of cold air, and ... then you were gone. Disappeared.*

Baladar had deep concern lining his eyes as he chimed in: "Finn got me out of bed, and when I got into your bedroom it reeked of dark magic. A magic which felt very similar to the dark book."

I ran a shaky hand through my hair. Damn. Somehow that bastard had figured out how to transport me from my bed and into his territory in the fae lands. "How is it even possible? How could he pull me into the Otherworld like that?"

There was a soft popping noise and then Violet was there, standing in her pajamas, hair a hot mess. "What happened?" she shouted as she looked around the room, focusing on something I couldn't see. "Holy dark magic." She waved her hand in the air above my head.

All of us were silent for a beat, which was pretty standard when Violet did her sudden appearance thing.

Baladar finally said, voice dry, "The Dark Fae Lord opened a portal and transported Arianna through it while she was asleep."

I squirmed out of Kade's grasp and scooted off the bed, needing to stand. My body temperature was finally beginning to return to normal, and with it came a frantic need to pace and throw my arms around. Pins and needles filled my feet, but at least I could feel them now.

Kade followed me, his eyes very dark and bear-like as he watched me closely. "Tell us what happened." His voice was bear-like too, growled out between clenched teeth. He was not happy, and he would be even less so when I filled them in on what had taken place.

I took a shaky breath, continued pacing, and left nothing out. I told them everything, even mentioned how the dark magic called to me. When I got to the part where the dark fae talked of us being together to rule in darkness, and how he'd eyed me in such an intimate way, fur began to break out on Kade's arms.

"I. Will. Kill. Him." Each word was said slowly, thudding across the room with the weight of Kade's fury.

I finished the rest quickly, my final line being, "So, he offered to call off the war if I promised to rule by his side."

Kade was now in his half bear shape, towering over everyone in the room. "What can we do to make sure he can never take her like that again?" He directed this blast of words at Baladar and Violet.

Violet was rubbing her chin. "Arianna can break spells, so that's why she was able to get out of there so easily."

The dark expression did not lift from Kade's face. "That doesn't answer my question."

Violet tried again. "He's a dark magic wielder, Kade, so we can't exactly keep him from doing his dark voodoo magic stuff, but I believe that if it happens again Ari can get out of it in the same way. She has incredible untapped power. If she trusts in her magic, no one can hold her against her will."

That seemed to calm my mate; fur disappeared, and he was back to being normal giant-sized Kade. Our hands reached out and found each other.

"Violet might be right. I'm just going to have to be more careful. Sleep with one eye open if possible."

It didn't sound possible to me right now. I was exhausted, cold, and wanted nothing more than to curl up with my mate and sleep for days.

Baladar frowned. "That won't work. He isn't physically coming into the room. He's pinpointing her essence and snatching her from her bed in a millisecond, pulling her through the magical ley lines, those which crisscross all the mecca stones. Obviously, he is able to tap his dark magic into that network too. The best thing we can do is train Ari's powers — teach her to hone her defensive skills."

Kade did not like the sound of that, ignoring Baladar to say, "I'll take first watch. Arianna, get some rest. The rest of you, we'll meet first thing in the morning for training."

I already knew that my sweet bear wouldn't be able to sleep again until the Dark Fae Lord was dead.

Baladar nodded. "As you wish."

Violet crossed the room and gave me one of her rare and brief hugs. "All spells are breakable," she whispered in my ear, and it gave me a small measure of comfort.

I just hoped I wasn't going to find myself on that frozen lake anytime soon. Or at least not before I got some more training with Rowan and Violet in. Alone in the room with just Kade and Finn, I sighed and walked over to my dresser to grab some socks. I slipped them on, and then my hiking boots for extra measure.

"What are you doing?" Kade asked, from where he stood beside the bed. Arms still crossed, face still frozen in lines of fury.

"Don't ask." I fell onto the pillow, pulling the covers up over me again.

If I was going to be caught on that frozen lake again, I sure as hell was going to have shoes this time. Kade curled himself around me, his warm palm stroking my back until I fell asleep.

I hadn't expected to, but my exhaustion got the best of me. I woke with the early morning light. Kade was hunched over at the foot of the bed, a deep snore rumbling from his chest. Poor guy, he would never be able to keep up with night watches. And I had a feeling Baladar was right. It wouldn't help either way. It looked like I was sleeping fully clothed from now on, shoes and all. Hell, I'd even sleep with my sword.

After a quick shower, I was dressed and ready for training. Kade was awake when I went back into the bedroom. I gave him a quick kiss and told him I was going to get breakfast.

"I'll go with you," he said in a husky voice.

With a shake of my head, I kissed him again, lingering for a few extra moments on his lips. "Get some sleep. If you insist on taking night

shifts, you're going to have to get some sleep during the day."

He didn't look convinced. "Promise me you'll stay with someone at all times, and don't leave the mansion without letting me know."

I wrinkled my nose at him. "You got it, boss."

He chuckled. "About time you realized who the boss was."

I pounced on him, wrestling him down, pinning his arms under my thighs. "You'll never tame me, King Kade."

His eyes were sparkling now, laughter bringing out some of the gold in them. "I would never want to change you, your fire or your fight. They're the things I love the most about you."

He flipped me over then, and I realized I didn't have him pinned at all. His huge body pressed into mine and a moan escaped from my lips as our mouths met in a fiery kiss. He was just wearing sleep shorts, which meant I had full access to all those bronzed muscles, running my hands across them as our kiss deepened.

Need slammed into me. The need to claim my mate, to brand our scents across each other. Kade must have felt the same way as he stripped my clothes off, his lips kissing along my jaw and down my collarbone as he moved. The dark fae was fighting a losing battle trying to coerce me to his side. There was literally nothing in any world, no power or stone, that could tear me away from Kade.

Nothing.

Later that morning, I got dressed for the second time, leaving a snoozing Kade in our bed. I'd lost some time with our morning love making, but even in the darkest of times one couldn't skip out on the beauty of life and love. None of us knew how many tomorrows we would get.

I made my way toward the main dining room, Victor, Jen, and Monica joining me. All of my guards took shifts through the night, making sure they were rested.

It would be a big day today. Blaine would have to go to the Otherworld; he'd already agreed he was the best candidate for the position. I still felt uneasy about it, but there was little I could do except have faith in him and his abilities. Kade also had to choose his representative today. We all knew it was a real priority now. Training with the fae, learning what to expect in the coming battle, and hopefully bridging the gap between our peoples.

When I walked into the dining area I was surprised to see Bianca, the Boston alpha sitting with Blaine and Violet, eating breakfast. The moment I saw her, an idea popped into my head.

"Your Majesty…" Bianca stood and gave a slight bow. Blaine and Violet just waved at me; protocol was long forgotten between us. Jen, Monica, and Victor joined the others at the table. They might protect me, but they were my family first. We all ate together.

"Bianca, lovely to see you again. To what do I owe the pleasure?" I sat on Violet's right and started to pile food onto my plate.

Bianca took her seat again. "I wanted to ask your permission to move my pack and dominants into the city. We would like to be stationed here to help until the threat is over."

She was a true alpha, one who pushed forward with the duty of her people in mind. If she had the proper lineage, she would have made a wonderful queen.

"Permission granted. Now I have a request I wanted to ask you," I told her.

"Anything," she answered readily.

"I'm sending Blaine to the Otherworld to train with our allies in the Summer Court. I think a second representative would be a great idea, someone else I can trust to be a liaison between our two peoples. I would like if it were you."

Her sharp gaze remained on me for a few long beats. I could tell she was analyzing what I had said, working out how she felt about it.

I decided to add, "I want you to know that this isn't an order. I know you're an alpha with your own pack. You're busy, and instrumental in this war, which are all the very reasons you would be my first choice to go with Blaine."

Her head bobbed a couple of times, and her expression softened. "I would be honored. My people will be fine without me, especially when they are here under your direct command."

I smiled. "I hear you have a very capable second-in-command."

She nodded. "Jason. Very dominant. I definitely trust him to keep the shifters in line."

Popping a piece of bacon into my mouth, I looked at Blaine. "Can you catch Bianca up on what to expect in the Otherworld? I need you both to leave tonight."

"Of course, Ari." Blaine's voice was rough with unconcealed emotions. Something was bothering him about all of this. I wished there was time for me to find out, but he was already rising and turning to Bianca.

"Shall we?"

She nodded, standing again and giving me one final bow, before they both left the room together. It was a good choice. I trusted no one more than I trusted Blaine. He was strong, skilled, and dominant. He would make sure we learned all we could from the fae. But a second voice was also important, especially a true alpha's.

Violet, who had just shoved a handful of grapes into her mouth, jumped to her feet as well. I tilted my head back to see her and she swallowed roughly, rasping out, "I'm going to round up Rowan. Meet us on the roof when you're done with breakfast."

With a shake of my head, I let out a chuckle. "One day you're going to choke."

Violet snorted as she left the room, taking her overwhelming energy with her.

Peering at Jen and Victor as they piled their plates high, I dived right into my breakfast, needing to fuel up my energy for the training I would undertake today. As I ate, my mind inevitably wandered to the Dark Fae Lord, that evil fae with the black-tipped horns. My road to being queen was already so rocky, it was hard to believe I was only a few months crowned. And while I might have taken care of Selene and her threat to our people, now it seemed I had three more adversaries to finish off before we all got our happily ever after. The winter queen, her son, and this dark fae ... they all needed to die. If they didn't, none of us would have a moment of peace.

The next few hours I spent getting beat down by Violet and Rowan. Their magic lessons were getting more grueling. I even lost the contents of my stomach after breaking a particularly complex spell — which didn't halt their torture in any way. They trapped me in boxes and held me under water. They called it an extra incentive to break the spells quickly. Which thankfully I did, because I was not a fan of drowning — not one of my preferred ways to go.

Exhausted and starving again, I hauled butt away from those two sadists and went to meet up with Kade for lunch. He wasn't in the main dining room, and after a few minutes searching I found him sitting in the magic library, on one of the old high wing-backed chairs. He looked stressed, leaning over the dark magic book, staring at the crystal on it, brows furrowed. Lying beside it was the cloth that Baladar had spelled to keep it contained.

"Hey, you all alone in here?" I asked, quickly glancing around the room.

He wasn't startled; no doubt he'd heard my footsteps from a long way away. When he turned, a slow smile crossed his face. It was the sort of smile he always reserved for me.

"Hey, how are you feeling?"

"Fine," I said, moving closer to him. "If you discount Rowan and Violet trying to kill me."

He chuckled, reaching out to pull me into his lap.

"How's it going with the book?" I was surprised he was in here with it alone, but maybe his unique way to read the mecca was involved. I knew he'd wanted to keep an eye on Baladar and Nikoli to make sure they didn't succumb to the book's powers.

He let out a ragged exhalation. "I've been trying to get a read on this dark energy. Usually energetic stuff comes easy to me, but this ... something about it feels different, and yet familiar." His hair was all messed up, like he had run his fingers through it repeatedly.

I felt the pull of the book's dark magic; it was strong. "Should you be so close to it?" I was half turned so I could run my fingers along his shoulders, hoping my touch would loosen the tight muscles there.

He pulled me even tighter against him. "I don't feel too much pull, so hopefully I'm managing to resist its draw."

I couldn't stop the flashback I had of the Dark Fae Lord. He had been a handsome male, just like Kade, until the dark crystal corrupted him. But ... he had sought out the power, Kade was already powerful from mecca and wanted nothing to do with the dark energy, so hopefully that would make a difference in Kade's ability to resist.

"Did you know that Violet popped in out of nowhere today and randomly told me that the dark crystal could bring people back from the dead? Then she left. A few moments later, Baladar showed up with the book and asked me to keep an eye on it until he got back."

I furrowed my brow. Why were magic born so freaking weird and cryptic? "I thought we were going to use the book to find the other crystal? Do you think they want us to try and figure out how to use this magic now? Like ... read the book? I'm not sure messing with darkness like this is a good idea."

Kade turned to look at me, his copper eyes swirling with concern. "I'm starting to worry that the reason Violet told me that is because she feels you might die in this war. Maybe I'm supposed to use this to save you."

I shook my head. "No one is dying. Violet is still recovering from her time in the Otherworld. She sees death everywhere. She worries a lot more now." I wasn't sure if I was saying this because I believed it or because I just wanted it to be true.

Kade's hand came up and wrapped around the back of my neck, pulling me closer, pressing his lips to mine. "Let's go out. Get pizza, go for a walk in Central Park or something normal."

I smiled. "That sounds perfect. Let's do it."

I missed normal. I would take any of it I could get.

Chapter Six

Who ordered the two large servings of rebellion?
Extra betrayal on the side.

KADE AND I decided to take Finn and Nix with us. They were our first and best line of defense in detecting an early fae attack. But more than that, we missed them. We had both been spending a lot of time away from our familiars. And to be separated from them for long periods of time, it was like being separated from a limb. Everything felt painful, awkward and difficult.

Victor, Jen, Monica, Violet, Nikoli, Calista, and Baladar were also coming along, which I wanted to object to, but I knew it was not in my best interest. These were our best soldiers, our strongest magic born, and we were their leaders. We needed protection, because if we were taken out early in the war, our people would fall apart. Mecca would leak everywhere. It would be a disaster.

But they were my family. I would not sacrifice them for my life, no matter the consequences. I just had to hope I was strong enough to keep all of us safe. Truthfully, between all of us—our power—we could take out a small army.

"Have you heard from Kian or Gerald?" I asked Kade as we waited in the front lobby of our Manhattan home for everyone to finish up their tasks and meet us.

Kian and Shelley went with Gerald to California. Only for a short period, as it was Kian's wish, to make sure everything was set up securely. And to settle their son. I wished I could go to Winnie, but there was no chance. At least I was getting updates through Annette.

"Yes, he sent a message. They have all arrived in California. Everything is secure and stable there. He'll return with Shelley in a few days."

Kade threaded his fingers through mine, and I snuggled closer. "That's good to know."

Footsteps sounded across the tiled hallway, and I felt the strong pulsing energy of multiple magic born. Violet, Baladar, Nikoli, and Rowan were coming toward us. Violet was in her usual medieval-style gown, a pretty turquoise color.

The others were dressed in form-fitting and dark clothing, like they were preparing for a fight.

I smiled at the fae. "I didn't know you were coming along. Violet said you were busy cooking up some new tortures for me."

Her elfin features lit up as a tinkling bell-like peal of laughter left her. "I wouldn't be much of a trainer if I let my charge go out without me. Even though we aren't in active war, it doesn't hurt to be prepared."

I straightened away from Kade. "Do you think it's unsafe for us to leave? I won't risk anyone because of my need for some normalcy. We can order pizza in. Or have the kitchen make it."

Rowan shook her head, her expression sobering again. "There are no guarantees, but I sense no reason we shouldn't get out for a little while. Sometimes the best thing you can do is have a few moments of normalcy. It makes the hard times a little easier to bear."

Calista nodded, coming over and giving me a hug. As she pulled back she said, "I think it's a great idea. You've been working so hard since gaining your crown back. Don't burn yourself out."

"We need you, Your Majesty," Baladar playfully added.

It was my turn to laugh now. "Okay, okay, you've all convinced me."

I felt Kade press his lips to the top of my head. It was such a sweet gesture that my eyes closed involuntarily at the perfect moment. By the time I had them opened again, the rest of our guard was there.

Victor gave me a low bow, followed by a fist bump. "Blaine said to bring him back a pizza with the works, and that they are pretty much ready to head across to the Otherworld. Bianca's people are all being housed in the Bronx right now."

"Great! We'll be back in time to send them across." I tilted my head up to Kade. "Did you choose a representative?"

He turned toward Nikoli, eyebrows slightly raised. The magic born gave a firm nod. "Yes, Luka has agreed to go into the Otherworld. He's one of our highly-trained soldiers, well respected by the rest of the army. They will follow his lead and teachings. He should be arriving here in the next hour or so."

It was nice to tick things off the to-do list, even though they all felt like Band-Aids over a bullet hole. At the end of the day, I had no idea if any of this would help to save us in this war, but all we could do was try.

The moment we walked into Vinnie's, my favorite pizza place, I smiled. That smell, the fresh dough, basil, and mozzarella, it permeated the air and made my stomach growl.

"This was a good idea," I told Kade.

The usually bustling place was pretty empty, and there was a sign hanging over the door. *Take away only. No dining.*

Just as disappointment hit me, Calista winked. "I called ahead," she said. "Thought we could use some privacy."

Thank the pizza gods for that.

There were a few shifters at the counter and they bent their heads low to me as I passed. The waitress came to seat us in the private back room and I caught sight of a familiar face in the kitchen as we passed. *Stan?* He was the last wolf I had expected to see in there.

Stan was an old wolf with old ideas. He had petitioned to not be made to mingle with the bears. Now here he stood in Manhattan, which was bear *and* wolf territory, holding a pizza box. I guess old habits died hard. Bronx pizza wasn't the same as Vinnie's.

I decided to let it go and let him have his pizza. Maybe he was coming around. I knew he and Vin had been old friends. It pained me that some of the shifters couldn't get past the ways of old. The last thing we needed right now was a division between ourselves.

"Something wrong?" Violet asked me. My friend was always in tune to what I was feeling.

I brushed it off. "Yes. I need a triple meat pizza with a side of jalapenos, STAT," I joked.

Violet and Kade both grinned. They knew I was not a woman to be messed with when hungry.

Victor, Monica, and Jen sat at a small table just outside the door that led to our private sitting room, guarding us, as always. In public they would be extra vigilant. Rowan, Violet, Nikoli, Calista, and Baladar, joined Kade and I, none of us speaking as we pretty much inhaled the most delicious pizza in New York City.

All good out there? I checked in with Finn. He was keeping watch outside with Nix, which was fine by me, but I would save him a few pieces of sausage.

All quiet. I have rarely seen the city so ... still.

Let me know if anything stirs up.

You got it. Now enjoy your pizza.

I disconnected from his mind, coming back to the table, Violet was telling Kade a funny story. Well, she had a lightly amused tone on, but there was sadness mingled there also.

"The kids would taunt me for having such light skin, and white hair, and white eyelashes," Violet explained, and I saw Nikoli nod in understanding. The fair look of the magic born was different, and different always invited ridicule with young children.

"I decided I was sick of getting picked on for my looks, and since Ari told me I couldn't spell everyone who pissed me off, I decided to dye my hair."

I smiled. I knew this story, and now I understood her amused tone.

Nikoli shook his head. "I'm pretty sure I know where this is going." He looked to be holding back laughter.

Kade's brows were bunched as he looked between the two of them. "What happened?"

Now I was trying not to laugh as I remembered how freaky she had looked.

Violet popped a pepperoni into her mouth. "Well, apparently, our hair is magic and cannot be dyed. Ever. It rejects all color, forever to be pigmentless."

My eyes flit across the table and I could see even Baladar was smiling. All of the magic born knew, except for Rowan. She seemed intrigued. Since I knew the winter queen had a black-haired magic born, I could only assume fae magic born were not exactly like the shifters.

Kade crossed his arms, leaning back in his chair. "Okay, so it didn't work..."

Violet leaned closer to him for full effect. "Not on my hair. But my skin..."

Kade's eyes widened, and a sparkle lit up their copper depths. "Seriously?"

"Yes!" Violet shouted. "The skin under my eyebrows and my scalp was black for a month! While my hair remained white as cotton. I looked like a Halloween creature, and I wasn't trained in magic then. Well, not enough to change it."

I couldn't hold it in anymore, laughter exploded out of me. "Why didn't you let me take a picture?" I said between my chuckles. "How much better would this story be with photographic evidence?"

She had genuinely looked horrifying. But it taught her something — and me too. Accept your natural beauty for what it is. Don't fight nature.

Violet rolled her eyes, at the same time leveling a vicious scowl in my direction. "Because at the time I was sure my life was over and a picture would just remind me of the time my life ended."

Her eyes shuttered, and I guessed she was back in the land of Faerie, remembering how her life had really almost ended. Perspective was a funny thing. She shook it off quickly though, smiling and joking with everyone around the table. I was pretty sure that only I noticed the weariness that remained deep in her eyes, in the tilt of her shoulders, in the tension of her hands.

She wasn't completely lost to me, though. She was improving, slowly coming back to us. Whatever the queen had done to her — taken from her — it was fixable.

"Dylan Mathews still asked you to the summer solstice that year," I reminded her.

Violet sat a little taller. "That he did. I was going to say no, because I thought it was a pity or dare thing, but you slapped me around a little and told me that some of us were just born to stand out."

Our eyes remained locked for a few long beats, and so much love and so many memories flashed between us in that time. "You could have dyed every part of your body, Vi. You would never have dulled your shine."

She looked like she was going to cry, and it was a relief when Kade broke the moment by saying, "Well, at least now we have a plan to scare off the winter queen and the dark fae. We just need Violet to try to dye her hair again."

That got Violet laughing again, and I was grateful for that. Baladar's booming voice echoed around the room as he launched into a story of his own.

Kade leaned over and kissed my cheek. "Be right back."

I lost track of Baladar's story as I let my focus rest on Kade. I couldn't believe at a moment

when the entire world was falling apart, I could still be so happy. It seemed ... wrong. But also, it was the best kind of right that had ever happened to me.

Kade paused briefly to chat with Victor, Monica, and Jen, and when they started to get up, he waved them off, no doubt reminding them he didn't need someone to hold his hand to the bathroom.

I love you. He was going to get a big head, considering how many times I'd told him that, but I would never stop.

His chuckle drifted through my mind, and the heat that followed was like a rush of warm water. *I love you, Ari. I'm going to tell you every single day. Multiple times a day. For the rest of our long lives.*

Fear trickled through the warmth of his love, and I pulled away to not only give him privacy, but to also hide my own growing anxiety. Those damn fae were trying to take away my happiness. We couldn't let that happen. I refused to give up. Not now. Not ever.

Calista leaned over to me and patted my hand. "We will win this war." Apparently, I was hiding none of my emotions today.

Before I could respond, I felt Finn's energy darken and then bristle with anxiety. *Kade's hurt.*

Those two words flushed ice water through my veins and I stood abruptly. Tapping into my bond with him again, I was immediately hit with sharp pain and anger. *Oh shit.*

"Kade's under attack!" I shouted.

Baladar stood, throwing his hands out. His magic slammed into all of us; it threw me back a few inches, but once it cleared I burst into action. What was it with the damn bathrooms here? Last time we were here I was attacked by a fae in the bathroom.

Baladar must have thought the same because he said, while running right behind me, "It isn't fae. That spell was designed to reveal all ... and I only sense our kind."

I was in the lead, and upon turning the corner, a rage so strong and potent I could taste it filled me. Six dominant wolves had Kade pinned down in the hallway, just outside the bathroom door. There was a blanket of magic over the top of him, and they were slashing out with weapons. I took a split-second to catalogue the scene for any other possible attacks, but the only other being in here was Vinnie, and he was knocked out in the corner.

I let out an enraged scream; my ice magic burst from me without thought, slamming the six wolves into the wall. The training I'd been doing with Rowan and Violet had helped immensely with tapping into it almost unconsciously. The shifters were back on their feet in seconds, turning to brandish their weapons at me.

I snarled, loud and animal-like. My wolf was prancing close to the surface, wanting to break free. *No, we need our magic.*

"You are all guilty of treason!" I said, my words slow and drawn out, my fury spilling over in each. "You have attacked your king."

Kade was still trapped under the magical netting, I had no idea where they had gotten such a thing, but I planned on breaking it. It also looked like they were outfitted with magically enhanced weaponry. That was the only way they could have gotten the drop on my mate, I knew that without a doubt.

I recognized them all; it was Stan and his inner circle. They had been very outspoken against Kade and I joining the two packs together. How had they known we were coming here tonight? Had it simply been that Stan had seen us and called in reinforcements? Or had we been betrayed once again?

Stan spat at my feet. "He's no king of ours, he's the enemy. You are the enemy also. A fae, mated to a bear … this is blasphemy. You both should die for what you've done to our world. You've destroyed the ways of old, and we will not stand for it."

He flung a knife at me; it must have been concealed in his free hand. Mecca and fae power burst from me, aiming to halt the blade. Only it wasn't halted; it cut through my magic with ease, almost like it had been designed to do that. A low groan escaped me as the blade slammed into my shoulder, all the way to the hilt. The pain burst across my senses, but it was dulled by my adrenalin and anger.

Kade roared from the floor. His huge body started to shift as he fought the netting.

I'm okay, I told him, but he was too enraged to hear.

"How did you know we were here?" I asked, uncaring which of the traitors answered.

Stan chuckled. "Everyone knows your love for Vinnie's. I figured it was only a matter of time. We've been hanging out here daily. You were too stupid to keep an eye on the wolves who did not want this new leadership."

Not stupid. Trusting. I was trying to appease both sides of the argument. Some days I understood why the Red Queen was so brutal with anyone who didn't fall under her rule. Look what happened when I tried to allow freedom from monarchy. I got anarchy.

"Those are pretty special weapons," I said, gritting my teeth against the throb in my shoulder. "Looks like you too, have aligned yourself with the fae?" I lowered my voice, letting my magic seep into it. I knew these weapons, and they were not of this world. I just hoped he would tell me who the hell gave them to him.

When the energy brushed against them, they slashed out with those weapons, dissipating the magic.

"They were left on our doorstep. Someone knew we would need them to kill you, fae-traitor-bitch," one of them sneered.

"Distract them," I murmured to Baladar, Violet, and Rowan, who were all standing around me.

The magic born didn't hesitate, they started blasting spells at the six wolves, most of which were deflected by their fancy weapons. Forcing myself to focus, I tapped into the pure fae power inside of me, specifically the energy I used to shatter spells. I directed it at the net holding Kade. It took quite a bit of my control; I had to funnel it for a minute or so, and only aim for the netting, but, eventually, with a push, it shattered into a thousand magical pieces.

The wolves should have taken more care to watch the threat behind them. They thought they had trapped Kade, that he was no threat. They were wrong.

In a flash, he was up on his hind legs, bear paws slashing through the six of them with ease. Body parts flew everywhere, and the rest of us took a step back so as not to accidentally get in the path of an enraged bear.

When the room was covered in blood and severed bodies, Kade stood there half shifted, his chest heaving as he fought the anger still riding him.

Kade, love, I'm okay.

His head shot up; his eyes locked me in place as he stalked slowly over the gory scene to me. I could barely make out his tawny skin he was so covered in the blood of our enemies, and for a brief second I almost wanted to run.

"You okay?" Violet eyed the knife in my shoulder.

I nodded. "I'm fine."

Ignoring me, she stepped forward, pulling a vial of a green swirling fluid from her pocket.

"Oh look, it's a bird!" Violet pointed to the ceiling.

"Wha — ow, muthaf — " My curse was cut off as I panted in and out, trying to calm my racing heart. She had just yanked the knife out, quickly murmuring a short incantation and pouring the green fluid into my open wound. My entire shoulder went ice cold then, before warming, and then the pain was gone.

"I'll look at it again later, but that should stop the pain and bleeding for now," she said.

"Thanks," I replied, before all of my focus went to Kade. He was breathing slowly, trying to find his humanity again.

"Okay. Call us if you need help. We're going to check around back and make sure there are no more attackers." Violet threw one last worried glance at the pile of bodies before she left with the others.

When Kade reached me, I was glad to see he had returned to his normal giant size, not that half-morphed bear he did so well. Uncaring about the blood, I reached out and placed my hand on his chest, right above his heart.

"I'm okay. I promise."

His eye flicked to the blood that had stained my dress.

"It's just a small wound," I said.

Some of the dark angles of his face softened, and he cupped my chin gently, rubbing his thumb across my cheek. "I got a bit of blood on you," he murmured, and I had to chuckle at that.

"You got a bit of blood on everything, mate. I think your lips are the only thing on your body not covered."

Kade bent down and picked up the blade that had been lodged in my shoulder and held it up for me to see. "Where have we seen weapons like these before?" he asked.

I looked a little closer. It was a dagger, smooth and white. The handle was a bone of some type — actually, the entire thing looked like it was carved from a bone — The handle was thick, with symbols etched into it, before it tapered up to a very sharp point.

"It's fae," I breathed, confirming my earlier suspicions, unease cramping my stomach. They often carved weapons from the bones of magical creatures. It made for quite the powerful piece, as had been demonstrated here today.

"Who would have dropped off fae weapons on their doorsteps?" I asked, trying to make out the other blades they had held.

Kade shook his head. "Someone who knew the wolves were looking for a chance to end us. Someone who also thought we would never suspect our own people and they would be able to get close."

"The winter queen," I snarled. That bitch. It had to be her, or the Dark Fae Lord. Either way, they were using far more underhanded methods than I had expected.

A groan from the corner distracted us both, and Kade stepped forward, his hands claws at his sides. I pushed past him when I realized it was just Vinnie. The older man was blinking rapidly, looking around as he tried to figure out what had happened. When he saw the state of the hallway to his bathroom, he went very pale.

I helped him sit up. "Are you okay?"

He nodded a few times, unable to look away from the bloody carnage Kade had left in his hallway.

"Glad to see you're okay, King Kade." He looked away finally, up to the bear shifter who was standing above me. "The way you held your cool, tried to reason with them. Well, it was nice to see a bear not just attack, even when you had all the right."

I freaking knew they wouldn't be able to get the drop on Kade. He had let them go, trying to stop a fight, trying not to hurt my people. And they had ambushed him with fae magic. Vinnie must have still been conscious for that part.

"Sorry about the mess, Vin. I'll have my magic born clean it up." I extended a hand and Vinnie took it, grunting as he lifted himself up.

"It's not a problem. Won't be much of my pizza place left if we don't win this war." He looked at the ground, trying to smooth out his features.

"We're going to win," I assured him. That was my place, to assure my people even if I wasn't sure myself.

The next few hours passed in a blur. Violet, Nikoli, and Rowan thoroughly checked the surrounding area for more rogue wolves, and thankfully there were none. Then they all worked with Baladar to fully clean and close my wound. Violet's temporary care had kept it pain free for a short while, before it started to weep and throb with pain again. Baladar was reasonably concerned about the weapon, and said he would do some research into what sort of bone it might be. I explained my theory about the winter fae leaving it there, which definitely increased his worry.

By the time we got back to the royal estate, there were no outward signs we had been attacked. Clothes were changed, blood cleaned, faces blank. Panicked shifters were the last thing I needed; they were already on edge. I would hide as much of this from them as I could.

I went straight up to my office, to find Blaine waiting there. He took one look at me and jumped up from his chair.

"Ari, what the hell happened?" His large hands wrapped around my biceps as he pulled me closer.

I collapsed a little into him, and in hurried whispers told him everything. By the end of the story, he was pacing back and forth across the room, looking far less cool and collected than usual. "Are you sure it's a good idea for me to go to the fae lands now? I don't want to leave you unprotected."

I sank into my office chair, thankful there was only the slightest twinge in my shoulder now. "I would love to keep you with me, mostly because I want to make sure you are safe." We had already lost too many of our inner circle. My dominants. With this new attack, I was rethinking everything. "But if the war is coming, we need to share information between our armies. I need someone I can trust in the Otherworld. Someone who can keep an eye on everything. That someone is you."

He didn't argue again, even though he didn't look particularly happy. A knock sounded against my door, and I called out, "Enter."

Rowan walked in. "I have opened the doorway to the Summer Court. It's time."

My chest tightened and I bit back the words that would stop Blaine from leaving. He was still staring at me, those intense green eyes locked on my face.

"Thanks, Rowan," I murmured. "We'll be right there."

She nodded, and then left the room. Standing again, I approached my old friend, and a million unsaid things drifted between us in a single look. "Be careful." I swallowed hard. "Report back to me via the flowers and magical mirrors whenever you can."

He gave me a firm nod, acting all business-like, until his arms swept around me and I was pulled into a tight hug. "Please don't die, Ari. I can't live in a world without you."

I let myself relax against him again, forgetting in that moment that I was the queen, with all the weight of my people's lives on my shoulders. Being with Blaine felt — at times — like stepping back to a more carefree Arianna.

After he left, I knew I was on the verge of freaking out, so I started to do some work. Which was the reason I told Kade I was going to my office in the first place. Catching up on some of my queenly duties.

Despite being late at night, everyone was busy. Working.

The magic born were working on the spell to find the dark crystals, Kade was dealing with his bear-king duties, and I was about to make multiple conference calls with other pack alphas, coordinating battle and attack plans, mobilizing our armies.

Sometimes it felt like being queen was all paperwork and phone calls.

Finn joined me at one point, resting his head on my thigh as I dealt with another set of

worried alpha wolves. By the time I hung up, my head was pretty much on my desk I was so tired.

Get your butt to bed, My Queen. Kade's voice in my head was a welcome relief, and I decided it was time to rest. A lot had happened today.

On my way.

Kade was in the room when Finn and I entered. I knew he'd only made it back just before me. "How did everything go with the bears?" I asked, kicking off my shoes as I walked. They flew across the room in different directions, but I was way too tired to care.

He met me halfway across the massive suite, his eyes dropping to my shoulder. "More importantly, how's the wound?" A murky energy still floated around him. I assumed it was lingering aggression from the fight.

Reaching up, I rubbed at it unconsciously. "It feels … okay. Nothing too crazy. I'll live."

I received an exasperated smile in return. "You better live. And the bears are all good now. We just had some disputes about who was in charge of the different dens. You'd think in times of war that sort of stupid shit would stop, but unfortunately it seems nothing ends the internal squabbling."

I almost laughed. I'd been dealing with similar things too, all the time wanting to tell them to get their acts together. My diplomacy was pretty much gone at the moment.

"You need to sleep." Kade's voice startled me, and I realized I'd drifted off.

I nodded. "Yes, sleep." I stumbled toward the bed, coming to a grinding halt. "Shoes! I need my shoes."

Kade didn't ask why. He found a pair of tennis shoes for me, which would be the easiest to sleep in. I also kept my jeans on, and strapped a blade to my thigh.

I wasn't going to let the Dark Fae Lord get the drop on me again.

Kade's voice washed over me: "Sleep. You'll heal faster. I'll keep watch." He stroked my injured arm, which felt amazing as I sank into a deep sleep.

It was dreamless at first, but all too soon the cold seeped in. Awareness returned in gradual increments until my eyelids snapped open. My feet slammed down onto the frozen lake at the same time I heard Kade yell my name.

I sensed the fae before he spoke. I was halfway through turning around when his voice washed over me. "I'd be careful with that book if I were you."

The dark fae stood tall, his antlers dripping black oil, a sneer on his face.

"Don't worry about me. Watch your own back," I spat, readying to break the spell and send myself back.

He held up a finger. "This is your last chance. Join me and I will spare your people."

I unhooked the dagger from my thigh sheath and he grinned as if it excited him.

"For the last time, no. I will never join you. And if you bring me here again I will cut those horns off with a blunt knife." I gathered up my fae magic and the Dark Fae Lord bared all of his teeth.

He had time to say, "You better pray you find that second stone before I do," before I threw my magic at him and the spell shattered, sending me shivering and gasping into Kade's arms, back in Manhattan.

"Did he hurt you?" Kade was inspecting me. I shook my head, too cold to talk. Finn crawled in on my other side and I threaded my fingers through his fur. I sensed my familiar was too furious for words, but just having him close was comforting.

Eventually, I rolled away and said to Kade, "He knows about the other stone. He's looking for it, too. It might be what they are waiting on to attack. We need to do that spell. Now." I sprang into action, climbing off the bed.

Kade remained where he was, no doubt trying to calm his rage. My poor mate; nothing worse than feeling helpless. Especially for someone used to taking charge.

Finally he said, "He already has one crystal. Why does he need another?"

Good question. "More power?"

Kade shook his head. "I think this is about the winter queen."

Isalinda. Of course. It actually made perfect sense. She was never satisfied with her lot in life, always wanting more. More power. More control. The dark fae wanted the Fall Court and the Earth side of the mecca. That I already knew, but I had never asked what the queen wanted. I assumed it was just his help in the war. Help to take me down. I also thought she was going to kill him after she got that help. But maybe what she wanted all along was some of the dark power.

"We can't forget that he sees us through the crystal, knows what we do." That unnerved me the most.

Kade stood and I could see the heaviness in his body from lack of sleep.

"Get rest. I'll come to you with news once I have some," I urged him.

He shook his head. "I'm fine. Just need some coffee."

I could have pushed further, but I knew it was futile.

"Alright, then. Let's wake the magic born." There was no way I was letting this creepy bastard get to the dark crystal before me.

Chapter Seven

Dark can taint the strongest light.

WE FOUND THE four magic born sprawled out across the floor of the main library, looking like they'd fallen asleep mid-research. I'd had all of the spell books transferred there, since it was a larger space to house everything. I felt a weird sense of relief having all of our resources in one place, like I could occasionally make a decent decision as an adult and queen.

We'd shut this room off to the rest of the staff at the estate as soon as all the books were inside, which no one seemed to mind. Seems the Red Queen had rarely let anyone in here anyway.

There were only a few lamps lit; it was early morning and dark still. I hit the switch for the

main lights, sending bright beams of illumination down the many rows of books.

"What the freak?" Violet was up, the pitch of her screech probably killing some of the pigeons outside. She had both hands out, and was breathing deeply, like her heart was beating a million miles an hour. When she saw me and Kade, her hands slowly lowered. I realized she had called magic to them when she initially jumped. Even in her sleep she was ready for an attack.

"Sorry," I said, my brow creasing as I walked toward her. "I should have … been more considerate."

In my impatience I forgot that Violet was recovering from an attack, and that the other three were no doubt as exhausted as Kade and me. "I just had some news to share, and hopefully you have some for us."

Baladar, Nikoli, and Rowan were up then too, all of us turning as a cheerfully humming Calista entered the library. She was wheeling a large tray covered in food and coffees. "Good morning. I thought we might all need some breakfast."

Was this woman a secret magic born? How had she known we were up? She had to have known before I even woke to have time to fetch a tray of food. She better not have security cameras in my suite. I wouldn't put it past her.

As she passed me, I got a firm hug. "Glad to see you're feeling better today."

"How ... how did you know we were here?"

She just shook her head, her beaming smile in place. "Never underestimate me, Ari. I see all."

No doubt my guards had reported to her, but still, she was amazing.

Her eyes flicked to my shoulder and I rubbed at the dull ache unconsciously. "I'm fine."

Some of her joy dulled, but as Baladar hurried over to her, declaring in a booming, desperate kind of tone that he loved her, she was soon back to her jolly self.

She let out a small snort-laugh, which was totally unlike her. "Those declarations of love would mean a lot more if you weren't staring at the coffee pot when you said them."

Baladar focused on her completely then, his icy eyes filled with shots of magic. Calista lasted all of two seconds before she was in his arms, getting her morning kiss. Those two made me happy. Turning away from their PDA, I noticed Violet still seemed a little twitchy. I plucked up a pink iced doughnut, which was one of her favorites, and passed it to her.

Some of her tension eased as she breathed in the sweet bread smell and took a huge bite. "Pink donuts are the best kind of fruit."

I snorted, because she had a crappy diet and she just did not care. And I was one to talk. Wrap it in bacon or smother it in mac and cheese and I was in love.

Kade, who had made himself comfortable in a large wingback armchair, was already on his second cup of coffee. He had some bagels on a plate too. I was glad to see some of the fatigue fading from his face, but with everything that was happening, him being attacked and partly-shifting, he was not even remotely getting enough sleep to restore his energy. I would have to make sure he slept first tonight.

"So, Arianna, what do you need to tell us?" Baladar looked completely unruffled, holding his mug in a refined manner.

I wasted no time on pleasantries, telling them everything about my unexpected kidnapping and what Kade and I thought the Dark Fae Lord wanted that second crystal for.

After I had finished, Baladar said, "What would you like us to do first?"

"First, some type of blocking spell. He sees everything we do, and if we're going to beat him to the stone, that has to stop." I paced the library as the magic born stared at me.

"It would be too hard to spell the entire royal estate and all of our energy signatures," Baladar started slowly.

My wolf rose up and the growl ripped from my mouth before I could stop it. *Dammit.* There was no way for us to plan anything if he could just see straight into our world.

Kade stood. He had finished his food and coffee now, and was looking alert. "Well, we'll just have to focus on us, and not the castle."

Baladar rubbed his chin. "Intriguing ... explain further."

"Well, I'm no magic born, but what if you could spell some jewelry or something and we could wear th—"

Violet leapt up. "Yes! It would take very little magic that way. We don't bother to hide the castle. We spell necklaces to shroud our energy signature from magical prying eyes. It will be simple. That way, if the Dark Fae Lord spies on the castle, he won't see what we're doing."

Baladar nodded. "We can hide the important people, and leave enough of the others around so he doesn't get too suspicious."

Yes, this was a plan I could work with. "He'll wonder where we have gone, and that should get him nice and nervous. Maybe he'll make a mistake." I pointed to Violet and Baladar. "Can you two please start on the necklaces? Nikoli, Rowan, and I will continue with the spell to find this dark crystal. We have to get to it before the dark fae."

No one argued. For once, they all acted like I was actually their queen, and hurried off to follow my orders.

Kade cleared his throat lightly. "I think you're forgetting someone."

I turned around and placed two hands on Kade's muscular chest. "You, My King, need to get a couple hours of sleep." His alertness would fade soon enough. He couldn't survive on coffee forever. "We have a crystal hunt to go on when you wake."

After a long pause, where he scrutinized me closely, he finally nodded. "Two hours. Not a minute longer."

I smiled. "Okay."

After Kade retreated out of sight, I sat down next to Rowan and Nikoli. "Okay, first thing. Can we do a temporary spell to hide us and this conversation?"

Rowan let out a chuckle. "You don't have to worry about it. This library is covered in fae magic. I'm not sure why, but long before we used this room, someone was hiding it from sight."

I echoed her chuckle, even though I knew exactly why this room was spelled. The Red Queen and Daddy Dearest. Pushing my parents back into the box of things I was never dealing with, I focused on the task.

"Alright, since our conversation should be private here, explain this magic to me. Why can't we find this other crystal? Can we just read the book? It's supposed to contain all the information we need to find and control the energy, right?"

Nikoli pulled the dark magic book out of the spelled cloth. The moment it was free, I felt its low hum of energy and those slivers of heavy, shadowy magic. It was muted, so whatever Baladar had done to the book was still working, but there was no doubting the strength of this sliver of crystal, or the dark information it contained.

Nikoli placed it between us all, careful not to touch the stone or open the pages.

"None of the magic born have opened the book, because we have no idea what is inside. We also have no idea what will happen if we read the words. This stone is pure dark magic. The only problem is, according to Baladar, the only way to learn how to trace or connect to the dark mecca is to read the spell inside. Only..."

"We don't want to turn evil..." I said, and he nodded.

"We don't want to turn evil, so none of us are willing to open the pages or connect to the stone. Who knows what might happen if we did."

Rowan was silent, staring in deep thought at the stone. "What if it were more ... familiar to us? What if we turned the black stone into something we knew, so we could connect with it briefly and read this spell ... trace it to its other half?"

Nikoli and I shared a look of confusion, and Rowan grinned like Violet often did. Like she knew something we didn't. "Mecca powder," she breathed. "If we coat this stone in mecca powder, it will mingle with the dark magic, temporarily bringing it closer to our purple mecca. That should limit the effect of the words inside, giving us enough time to see what information it's hiding."

I wasn't a magic born, so it didn't make sense to me, but it sounded like a decent idea. The mecca powder had certainly done some incredible things the times I'd seen it at work. "What are the odds it could backfire and make all of my magic born go dark?" I asked seriously.

Rowan's shoulders drooped forward a little. "High. That's why only one of us should do it. Just in case."

Damn.

Nikoli nodded. "Baladar is too valuable to lose, Violet is too fragile after her time as prisoner with the Winter Court. Queen Arianna and King

Kade are way too important to risk ... so, I'll do it."

"I can do it," Rowan offered. Her beautiful pixie features were smooth. She didn't seem too worried.

"You're our only fae knowledge base. And you are valuable to the Summer Court. We definitely don't want to upset them by turning their magic born dark." He shook his head. "No, it has to be me."

He was confident and sure, unwilling to risk anyone else on this task. I was touched.

"Nikoli, you are a treasured friend and magic born. Thank you," I told him, and he simply nodded.

I stood. "Alright, get ready for the spell. We'll do it in two hours when Kade is awake to make sure the energy can be controlled. We will all have our magic necklaces by then, so the dark fae will have no idea where we are."

It was a plan ... a sort of scary one, but the best we could hope for. Part of me was worried about Nikoli. We couldn't afford to lose any of the magic born ... Violet especially. But this was war, and there was no way for me to keep my loved ones safe. We just had to hope for the best, and try to wipe those fae out before they got us.

Two hours later, we were all gathered in the basement, the place where I had defeated Selene—twice. The large room would be able to handle a reasonable amount of magical blowback. We couldn't use the library; Rowan said that whatever magic hid it from prying eyes might interfere in our spell.

We all wore the necklaces. They were simple-looking: a plain brown leather string with a white crystal shard hanging from it. But the moment I touched it, I knew it was anything but simple. An energy bubble had been placed over me.

"So you can't see my energy at all?" I asked Violet for the third time. Ever since my winter magic had been unlocked, I had been like a shining beacon to her.

"Nothing. I don't even pick up a human level of energy. It's like you have ceased to exist ... in energy anyway."

"Will it affect my magic?" I added.

She shook her head. "Nope. Just hide you from prying eyes."

Whoa. I looked at the little crystal with newfound respect. At least part one of our plan was a success. I tried to stop fidgeting while the others finished setting up the dark crystal spell. I was scared. What if mixing the mecca power with the dark crystal caused some kind of explosion? Or turned all of us dark and we joined the dark fae? What if it tainted the mecca itself? There were so many risks.

Violet reached out and briefly swiped her hand across mine, only enough contact for a fleeting spark between us. "Baladar said it was a good plan. I trust him."

I nodded, managing to keep my feet still. I trusted Baladar too, but it was a queen's job to worry about her people.

Violet crossed over to Nikoli. He turned straight to her, as if he'd been aware of what she was doing the entire time. She leaned into him.

"Are you sure?" she whispered.

He nodded, his expression softening. Violet's did the opposite. Her back straightened and she shifted away from him, stepping back. Her face was carefully blank — she was shutting him out, afraid of losing him, which was very unlike Violet. She normally threw caution to the wind. Her time in the Winter Court had destroyed a piece of her childlike innocence, the part of her I'd always adored the most. Instinct was telling me that I needed to have a heart-to-heart with my best friend; she couldn't keep burying it inside.

After we survived this, of course.

Kade's comforting presence pressed in behind me, and I was thankful that the necklaces didn't seem to interfere in our bond. I could still feel him as strong as always in my mind. Gently spinning me around, he cupped my face with both hands, pressing a kiss to my forehead. It was so sweet that I let out a deep sigh, enjoying that moment of pure bliss.

As he pulled back he said, "I'll stay close to Nikoli, in case he needs help controlling the mecca."

I wasn't at all surprised. Nikoli was a close friend of his. Like me and Violet, they had known each other most of their lives. He would not let his friend face the darkness alone. His ability to filter mecca, allowing only little pieces to leak through, was a powerful weapon. It still made me nervous, though.

"Be careful. If it's gets too crazy, just stop. We will find another way. There is always another way." Both of my hands lifted to press against his, which were still on my face.

He nodded, but before he could say anything more, Baladar's voice boomed across the large room. "Okay, time for you all to leave and wait in the hall. Kade and Nikoli are the only ones to remain in here." He moved away from his position behind the round copper pot; the book was inside it, just waiting for the powder to be added.

All of us leaving had been Kade's idea, in case the spell went awry and lashed out. It was smart, but shutting those doors on my mate and his magic born, leaving them with that evil book, was physically painful. I blew Kade one last kiss and he gave me a wink. I loved his confidence; it always seemed to make my worries lessen. But ... there was nothing that could make them disappear completely.

Especially when he shut off the bond between us, erecting those mental blocks we rarely used.

We walked a few feet down the hall. I wanted to be close enough to get to them quickly if they needed help. Minutes passed with no sound, no change in the energy around us ... not even a change in scent. Then a pop ripped through the air and a heaviness pressed into me. Baladar's eyes widened and Violet took a protective stance in front of me. I quickly quieted my frantic mind and attempted to push into Kade's mind through our bond. He was still shielding me, so I couldn't tell exactly what was going on, but I felt pain and darkness. And a bone chilling evil washing over my mate.

"No!" I screamed, pushing through my friends without thought. I was not letting my mate succumb to that darkness. What I had just felt, that inkling of the dark stone, absolutely terrified

me. It was as bad as being in the presence of the dark fae.

Worse actually, because this time, it was Kade who felt like the Dark Fae Lord.

Violet latched on to my arm, trying to hold me back. "Let go, Vi!" I gave her a look that said if she didn't let me go I would never forgive her. Her eyes locked on mine for a few long moments, and she swallowed hard, loosening her grip on me. I ran for the double doors, kicking them open. I felt for that wild magic inside of me, bringing it closer to the surface as I readied myself for anything.

Nikoli was hunched over the book on the ground and Kade stood behind him, his back to me, and both of his arms in the air. Every vein and muscle in Kade's back and arms were bulging as he used all of the strength within him to contain the giant, black, oily ball of hell that had opened above Nikoli's head. Nikoli was chanting, and with a final word he slammed the book shut and the black oil pushed against my mate.

Kade's feet began dragging backwards as if someone were bulldozing him across the room. I stood there frozen, terrified, and unsure of what to do. It was only when Nikoli turned around and looked up at the blob, muttering a curse word, that I spurred into action.

My magic vibrated inside of me, so alive I could feel it like a tangible thing, with a scream I threw everything I had at the ball, focusing mostly on the spell-breaking side, since I had no idea what this ball of darkness was — but it felt like a spell.

Baladar, who must have followed me in, did the same. The mixed hues of purple and deep blue of my magic lashed out and saturated the dark mass, covering it like a magical cocoon. I stumbled as the room shook, a roaring filling my ears until I could hear nothing else. Somehow I stayed on my feet, funneling more of my magic at the thing. The roar then turned to a shrill whine. I was about to cover my ears when all noise abruptly cut off. There was an eerie silence for two heartbeats ... then the ball exploded.

Kade was blown backwards, and using every ounce of my shifter abilities — howls rocked my chest as my wolf rose up, ready to save her mate — I sprinted and dived forward just in time to break his fall with my body. He slammed into me with such force that it knocked the wind out of me.

He was off me in a moment, and I reached across his chest to take his face in my hands. "Are you okay?" I asked him frantically, searching for any injuries.

A shadow moved across those stunning eyes, and for a moment the color wavered from its normal bronze to something more like a murky brown. By the time I blinked again it was gone, and the swirling copper tones were back.

"I'm fine, Ari," he said, almost breathless. That dark mass had exploded with such huge force, he'd been launched across the room. My aching ribs could attest to that.

Needing more confirmation, I latched onto the mate bond again, pressing into Kade's energy. The block between us had eased, but he wasn't completely open either. From the flickers of information I was getting, he did seem to be okay. I couldn't sense any major injury or pain, so ... I'd accept what he said. For now.

Baladar knelt down and ran a hand up Kade's arm, but before he got further than the bear's shoulder, Kade pushed him away. "I'm fine. I promise." He dismissed us by turning to Nikoli.

"Did you get a location on the stone?"

I exchanged a quick glance with Baladar. The ancient magic born wore a blank expression. Something told me he had as many thoughts and worries going on as I did.

Nikoli, whose face was pale and strained, nodded. "The other crystal is in Boston, but so is the Dark Fae Lord. He's one step ahead of us."

Shit.

None of us wasted another second. We grabbed whatever stuff we thought we would need for a few days and we piled into a black Suburban.

"We'll keep an eye on everything here," Baladar said to me through the car window. There had been an argument about who was staying behind. No one wanted that job, but it was almost as important to keep an eye on the royal estate. Calista and Baladar eventually took the role.

As hard as it was to leave the powerful magic born behind, I needed him to protect Calista and my city. Normally, it was a three to four hour drive to Boston. The speed we were planning on going, it would likely be much faster. But still, I wouldn't get back quickly if anything happened.

"Hopefully we'll return home by tomorrow at the latest," I said to my advisor, who had a worried look in her eyes. She leaned in and gave me a kiss on the cheek, stepping back so that Kade could back the car out of the huge underground garage.

Jen, Monica, and Victor waved from where they stood with Baladar. It had been hard to convince them to stay behind too, but with this being a magical matter, facing a dark fae and all, I thought it best to keep our group small, limited to those who could harness the mecca. Even though mecca magic didn't work directly on the dark fae, there were other things they could do to help me. They could also defend themselves against any others who might be waiting to attack.

I refused to lose any more of my dominants. Not today. I would just have to hope that between Kade, Violet, Nikoli, Rowan, Finn, Nix, and me we had enough firepower.

Thankfully, we beat the traffic and made great time. Conversation was stilted, most of us lost in our own thoughts. Finn snoozed in the back; Nix was travelling in the air since a giant eagle was one too many in the SUV.

When we were about ten minutes outside of Boston on the I-93, Kade met Nikoli's eyes in the rearview. "Where to now?" he asked.

Kade had been quiet and closed off the entire drive, even more so than the rest of us. Which I chalked up to lack of sleep and stress. The bond between us was open … kinda. I could feel him there, and everything seemed okay. Sleep and stress, it had to be that.

Nikoli leaned forward. "In the town of Somerville there's a park called Baxter Riverfront Park. It's right on the Mystic River. The crystal is in the water there."

An apt name for a river hiding a magical crystal.

I turned to see him better. "So it's actually *in* the water?" I remembered the wolf council telling me that the original queen found our mecca stone in the water too.

He nodded. "Apparently everyone knows better than to swim in this river. It has claimed multiple lives, and the water is said to be tainted."

Sounded about right. And it looked like one of us was going to have to go swimming in broad daylight in front of a bunch of humans to retrieve this thing. And if it was anything like the crystal in the book, it was going to be evil and try to corrupt us all.

Violet had been in the back, squished next to Finn for the entire drive, working on some type of protective magical case for it, but we had to get it out of the water first.

"You think it's possible the fae lord already has it?" I pondered aloud.

Kade was the one to answer. "No. He has a general idea of the area, but is waiting for us to show up for its exact location."

I gave my mate a side glance. He had sounded so sure when he said that, like he … knew. But how could he possibly know that? His instincts were sharp, of course, but this felt like more than instinct.

"I hope you're wrong about part of that at least," I finally said, trying to swallow my unease. I didn't address the fact that Kade was not acting like himself, because I was afraid deep down to acknowledge that this might be fallout from filtering the dark energy.

Kade nodded. "I hope he's not there too. It would be nice to get in and out without drama."

He reached forward and plugged the Baxter Riverfront Park into the GPS. As we drove through the city, passing families and young children, a thought came to me.

I spun around and faced Rowan just as Kade was pulling the large SUV into a parking spot at the park. "When we do our training, you create a dome so the humans can't see. Is there any chance you can make one big enough to hide us today?"

Rowan smiled. "No problem."

I exhaled the breath I had been holding. If the Dark Fae Lord showed up and there was a fight in broad daylight, in public, it could turn into a magical bloodbath. I needed to hide us, and protect the humans. We couldn't be worrying about that when we were fighting for our lives.

Luckily, the park and the bridge that looked over the Mystic River were pretty deserted, and as soon as I opened the door I knew why. It was freezing outside. Fall had descended on the east coast, and mercifully made this park uninhabited for our excursion, deserted except for an old man fishing on a bench. A quick scan told me that no stag-horned dark fae was milling about, but the knot in my stomach didn't ease. As we all huddled together, Kade wrapped an arm around me; his warmth was like plunging into a bath.

Thanks, mate. I used our bond.

Always.

Well, that was more like my Kade. Maybe the dark energy that had been bothering him was dissipating. It made sense that it would take some time to be cleansed fully from his aura.

I patted my blade, relieved to feel it in my thigh holster. I also had a gun tucked in my waistband. All hidden by my thick trench coat. The weapons would do little against the Dark Fae Lord, but just having them on me made me feel more secure, more in control.

Kade straightened, and turned to look out over the water. "I sense it," he growled. That sick feeling in my gut flared to life.

"What?" My voice was low and controlled, but on the inside I was screaming. "What do you mean you *sense* it?"

Rowan and Violet were already moving to start the wards to block us from everyone except the man fishing on the bench. He was too close and would be inside our barrier, so he would see whatever he saw, and there was nothing we could do about that.

Kade broke his trance with the lake and met my eyes. "It has an energy signature similar to the mecca. Now that I've connected once, I can feel it."

What he said sounded logical, but ... I was still worried.

"Then lead the way." I shrugged, acting as nonchalant as him. The sooner we got the stone, the sooner we could get the hell out of here.

Kade walked slowly along the river's edge with his left hand out, as if he was skimming the energy of the water.

"It's powerful," he said, and I didn't like the tone of his voice. It wasn't fear I detected, it was interest. He was intrigued with this power, and I was really starting to regret our plan to read the book. We had no choice now, we had to follow through and get that stone first, but that didn't mean I was happy about it all.

Violet peeked over my shoulder. "I can probably do a spell to bring it up out of the water, so no one has to go swimming."

Just as I was thinking that was a fantastic idea, Nikoli interjected: "No, it's far too dangerous. I won't risk you."

Violet put a hand on her hip. "Do you know any water retrieval spells?"

Nikoli's jaw hardened; he stared her down for a few moments, before finally saying, "No."

Violet looked to Rowan. "You?"

Rowan shrugged. "I can make portals in water, but I can't pull up objects I haven't seen or touched."

Violet smiled. "Then it's settled."

That was my best friend. Not exactly humble in her gifts. "Be careful, Vi," I told her.

After seeing that giant blob of darkness, and how it had pushed my mountain of a mate across the room, it gave me the chills to think of Violet using her magic to connect with it. But if she wanted to try, I wasn't going to stop her. Nikoli was going to learn something I already knew: Violet wasn't a fan of being told what to do.

He still tried one final time. "If you absolutely insist on this, then ... pull it up, but please don't touch it. You're ... too important."

A man telling Violet what to do would normally earn them a black eye, but not this man. Her face softened the slightest bit and I knew his concern had touched her.

"Fine." She gestured to the case she had in her other hand. "I'll guide Lucifer right in here and won't touch it."

A garbled laugh mixed with a snort escaped me. "Lucifer?"

Violet smirked. "We need to name it, right? Seems fitting."

It was fitting and depressing. We were pulling a crystal that had earned the name Lucifer out of the lake. Life had really reached a low point. Violet and Kade started to walk toward a bridge that went out onto the water. The rest of us followed but stayed on the shore, keeping an eye out for the fae lord.

I leaned into Rowan. "Do you sense him?" I was pretty sure I'd pick up on his unique, frosty energy. It had a heaviness to it that acted like chloroform on my aura, suppressing it.

She looked around, unsure. "I sense a lot of dark fae magic in that water. It could be him or the crystal."

I was sensing the same thing. At least it appeared the fishing man had packed up and left. Now there were no onlookers, I felt safe in unhooking my blade, settling it comfortably into my right hand. It eased my nerves the slightest bit, even if the weapon was useless. Violet was standing halfway along the bridge now, hands outstretched. Kade was directing her by pointing to something in the water. Violet had an affinity for water magic. She'd been the genius to think up the spell to enchant the water around the royal houses so the fae could not use them as portals. I hoped she knew what she was doing now, because I had the horrible feeling we were making all kinds of wrong decisions when it came to this darkness.

"Was there anything else in the book?" I asked Nikoli, who had his gaze pinned on Violet.

"No," he said without turning away, "there was only the spell of location retrieval. All of the other pages were blank. It was like … it only showed me what it believed I needed to know."

I shivered. That was really creepy. I didn't like it when magic objects thought for themselves. Too unpredictable. Unable to stand still, I crossed even closer to the bridge, and just as I was about to step onto it I felt a new cold darkness sweep in. Rowan met my gaze, and I gave her a nod. It was the Dark Fae Lord.

Doing a half spin, I looked all around the park and the adjoining water, and saw no one. Nix screeched in the sky and I was reminded that our familiars were doing patrol. I connected to Finn.

Anything out there, buddy?

His reply was instant. *Negative. And Nix says the sky is clear. All areas of the perimeter are secure. But I sense a dark energy coming from the lake.*

Shit.

Be careful. I'll be there in a moment. He ended our mental conversation.

I turned my attention to the lake. "He's in the water," I murmured to those around me.

All of us took a step forward, the icy water lapping close to our feet. I wasn't sure who saw it first, but as soon as the water's ripples grew in size, all of us were paying close attention. The dark energy was getting stronger. I let out a yell as two horns broke the lake's surface.

"Kade … Vi … you better hurry up!" I shouted, not taking my eyes off those growing swells.

I already had my fae and mecca energy mingling ferociously within me, my wolf inside pressing her own brand of energy to the front as well. Even though I was stronger in my human form when it came to magic, her strength still helped fuel me.

Rowan and Nikoli stepped in on either side of me.

"We need to keep him away from them," I said, as more of his head appeared. He slowly rose, water trailing off him, his long black robes flowing out behind him, swirling through the dark icy water. He held his staff, the black crystal at the top sparkling in the dull light.

His eyes locked on Violet, who was churning energy through the water, causing a small whirlpool.

"Hey!" I shouted, bringing his gaze to me. "You and I have a little score to settle."

Chapter Eight

Who you gonna call? Darkness Destroyer.

HE STARED AT me, and I wasted no time slapping out with my energy the way I had been learning with Rowan, letting my fae-side take the lead, because mecca magic had no effect on him. The dark fae faced me fully, so at least none of his attention was on Kade and Violet.

He jabbed forward with his staff, countering my attack with one of his own. Our energy met in the middle, sending out an explosion of light and power.

Ari, be careful! Kade's voice was briefly in my head, but there was no time to reply.

Two erchos burst from the water on either side of the dark fae, hovering in the air. *Well, shit.* Things just got real. Rowan, Nikoli, and I ran along the bridge, heading closer to Kade and Violet so we could defend them.

The erchos let out a screech, which sent waves of pain through my ears, but Nikoli, after muttering a spell, did something that dulled some of the effect. I kept half of my attention locked on their dark oiliness — a blot in the gray skies. The other half was on the Dark Fae Lord. He had a grin on his face now, that creepy, sardonic, psycho smile he did so well.

"Last chance to join me, Ari."

His shout echoed across the water, and I responded with another blast of energy, which he lazily blocked. He then waved his two creatures on. They came straight for us, but thankfully, we had reached the others by now. We could stop running, and start fighting.

"Remember that drill we practiced, Arianna," Rowan said in a rush. "Where I boost your powers with my own for an attack spell."

I nodded, understanding immediately where she was going. This was what Violet did in the Otherworld, when she had made the eternal fire. We had been practicing this as well as spell breaking.

I summoned my winter fae magic, focusing on filling my center with ice, and just as I was about to fling it free, Rowan latched onto my forearm. The moment she wrapped her hands around me, it was like I had stuck my hand onto a pure source of power. It jolted through my veins and I released the spell, aiming for the two erchos. They tried to avoid my blast, but with the extra boost, my range was wide, spreading out across the water. There was nowhere for them to go.

I wasn't sure what to expect. I had refused to freeze any living beings when we practiced. It had been a potted plant, a few stuffed animals, and the pool. All of which had been a success — after a few attempts.

I didn't have a few attempts this time, so I sent everything I had at them. Thankfully, the ice wrapped around them as I had hoped would happen, freezing both of them in the air. I held the magic for a few beats, letting them plunge deep into the water. I had no idea if they could withstand a full body freezing ... or hold their breath indefinitely ... but I had bought us some time at least.

The Dark Fae Lord looked unperturbed, walking along the top of the water, closing the distance to Violet's swirling portal. My friend's face was lined with strain, veins standing out across her pale skin, even throbbing in her forehead. I leaned closer, careful not to touch her. The second crystal was visible just below the surface of the murky lake; whatever she was doing was working. Slowly.

As more of it emerged, I realized that it wasn't just a dark crystal. It was another staff. There was a gold filigree of vines wrapped around the base of the stone, and it looked like that gold metal extended down into the water.

The dark fae eyed the second staff greedily, looking between it and his own dark piece over and over. So there were two staffs and two books. Seemed someone had created these weapons long ago, and left the books with the unique slivers of stone so that if the staff was ever lost, someone could find it. *Evil bastard.*

Was this the work of the God obsessed with fairness? Was he represented by the inverted tree carved into the book? Or was there another being from long ago who created the staffs? How had the Red Queen even gotten the book? I felt like these were questions I would never have the answers to. And in reality, it didn't matter. All that mattered was that the staffs existed, and one of them was being used to threaten my people.

I could not let him have the other one.

My fae energy had frozen the part of the river where the erchos had fallen. The Dark Fae Lord stepped on that ice, moving more rapidly as the second staff broke the surface of the water. It seemed the more of it that emerged, the harder Violet was having to work to lift it.

Violet groaned. "It's stuck. He's countering me."

"We need to get that staff before he does," I said, positioning myself in front of her. "It could be the difference in our success or failure in this war."

Kade was still on her other side, helping direct her energy. "We won't let him have it," he said, and before I could stop him he chucked off his jacket and dove into the water.

"No, Kade!" I screamed. No, no, no! What the heck was he doing? If the Dark Fae Lord didn't kill him, I might after he pulled that stunt.

The dark fae paused, hovering above the water, only a dozen or so feet from us. He seemed to be staring down into the shadowy churning water, clearly waiting for the bear shifter to appear. We were all waiting, but the water was dark and choppy, and the waves my mate had created when he had jumped had obscured the staff.

"What is he doing?" Violet sounded mildly panicked; I could see she was losing her magical control on the staff. The strain on her face was increasing, until all of a sudden she stumbled back, her hands falling to her sides.

She turned wide, unblinking eyes on me.

"What!" I asked her panicked.

"Kade has the staff." The words had barely left her lips when Kade broke the surface of the water, staff in hand.

What in the hell? I'd said we needed the staff because I wanted everyone to be prepared for a fight. Not because I wanted my idiot mate to jump in and grab it with his bare hands.

What are you doing? I asked through our bond, receiving no answer. From what I could sense, all of his concentration was on holding that staff and trying to swim at the same time.

The dark fae grinned and held his free hand out, raising it up into the air. My mate rose up out of the water. *Oh shit.* Kade had no idea how to control the dark magic contained within that staff, but this fae had a lot of practice, and he currently had control over my mate.

Before I could freak out completely, Rowan leaned in and whispered, "I can create a portal behind the fae if you can get Kade to shove him in."

I nodded, my movements jagged, before I mentally reached for my bond with Kade. Chills broke out on my arms. In the few seconds since I had checked last, there was now a dark cloying energy coating his end of our bond. It was not hugely surprising, considering he was holding a dark magical staff, but it had infiltrated rather quickly. I pushed through the darkness, feeling it reaching out for me.

Kade, drop that thing.

No. We need it, was his short reply.

He was right, but what if he was inviting the darkness in permanently? We didn't need it that bad that I would sacrifice any part of Kade's goodness for it.

Rowan is opening a portal behind him. You need to push the fae into it, I said. The sooner he got rid of the dark fae, the sooner he could let that staff go.

Kade just nodded before kicking me out and closing our bond down tight. A damp heat sprang to my eyes, my throat and chest tight as I rasped in a breath. He'd never done that before, kicked me out so violently. I knew it was to protect me but ... it hurt. It physically and mentally hurt.

I recovered with a few deep breaths, ignoring the lingering twinges of pain to focus on the scene in the water. The fae, who still had his power wrapped around Kade, closed his hands into tight fists, and Kade's feet skimmed across the water, gliding towards the fae at an alarming speed.

I could have used my ability to break spells and free my mate, but he needed to get closer to the fae to knock him in. So all I could do was watch. I saw Kade's hand slip up behind his shirt, pulling free his twelve-inch serrated hunting blade. His other hand was still grasping the staff.

Rowan was spinning her hands next to me, murmuring low words. A swirling circle was opening up just behind the dark fae's feet, partially hidden by the choppy waters. Kade, was now mere feet from the Dark Fae Lord.

"I believe you have something that belongs to me," the dark fae told Kade.

The bear let out a low growl, swinging his knife around and slashing out at the fae's neck. The Dark Fae Lord must have seen the blade coming, because he ducked his head down, jerking it toward my mate, goring him in the rib cage with one of his horns. Kade's knife sliced right through the other one of the horns; black oil spilled out of the severed end. Kade had to drop the blade as the fae grabbed for the staff, both of them struggling with it.

Kade had the advantage, physical strength far beyond the fae. But the fae had the other staff, and he was still using it to limit Kade's movement.

I gathered as much of my winter magic as I could, feeling the slightest tendrils of fatigue kicking in. I had used a lot of energy already today, and we had barely started. I aimed for the Dark Fae Lord's staff, letting my icy energy fly. The second it slammed into the dark crystal, breaking the spell holding Kade in place, I shouted, "Kick him in!"

The ice on the lake was pretty much gone now; it had only been the fae lord keeping them above the water. When I broke the spell, Kade immediately started to sink, but he had enough time to lift his big foot and connect with the fae's stomach, sending him flying backward into the open portal. With a loud yell, the Fae Lord cursed as he fell through, and immediately the portal sealed.

Kade groaned, and my wolf almost burst free from my chest when he clutched his stomach and disappeared into the frigid water.

I leapt off the bridge without a second thought; the moment the icy water hit my skin I had to fight the urge to take in a deep breath out of shock from the cold.

Pulling myself together, I ignored the calls of my friends and Finn in my head, and instead headed straight for the last place I'd seen Kade. Following the trail of blood and oil that coated the surface of the lake in that spot.

The water was deep, and I had almost no visibility when I was a few feet down. I kicked and pushed harder, blindly feeling around for Kade. Just when I thought I was going to have to surface again, my lungs screaming for air, my hands brushed against something solid. Hoping whatever I was holding was Kade and not a piece of trash or wood, I sent some fae and mecca magic out, using it to propel us to the surface.

When my head broke through, I took in a huge gasping breath, hauling the heavy weight up. Relief and panic warred within me as Kade's pale features became visible. Mercifully, he coughed out a mouthful of water, but was still unconscious. I could feel the pulsing of dark energy within him, and as I pulled him farther up, the staff popped up at his side. It was hooked in the arm of his sleeve, floating along beside him.

Well, that was a lucky break. With the last of my energy, I towed him to the shore, where our friends were waiting. Nikoli and Violet pulled him up and I crawled out of the water, teeth chattering.

"W-w-why is he unconscious?" I asked Violet. "We need to wake him, t-t-the d-d-d—"

The chattering got so bad I couldn't get words "Dark Fae Lord" out. But everyone understood.

"The wound." Violet turned worried eyes on me. "He's fighting it. His body has shut down to try and expel the dark energy."

The wound inflicted from the oily horn. Violet slammed her hands down on his chest, sending out a burst of energy, like a defibrillator to his heart. Kade's eyes shot open, then with a roar he was on his feet, icy water flinging off him in large arcs. Violet stumbled back; Nikoli caught her before she hit the ground.

I stood in front of them both, in case Kade was about to lose it. He had the staff in his hand again. Somehow he had snatched it up from where it lay beside him as he jumped.

"What happened? Where is the dark fae?" he asked, and I was relieved that his voice sounded somewhat normal, not as rage-filled as that bellow.

"Y-y-you pushed him into Rowan's portal," I reminded him

Violet stepped forward, and I felt her hand press into my back. A wave of heat filled me. My clothes dried in an instant, and I was warm enough to be able to halt my chattering teeth. I still felt the chill to my bones, but I could at least talk now. "What happened, Kade? Why did you drop in the water?"

He shook his head a few times, his face crumpling as he lifted his free hand to rub at his forehead. "I can't remember ... he gored me, and then my head went cloudy."

"I think you need to drop that stone now." Rowan was moving cautiously, acting almost as worried as she had been with the dark fae.

Kade's eyes flicked to the staff, moving up to the stone at the top. It was like he had forgotten

he was holding it. "Shouldn't I keep a hold of it until we can get it back to the royal estate? He might return for it."

"You need to drop it," Rowan said again, and I was silently begging him to hand it over. He had to be able to let it go. I felt it in my soul that if he couldn't, we would be in trouble. Some of the agony on my face must have registered with him. He watched me for a few moments, then he slowly lowered the staff.

The moment he lost contact with it, he seemed to lose the small amount of strength he had, crumpling to the ground. Violet hurried to him, pulling her special box from a bag she had slung across her body. It was only large enough to enclose the head of the staff, but hopefully was enough to keep the evil somewhat contained.

"Are you okay?" I dropped to his side, and he let out a pained chuckle, reaching up to push back a few strands of my now dry hair.

I didn't like how pale his bronze skin was looking, chalky almost.

Violet flung herself down beside us, drying his clothes at the same time she said, "That's a dark magic wound. I can't heal it until we get back to the castle, but ... at the rate it's advancing, it will kill him long before then."

No!

"How much time do I have?" Kade rasped out.

Violet lifted his shirt, exposing the deep ragged gash. It was seeping a black and fizzing fluid, like his blood was having a chemical reaction to the darkness.

She shook her head. "I'm not sure. This is like nothing I've seen before. Maybe a few minutes. *Shit...*" she cursed. "I need this special powder I have back at home. It's the only thing I can think of which might save him. Counteract the dark poison."

"We're hours from home," I told her, panicking as more color drained from Kade's face. Magic born had limits on how far they could zap themselves, Violet wouldn't make it in time.

Finn pressed to my side, and I dropped my hand into his fur, seeking his comfort. In the air I could hear Nix's call. She sounded like she was weakening also.

Rowan stepped forward. "I can open a temporary portal back to the castle."

Relief flooded through me. It felt like she was offering me a miracle. "Do it, do whatever you need to save him," I said, one of my hands tightly wrapped around Kade's, the other still in Finn's fur.

Violet stood, moving to Rowan's side. Nikoli stepped in on the other side.

"I'll need you to direct me," Rowan added. "I don't know the royal estate like you do, and there will be securities in place to stop what I'm about to try."

Violet nodded. "It's not something a single magic born could do on their own, which is why I didn't think of it, but together we might be able to."

Luckily, the fae seemed to have a special affinity for portals. And I knew these three would come through. They had to. Losing Kade was not an option.

"I will use my magic to open the portal," Rowan instructed. "You can direct the energy to a safe place."

Rowan already had her hands out. Violet touched her arm, then a swirling oval started to form in the air. I was distracted as Kade let out a choked cough.

"I got you, mate," I murmured into his ear. "You just need to hold on a little longer."

In a desperate attempt to stop the dark wound from killing him, I placed my hand over the injury, and sent a few bursts of ice magic into it. Ice would slow the darkness, right? It was the only thing I could think of.

Kade let out a low groan as the blue energy slipped into the cut. A coating of frost formed over the top of the black blood, halting the oozing.

"Portal is ready," Nikoli said. Between the two of us, we got Kade to his feet, Nikoli taking most of his weight.

Kade shook his head; his words were labored. "Still ... kick your ass, Nik."

"Sure, sure," the magic born teased him as the two of us half-carried Kade toward the shimmery portal. I appreciated the little banter, even though I was still internally freaking out. *What if Violet can't find the powder? What if it doesn't work? What if the dark fae have some sort of special, never-before-seen darkness?* The worries spun round and round in my head, and even being warm and dry again, thanks to Violet's magic, the chilling my veins persisted.

Rowan and Violet stood on either side of the portal, clearly waiting for us to go through first.

"Good idea with the ice magic," Violet said, leaning forward to probe the wound through the hole in his shirt. "It has slowed the darkness. We should have time."

We'd better have time. I was not accepting any other outcome. By the time we stepped through the magic and out into my office, Nikoli and I were carrying Kade completely. I only made it a few more steps before we had to lower him to the ground.

"Dude has to be three hundred pounds of muscle, doesn't he?" I groaned.

Kade's lips twitched; sweat had broken out along his brow and neck.

"I'll be right back," Violet shouted as she disappeared in an instant. I hadn't even seen her exit the portal.

Finn, with Nix on his back, waited on the edge of the room, both watching with their calm, ancient eyes. Rowan immediately dropped down to Kade's side. She held her hands out over him, hovering a few inches from his chest, before closing her eyes and breathing in and out slowly.

"We're losing him," she said a minute later. "You're going to have to send more ice into his veins. The ice magic can counteract the darkness. It's a myth that winter magic is evil. It is neutral, like most energy. It depends on the wielder. Ice magic can be a very positive force in the universe."

I swallowed hard, my throat and mouth dry. "How do I help him without hurting him?" Freezing him to death was as big a problem as the darkness killing him.

"Like in training, you need to send out the magic and guide it through Kade. Sense his inner power, find his energy within, and chase the darkness out. Freeze it from affecting him further."

Oh sure. Easy peasy. I might be learning how to control the magic, but I was still rough. This would require finesse and precision, and since it was Kade's life I was messing with, I could not screw it up. After a really quick internal pep talk, I reached out and placed my hands on Kade's chest.

The darkness felt like it was everywhere now, which was no doubt why he was fading away.

Stay with me, baby.

It was becoming so easy to push the mecca down now, to capture only that part of my power that had been unlocked in the Otherworld. The icy energy responded in an instant, gliding with a wisp of frost through my body and into my hands.

"You know you could have countered the chill of that icy water," said Rowan, surprising me. My eyes flew open to meet hers. "You have to embrace that side of yourself. You never need to fear the cold again."

Good to know, but not today. Today I needed to deal with Kade. She apologized for interrupting me, and I gave her a nod, closing my eyes again. I could tell the thought had randomly come to mind and she'd done a Violet with blurting it out.

Breathing deeply, I let the chilly magic seep out of my body and into Kade. I used our bond to follow the path of darkness through his bright inner essence. I fought back tears when I

brushed against the black energy. It was like a spider web, sticky, connected in multiple parts.

I sent my power into the main gathering of darkness and his body jerked, before settling down again. Remaining connected to his chest, and to my magic, I continued to pour my power into him, following as it slipped through his chest and deeper into his body.

I brushed against familiar energy – his mecca power. Our mate bond was thrumming in that part of his center. My chest ached so badly that it felt like someone had just stabbed me in it. Being shut away from him, feeling the faltering beats of his heart, I could barely function.

But I needed to, for Kade.

More darkness brushed across my power then, and I immediately reacted with force, slapping out, using an attack of ice to send it reeling away. I followed as it fled, and as I closed in on Kade's center, I realized there was an even larger mass of black, oily energy there. It was sending those tendrils all through Kade's body, cutting off his organs, tainting his blood to a thick, dark sludge.

NO! I screamed through our bond. *You cannot have him. He's mine.*

I pushed at the energy, trying to dislodge it from him, but there was nowhere for it to go. If anything, I was sending it closer to the bright light that made up my mate's soul. I stopped pushing, knowing that chasing the energy around was not going to save him. I needed to remove it from him. Somehow.

Maybe instead of pushing ... I could pull it from him. Siphon some of the darkness into myself. Knowing time was running out, his breathing ragged and weak, I reversed my tactic and latched onto the darkness, freezing it to my magic and pulling it through the bond back into me. I thought it would resist me, wanting to stay with Kade, but it slid easily from his energy center to mine. The moment it touched my magical essence, I flinched. This darkness felt foreign ... the complete opposite of the light which my mecca and fae magic was built on. My instinct was to stop, bring no more of that tainted energy into me, but I had to save Kade. With gritted teeth, I fought on, pulling it deeper into me. In a surge of power, my winter and mecca magic rose up around the inky tendrils and it ... disappeared. My icy fae magic was consuming it, transmuting it into ... nothing.

"I got it!" Violet screamed, jarring me. My eyes snapped open and my hands fell from Kade.

I immediately ran my gaze across his face, relieved to see his coloring was better, less pale, and he was no longer sweating. His breathing even seemed smoother. I searched inside of myself and didn't sense any lingering darkness. What had I done? Had I really just brought some of the darkness into myself and ... consumed it? Or did I heal it? Transform it into light? Was any of that possible?

Violet was already crouched by Kade, popping the top off a vial of swirling pink potion. She pinched his jaw and poured the concoction into his mouth, leaving a few drops in the bottom to pour over his wound. Then she placed a hand to his chest, closing her eyes briefly. "I sense that it's less serious than I originally feared." She sounded surprised. "With his strength, he should recover easily."

I didn't say anything because my emotions were a mess of shock and disbelief. Had I actually done that to the darkness? How was it even possible? Maybe I was just in the right place at the right time. I would hate for everyone to rely on me to do something like that again. It could have been a fluke.

I decided it was better to keep it to myself until I had time to explore it further.

Moments passed, none of us taking our eyes from Kade, and I thought I would go mad waiting for him to wake. I felt him in our bond a moment before he took a deep, gasping breath, and his eyes snapped open.

"Ari..."

My name was a breathless sigh on his lips. My heart clenched, and the thought of how close I had come to losing him to the darkness had a hot dampness filling my eyes.

"I'm here," I whispered, forcing myself to hold back those tears.

Violet ripped Kade's shirt open, exposing the tan muscled flesh there. I was relieved to see that besides a small section of frostbitten skin, there was no more leaking darkness. Violet let out a happy sigh, and I took that as a good sign.

Kade, who was yet to take his eyes from me, reached out and pulled me gently into him. He took a big whiff of my hair, his voice hoarse as he said, "I couldn't smell you. Couldn't sense you. I was..."

"Shhh," I said, before pressing my lips to his over and over. He returned the kisses as frantically. "You're okay. You're okay." I continued murmuring, unable to calm my frazzled brain. I had almost lost my mate. It was not something I could compute.

Eventually I helped Kade sit up. His color continued to improve, and by the time he was propped against a nearby wall, he almost looked to be back to his robust self. He turned toward Nix and she took flight, which caused a gust of wind in the small space. She landed on his bare outstretched arm and immediately nuzzled her giant beaked head into his neck.

I knew they were having their own private conversation. No one said a word. They needed this moment. Eventually, Kade turned back and looked at Violet. "Where's the crystal staff?" he asked.

Violet raised one eyebrow. "Eager to be near death again?"

He gave her an exasperated kind of stare. "Ha. Ha. No. I'm eager to learn how to control it so we can destroy that fae lord and then destroy the staffs. I already have a pretty good idea of what I need to do to learn how to control it. Something about its magic is similar to the mecca. I just need a decent amount of time working with it."

His desire made me uncomfortable. I didn't want him anywhere near that thing. Who knew if all that darkness inside was just from being gored by the Dark Fae Lord. What if the staff contributed too?

"So you plan to destroy it?" I questioned him.

Kade met my stare without flinching. "Yes, but no doubt I will have to use it first. We need it to defeat the dark fae."

Nikoli clapped a hand on Kade's back. "That's dangerous, My King. I must advise against it."

I breathed a sigh of relief, glad I wasn't the only one who had a problem with this.

Kade's features flattened into hard lines, the look he wore when someone was pissing him off and he was about to go all king on their ass. "Advisement noted." His words were clipped. "But the next time the fae lord shows up and controls my entire body with the flick of his wrist, I'm going to be able to fight back."

"He's right." Baladar's voice came from behind us and I wondered how long he had been standing there. "This staff ... controlling it ... may be our only chance to truly defeat the Dark Fae Lord."

I wanted to argue, but I sensed that now wasn't the time. Besides, Baladar was probably right. Still, why did it have to be Kade?

As if he had heard me, Kade directed his next words at me: "I will focus on killing the Dark Fae Lord with the staff. You focus on destroying the winter queen with your magic. It's the only way we can win this war and live in happiness with Winnie."

His mention of my little sister hit me like he had punched me in the chest. The picture he painted left an aching need in its wake. I wanted that happy ending for all of us.

"Okay," I said, resigned.

"I'll work with him," Baladar stated. "We will not let the fae lord, or the dark crystal, win."

I trusted Baladar, he knew a lot about dark magic, and his reassurance made me feel a little less anxious about the entire thing. In all honesty, we needed someone to match the Dark Fae Lord's strength, and if anyone could do it, it was Kade. He would pay whatever cost for the chance to save us all. But I wasn't okay with that. There had to be a way for us to win without sacrificing our souls. I would keep Kade protected while he was busy protecting everyone else.

Calista popped up in the doorway, her eyes finding mine. "Sorry for the interruption, but I need to speak with Arianna." She sounded so formal I nearly laughed. All protocol had gone out the window lately, but Calista was finding it a hard habit to break.

I reached over and squeezed Kade's hand. "You okay?"

He nodded. "I'm fine. Go. I'll be with Baladar in the basement."

I tried not to sigh. For now, I had no choice but to trust in my mate and the powerful magic born. Trust that they would respect their limits when playing with darkness. And basically hope for the best.

I followed Calista out of the room and she didn't say a word. We walked in silence until we were alone in the far corridor.

"What is it?" Now I was nervous because my advisor was acting strange. She finally turned to me, a serious expression creasing her face. "It's just a hunch, Ari, but I have this nagging feeling..."

My pulse picked up at the tone in her voice. "Spit it out. You're freaking me out."

Calista started pacing. "I sense that we are making a mistake just waiting for the fae to attack. We're giving them too much power, playing the submissive role. I feel it will be much worse if we keep waiting."

I focused with a hundred percent of my attention. Calista had taught me everything she knew about strategy. She was the best, and her instincts were always spot on. "I think so too," I admitted. "I have been worried about this delay of any sort of serious attack, especially when Prince Caspien has no idea what they are up to."

Calista nodded a few times. "A part of me believes they are gathering intel, maybe sending out a few assassins like those in the pizza shop ... testing the waters ... perfecting their attack."

I interrupted as a thought sprang to mind. "The Dark Fae Lord did say that he wanted to punish the Fall Court. What if he wants to use the shifters to do it? Maybe they're hoping to take Kade and I out behind the scenes, so to speak, and just step into the role of leaders."

Calista tilted her head, not looking convinced. "It's possible. I feel as if the pizza one was designed to make you nervous. Throw you off your game."

Well, it had certainly done that.

"So what should I do?" I asked her. "Should we march our army on the Otherworld? Take our strongest and join the Summer Court? Cut those bastards off before they can get to us, or before they can corrupt our people?"

She looked torn, her eyes drifting to a spot behind me. I knew she'd be running all of the possible scenarios through her head.

"Maybe ... maybe the answer has been there all along," I mused, not giving her time to reply. "Maybe instead of our army going, I go alone into the Otherworld and take their leaders out. Cut off the head, the body will fall too."

Something crazy must have gleamed in my eyes, because Calista sucked in a deep breath. "That's too dangerous, Ari." She shook her head. "I feel like we are missing something important here. A huge piece of the puzzle. If they are trying to take you out, how do they plan on making the shifters fall in line? None of them are going to follow a fae leader who killed their monarch. There has to be another piece."

"There probably is," I growled out, my wolf unhappy. "But I don't think I can wait around any longer to find out."

I continued working through my messy thoughts, letting all of the information mesh in my head. Part of me wished there was someone with more experience I could turn to. Maybe we could phone and ask Annette; she had ruled with her mate for a long time — before he was killed. She was a little too peace-loving though. I needed someone well versed in battle strategy.

I paused. The best person to ask would have been ... the Red Queen. She had been brilliant at battle. It was something she was lauded for daily. Maybe ... there was a way.

"Send Violet to the small library room, please," I said to Calista. She gave me an inquisitive look but I was already moving. "I'm going to see the Red Queen," I called over my shoulder. If she was still trapped in the mecca and I could talk to her through the crystal, then maybe I could get the upper hand in this war.

Chapter Nine

Only losers play the waiting game.

I GOT TO the hall of the small library that hid the mecca stone in no time. The two guards posted outside gave me a half bow and then opened the double doors for me. They were under strict instructions not to let anyone but my core group inside. This stone had to be protected above all else. It might be our greatest weapon in this war.

When the door shut behind me, I took a deep cleansing breath and walked over to pull the book down. I entered the secret passage, making sure to close the door firmly behind me. Now that the balance had been restored, it was almost easy to walk to the stone. Not to mention I was a hell of a lot stronger than I used to be. The pulse of energy within the stone called to me like an old friend, but I resisted the impulse to touch it. I needed Violet here to make sure nothing went wrong, to help me out with transitioning between this world and the mecca one.

I probably didn't really need her help now. I was not a regular shifter, but another thing I had decided to change this time around as queen was acting like I was an island, always having to do it alone.

"Ari!" Violet's voice echoed down the secret tunnel before she emerged in a flurry of orange silk. She must have changed after the lake incident. Her dress was simple but stunning; rows of pearls lined the bodice and extended down through the long lengths. "What are we doing?"

Her eyes were sparkling. Actual real sparkles. It felt like a million years since I had seen true excitement from her. It reminded me I still needed to talk to her about the Otherworld, about everything that had happened, and what she went through. I was determined to make time for it, she was one of my priorities. Maybe after our little journey into the world of mecca.

"I want to contact the Red Queen," I said to her. "Calista and I are worried about this delay from the fae, and frankly I'm done waiting. I want Winnie back. I want to focus on problems of the bear and wolf variety."

Violet nodded slowly. "The delay is kind of weird, but I just figured the fae are weird. That's how I explain everything they do."

"Do you have any idea what Isalinda is up to? Did she ever mention anything..." I was hesitant to ask, not wanting to remind my friend of her time in the Otherworld. But she had the most experience with the winter psychopath.

Violet rubbed her eyes, looking tired and defeated. The sparkle was most definitely gone now. "Honestly, restraint didn't seem to be something she possessed a lot of. She's narcissistic, used to everything being about her. Everything in that court is about her, after all, and she has no concept of others. But ... I believe she wants that dark weapon, and she is clearly prepared to work with the crazy horned fae to get it."

"So she's going to have to act out of character. Follow some of his leads," I mused. I then hurried on and explained my theory about the Dark Fae Lord wanting a shifter army to take out the Fall Court.

"He really hates them, Vi. You should have seen the fury in his eyes."

She sucked in a deep breath, bobbing her head a few times. "Yes, that's got to be it. They're planning something big that will take out you and Kade, all the while trapping the shifters in their sticky web."

Which is why I had to go to them first, take them by surprise. I was just opening my mouth to explain the assassination plan, and why I wanted to try to talk to the Red Queen again, when Violet got distracted by the stone. "Its call is not as strong. It feels … more stable." She took a step closer, placing her hand right onto the faceted side.

Her eyes fluttered closed. "The power is addictive," she murmured.

When she opened her eyes again, she blindsided me with a question. "What if this delay is more than just the fae lord finalizing his plan to puppet our shifters to form an army? What if the winter queen is afraid of taking you head on? She knew something about your power, something which made her want it really badly." Her gaze turned very shrewd. "Did you do something to the darkness inside of Kade?"

I should have known I wouldn't be able to hide that from Violet. She'd clearly put all the information together, and reached a logical conclusion. Pressing my lips tightly together, I wondered how much I should tell her. Judging by the look on her face, I wasn't going to get away with a half answer.

"I don't know what happened, Vi. It kind of seemed like I somehow pulled the dark energy into myself and dissolved it, but ... I'm not sure if that's right or not. Which is why I didn't mention it. I don't want everyone to think I can eat dark energy. I want them to all be cautious around the dark fae and his power."

Her expression didn't change, but her eyes widened. "I have never heard of someone being able to dissolve energy like that ... good or bad. Energy can be shifted, but it never disappears."

I nodded. "I know, which is why there has to be another explanation."

She reached out and almost grabbed my hand, stopping at the last second. We were too close to the mecca stone to have our powers bouncing off each other. "We need to explore this further."

I swallowed hard and nodded. "Yes, I know. But right now I need some advice from the most ruthless leader I have ever known."

We both turned to the stone, and with a deep breath I reached out and placed my hand on it. A burst of familiar mecca power crashed into my center and I felt it swell up within me. I sent my essence into the stone, and from there I could feel all of the lines that connected the mecca to the other stones across this world and the Otherworld.

They were strong and powerful. No more frail, power-drained connections.

"Ignore those lines," Violet advised me. "Search for the heart of this mecca stone. This is the one she tied herself to, this is where the Red Queen is."

The heart? How was I supposed to find that? I brought my focus back to the stone itself, to the point where all lines converged. There was a small shimmery center there, which had caught my eye before. I didn't hesitate; there wasn't time for any sort of uncertainty. I reached out and grabbed Violet's hand, both of us jerking at the shock of power that zipped between us. I was trying to figure out how to plunge myself into that center when something tugged on my energy. It was not a gentle tug either; it whipped me forward, and with a popping sound, a veil of purple washed over my vision. When I opened my eyes again, I was standing on the mecca beach, Violet at my side, our hands still clasped together.

"Holy shifter gods, I'm in a freaking mecca stone." Violet's wide eyes were unblinking as she spun to take in the full scale of the purple landscape. Purple clouds of mecca were washing through us. Waves of purple water crashed on the white sandy beach to my left.

Knowing time was of the essence, I called out, "Red Queen!"

"Ari, maybe—" Violet was cut off by a vision of red coming towards us. The queen looked regal in her flowing red silk dress. The train must have been ten feet long, billowing out behind her. It was a different dress than last time; she clearly had some control over her appearance.

As she got closer she smiled. "You came back," she breathed. I realized then how lonely she must be, stuck here for eternity.

Violet just watched her, mouth agape.

"Yes. I need your advice," I told her honestly.

She was close enough that I could smell her lavender perfume. Everything about her seemed so real. It felt as if we were both alive, just standing on a beach having a conversation.

She reached out as if she wanted to touch me, but then pulled her hand back at the last moment.

"Tell me, child."

I jumped right in. "The winter queen and the Dark Fae Lord have teamed up. They want to take over the Earth-side mecca. We have been waiting for their attack, preparing for a war, but they haven't made a move yet. This is worrying me. I feel as if we are giving them time to set some huge plan into motion."

The Red Queen's face went from ethereal beauty to enraged monarch in seconds. That look was more like the woman I remembered. "How long have you been waiting for this attack?"

"Almost a month," I told her.

A cunning light flickered across her eyes. "You cannot give them any more time. If they are taking this long, then they have much more than a battle planned. You need to go to the Otherworld. You need to take them out first before they succeed at whatever they are working toward."

I wasn't shocked by her advice. It had been what I was thinking all along. I had needed her reassurance, though, that I wasn't acting rashly, that my actions would not end up making it worse for everyone. I wasn't the same sort of ruler the Red Queen was, but that didn't mean her years of experience were not valuable. If she thought seeking to take them out first was a viable option, then it was one worth considering.

Violet paled, as if that was possible, and I could feel her shaking next to me. "No! There has to be another way. We can't go back there! That land is…" Her voice cracked.

Violet went through some horrific torture at the hands of the winter queen. I had seen some of it in our dream sharing. But, in moments like

this, with pain and fear shining in those pale eyes, I saw the true depth of her scars.

I wasn't sure if I should touch her or not, but my arms ached with the need to comfort her. "It's okay, Vi. You don't have to come. I would never expect you to go back there again. You have spent enough time in that world."

She fell silent, wrapping her arms around herself while she looked down at her feet. A pure sort of fury ripped through me. This was what abuse did. It crushed strong and vibrant people into quivering shells. The winter queen did this! She broke the light within my most cherished friend. She would do that to all of my people if I let her, her and the Dark Fae Lord. They would break them all down, crush their souls and spirits. I could never let that happen.

I looked up at the Red Queen and gave her a tight smile. "Thank you. I agree with you, this is the best plan. I must take her out before she has a chance to bring her plan to fruition. Before she has a chance to harm any more of my people."

I would never let them touch my city. My mecca. My shifters. I was going to kill them both. I didn't take murder lightly, but I had to do this for my people. To save us all. Violet shifted her gaze from her feet to the ocean, arms still wrapped around herself. As soon as we got out of here, we were going to have that long conversation. It was time for her to share the burden.

I turned back to the Red Queen. "Thank you for your advice. We must go now. I have an assassination to plan."

Her face was smooth again, but dark shadows slithered across her eyes. I found myself asking, "Are you happy here?"

Some of the passivity faded from her face; she blinked rapidly as if trying to compose herself again. "I thought I would be. To live forever, even if in this state, but..." She let the sentence linger and I nodded.

"If I can find a way to free you ... to set your soul free, I will." I didn't love her. I didn't know her well enough to love her, but she was my biological mother. And she had done more than I realized for me in my life. She had loved me in her own weird way.

She looked taken aback, an expression I had never seen on her face before. I marveled at how different she appeared to be ... less robotic ... less cold. Maybe being stuck here had given her time to reflect on who she was. It was a shame our people couldn't have seen some of her warmer side.

Sucking in a deep breath for fortitude, I turned to Violet. "It's time to go home, Vi."

She pulled her gaze from the ocean, returning from whatever horror was holding her captive in her mind. Her eyes were shadowed and haunted, but she didn't hesitate to reach out and touch me. When her hand came around my forearm, we were pulled back into the mecca crystal room.

Without a word, Violet turned and walked away from the stone, disappearing out into the library room. I followed her.

"Violet," I said, but she continued walking fast toward the door. "Violet!" I shouted this time. She paused, her back rigid as her shoulders shook. Finally she turned to face me, tears spilling down her cheeks.

My heart was aching so hard it felt like someone had punched my chest in. "Tell me," I begged her.

She bit her bottom lip and stared at me, those tears still silently tracing her porcelain cheeks. When her breathing turned into ragged gasps, I stepped forward and pulled her into my arms. She collapsed against me, her body shaking so hard I almost couldn't keep her upright. Our energy crashed together, but for once neither of us cared.

"I still see it in my head," she said in a broken whisper. "Every time I close my eyes, I have to relive the days I spent in the Otherworld."

I rubbed her back gently, pulling away so I could lead her to two high-backed armchairs. When we were sitting, facing each other, I reached out and grasped her hands. "You don't have to talk about it, Vi, but ... I'm here, and it might help. Maybe part of the reason you're being haunted is because you're holding it all inside. Pretending it didn't happen."

She swallowed hard, stray tears still sprinkling her eyelashes. "I thought if I just acted normal, then eventually I would feel normal. And to a certain degree that has worked. I'm genuinely happy with Nikoli, happy when I'm around you and Kade, and all your overabundance of love. But ... at night, I can't escape. I've barely slept since we got back."

I waited, sensing she had more to say. Her next words came out in a big rush.

"The winter queen tortured me, which was fine. The physical cruelty barely even bothered me. I have a high tolerance for pain, as you well know." Her breath caught in her throat as she choked out the next part. "But, it wasn't just physical torture. She's an expert at the psychological too. She got in my head..." A ragged whisper of words: "You, and Blaine, and Winnie ... you died, over and over again, in a different way every day. Nothing I did could ever save you. There was no way for me to tell it wasn't real. I had to live it, it was ... I also died a million times, holding your bodies in my arms."

Oh, holy gods. If I had to live through Calista, Violet, Winnie, or Kade's death even once, I would have lost my mind. Ben and Derek's deaths had almost broken me, and they were not quite the same level as the other four. I had no idea how she had stayed so strong for so long. But I had even more respect and love for her.

I moved forward to pull her closer, wanting to reassure her that I was here, but she put out a hand to stop me. "By the end, when you came to rescue me, I couldn't tell what was real anymore. The only thing which kept my mind from shattering completely, was my one goal of preventing her from taking your fae essence."

Tears were splashing down my cheeks as I witnessed my friend crack into a million pieces. All of her broken parts were out in the open now, the pain she held inside her heart finally revealed.

"I wish I could take all of that away from you," I said, my words husky with emotion. "I would have taken your place if I could. You should have never had to go through that." She had protected me, almost at the cost of her own sanity. "I love you," I choked out. "And I am not going to let her win. I will destroy the winter queen."

Violet's sobs were loud and violent, and in a move I did not expect, she leaned forward and wrapped me tightly in her arms. "I love you, too. I would take the torture again if it meant you were safe ... that you had the power which was rightfully yours."

I pressed myself into her shoulder, absorbing the strength of her magic, relishing her heart beating so strongly. This was a rare thing, to be hugged so tightly by her. I was going to take every second of it I could get. "I will always come for you. Always," I told her.

Violet nodded into my shoulder and pulled away, wiping her eyes. We sat in our chairs, staring at each other for a few long moments.

Then she smiled at me, and for a second it felt like everything was right in the world.

She nodded a few times, that smile going nowhere. "Wow." She breathed, surprise lighting up her wide eyes.

"What?" I asked, leaning forward, drawn to her happiness.

She took in a deep breath and then exhaled. "I ... actually feel so much lighter. She's going to lose her grip on me, if it's the last thing I do."

I smiled. "Oh, yes, she definitely is."

We sat there for a few more moments, in the sort of comfortable silence that had been missing from our relationship of late.

Violet was the one to break it, a quirk of a smile lighting up her wan face. "So ... I couldn't help but think that our trip into the mecca world was a little ... unnecessary. You and Calista are the best at strategy. No one beats you at mecca chess. No one. You even have Kade to run things past, and he is hot, smart and built like a linebacker, the bastard. So ... was there another reason for this visit?"

Her question took me by surprise, and my immediate reaction was defensive. I opened my mouth to justify myself ... I had only been queen for what felt like all of five minutes, and four of those I had been dethroned, so, I wasn't sure I was exactly making fantastic decisions lately. I was desperately in need of guidance. Still, I couldn't ignore the part of me that agreed with her.

"I think, maybe, I was looking for an excuse to see her again. Without even realizing it." I was hesitant, pretty much working out the motivations for my actions as I put the sentence together. But the moment I said it, I knew that was the truth. I finished in a rush: "Ever since I found out she was my mother, it has been this niggling thing in the back of my mind. Because I know she is still sort of accessible to me."

There was no judgment on Violet's face. None. The only thing shining from her was a deep understanding. "It would be a lot for anyone to take. You're handling it all pretty friggin' well, if you ask me."

I swallowed the lump in my throat, hoping it would ease the roughness in my chest. "I'm just taking it day by day." I jumped to my feet, needing an ease of the emotion overload. "But, since we now have an attack to plan, I'm quite excited to be moving ahead. I'm ready to have it all be over. I'm ready to end this."

Violet joined me, determination shadowing the planes of her face. "Right there with you, sister. Let's go and plan an assassination." She paused. "Again."

I couldn't help but laugh. When had this become our lives?

I faced Kade in the basement. He had the staff in one hand, the other hanging loosely at his side. He wore a look of absolute fury. "Tell me you're kidding!" His scowl deepened as he stared me down. "No, Arianna, be reasonable. I almost lost you to her once. What do you think will happen if she gets her hands on you a second time?"

I fought to keep my own anger from rising. I knew he was just stressed and worried. I completely understood after just watching him almost die. But I didn't have a choice.

"We have waited long enough, playing the submissive, waiting for her to attack. It's time for us to take the fight to her, end this once and for all."

He slammed the staff into the ground, and by instinct I reached through our bond. The darkness he was handling still worried me. Thankfully, there was only normal purple mecca energy flowing through his body. "Why does it have to be you, Ari? There are plenty of shifters trained in the art of assassination in both of our packs. Hell, I could have ten here in the next hour."

I snorted. "Yes, Almighty One, I know you are the king of the assassins." They had been dormant for a few years, no longer actively training, but bears and wolves both used to have special leagues of warriors specifically skilled in the art of murder. Blaine actually had some of that specific training; it was what made him a lethal warrior. The others were scattered around, lost to time and history. But clearly, Kade thought he could dig them up.

"It needs to be me," I said quietly. "She has ice magic and so do I. No one else can rival her. I'm also the only one with magic that can counter the Dark Fae Lord, since Earth-side mecca doesn't work on him. Besides, you know there are very few who can stand against the power of a monarch." There was a reason I always sent my queen out to battle in mecca chess.

"Except another monarch," Kade finished.

I nodded. "Exactly. Either they are building up to some big assassination plan of their own, or something more sinister, but now is the time for us to act — before they decide to get really serious about it."

Kade's fists tightened on the staff, and despite its power I could have sworn it started to bend. "You won't go alone. I need to be there, to keep you safe. I can wield this staff. I can take down the Dark Fae Lord."

I wanted to argue. The entire point of a stealth attack was that you went in quietly and got the job done. But we were stronger as a team, and I was also coming to terms with the fact that I might have been able to fight the fae lord, but Kade was probably the only one who could use the weapon that would actually kill him.

"Okay." I nodded. "Just you and me. And ... I think we should only tell a few people. Keep it under wraps as much as possible."

He didn't argue, and his grip eased on the staff as he said, "Maybe we should have Violet spell two shifters, create an illusion of us in the mansion. It would be dangerous for whatever shifter they use, but it's important the fae spies don't report our disappearance."

I agreed. Even though I didn't like putting that sort of target on any of our people, it needed to be done. It would be hard enough to fight Isalinda and the Dark Fae Lord without giving them a heads-up that we were coming for them.

Kade continued: "There's a low-ranking bear shifter in my royal guard on the Island. We are often told of our likeness in looks."

My mind searched for someone I could trust that was tall and blond and ... *Jen*. She would need whiter hair, but that could be changed easily enough; Violet's magic could take care of the rest. "Jen can be my lookalike. They will keep up appearances here, while we go in and take out the winter queen and the Dark Fae Lord. End this war before it starts."

Kade's eyes deepened to a dark brown and a frown touched his lips. "What if we don't make it back?"

I sighed. It was a damn good question, just not one I wanted to think about. "You owe me a wedding and babies. We're making it back. You have forty-eight hours to master that staff. We leave in two days."

The mention of future babies had a soft sort of grin lifting his cheeks. "With that sort of motivation, how can I refuse?"

I smiled lightly and stood on my tiptoes to kiss his warm lips. Times were never so dire that there was no time for kissing. "I'll prepare for our trip," I told him after I pulled away.

"Two days." He confirmed with a nod, then turned and bellowed out in the hallway, "Baladar, get your ass back in here."

No doubt they would have it mastered in that time. I could sense his determination.

The next two days were filled with training, strategy, and planning. Calista unearthed some ancient books on the Tuatha de Danann, which had a rough map of the entire world. The Dark Fae Lord's territory was not on there, but it was fascinating to see the huge scale of their realm. I had explored such a small part. She made me learn as much as I could, both of us hoping the landscape hadn't changed over the years.

I had explained to her that we were starting in the Summer Court, that hopefully they would point us in the direction we needed to go. When Calista wasn't grilling me, I trained with Kade. He threw dark magic at me with the staff, which was helping him get the hang of it, and me to get the hang of fighting the dark magic it held.

The stone atop his staff was absolutely fascinating to me. I was drawn to it, the same way I was with the purple mecca, but it also left a weird residue of oiliness on my tongue. There

was a wrongness about it I couldn't get past, even though it didn't seem to bother Kade.

At least — besides a couple of mishaps — I successfully broke any and all dark spells. I was as ready as I would ever be. Violet, Calista, Jen, Kevin — Kade's bear lookalike — Finn, and Nix were the sole bearers of our secret. The others believed they were training us for the war. After we left, Violet would break the news to the rest of our inner circle. We argued about whether this was the right thing to do. Kade was worried our family wouldn't be able to keep up a convincing act with our spelled lookalikes if they knew it wasn't us, but I refused to deceive everyone in that way. I wouldn't let them believe that Kevin and Jen were really us.

Our doppelgängers were already situated in the far west wing of the royal estate; both had been thrilled to be able to help us with this. Neither cared about the danger, even after I explained it to them. I felt it was an essential part of our plan that if the winter queen or Dark Fae Lord were watching the castle, they would still see us in the residence.

Finn had halted his perimeter excursions, sticking by my side as much as possible. The morning before we were about to leave, he bumped his head into me. *I still think I should come with you. Being separated like this ... it's not right.*

I dropped to my knees, wrapping my arms tightly around his middle. *I know, I want you there more than anyone. But ... you stand out too much. Nix stands out too much. It's safer if you stay here, keep an eye on the city, and tell me everything that's happening. You can pass on information if needed.*

His chest rumbled under my hold, his next words hard: *We don't know that we can communicate between the worlds. What if you can't hear me?*

I sighed. *We'll figure out a way.*

War was taking a toll on all of us, and it hadn't even started yet.

After much discussion, Kade and I felt it was the best move politically to take a portal into the Summer Court and briefly talk with Blaine and Bianca before moving to a private meeting with the king and prince. They would be the only ones to know of our plans. Gossip no doubt spread as rapidly there as it did here, and we wanted to contain it at all costs.

I wished there was no need to tell anyone, but it wouldn't be right to sneak into their lands, and hopefully they could offer us some guidance in the direction of Isalinda and the Dark Fae Lord.

"Ready?" Violet whispered.

I nodded. "Yep, can't wait." My voice was light, no real emotion.

It was near midnight and the entire house was sleeping except for Kade, Violet, Rowan, and me. We'd told Rowan we were going to have a meeting with her king — which wasn't a total lie. We were still trying to keep everything under wraps, but I think she knew something else was up, because she eyed our heavily-laden packs and Kade's dark staff with wary eyes.

"Worried about running into trouble in the Summer Court?" she asked, as she prepared to make a portal into the Otherworld.

"Hopefully not," I answered honestly.

Rowan just shook her head, the slightest of smiles tipping up her lips. Then she smoothed her coat, and in a flash pulled out a small shimmering vial. It was the mecca dust we'd been gifted. A second bottle. She pressed it into my hand. "In case you're in trouble. Mecca powder needs only to be given direction, and then it can accomplish almost any spell."

Our gazes clashed; the tiny fae nodded once, and I knew that she knew what we were up to. She knew and she supported it. For some reason, that made me feel a little better about the plan. I met Violet face to face. Her eyes were swimming with so much emotion.

"I should be with you," she finally said aloud. I shook my head. "I want you there so badly, but I have Kade. We have to do this together."

Kade's strong hand rested on my shoulder and he met Violet's gaze. "I will put Arianna's life before my own. Always."

His assurance sent trills of fear through me, but I saw that Violet relaxed somewhat. Her clenched fists eased. There was still a heaviness across her brow and around her eyes; my trip was bringing back memories for her. But it was clear she was grateful Kade was along to help.

She hugged me tightly. I was lucky, two of these hugs in as many days. I breathed in her scent, committing it to memory and praying this wasn't the last time I would see my best friend. Rowan and Violet took a few minutes to swirl enough energy to create the portal. As the warm floral-scented winds of the fae lands filtered through, Kade's body shifted in that direction, his entire demeanor softening. He was born of the Summer Court and I knew going there would give him strength. I, however, seemed to fare better in the Winter Court, which was possibly our eventual destination.

"See you soon," I told the two magic born as they held the portal open.

They both looked stressed, unsure but supportive.

"See you soon," Violet echoed.

"Kade!"

A deep voice had us all spinning around, Kade naturally falling into a protective stance in front of me. He relaxed when Kian's face popped into view, Shelley's beautiful features appearing from behind him as they both walked through the doorway.

"Brother!" Kade exclaimed, crossing to clasp hands before they embraced. "Are the children okay?"

Kian and Shelley were supposed to have been back a few days ago, but had decided to stay a little longer, reluctant to leave Nathaniel, which I completely understood. If I wasn't the queen, I would have been tied to Winnie's side.

"They're all very safe," Shelley said, her soft voice ringing across the room. "It's certainly a battle keeping that many little ones entertained, breaking up the fights and feeding their hungry bellies. But the people you sent are more than handling it."

"How's Winnie?" I asked, desperate for news about my baby sister.

Kian and Shelley both grinned broadly. "She's amazing. Rules the other kids — or should I say pirate clans — with an iron fist."

I wasn't surprised about that at all.

"She's telling anyone who will listen that her family is going to end this war, so they don't have to worry. She has a lot of faith in you two," Kian added.

My throat got really tight then. I had to swallow a few times to clear it. "Gods, I miss her so much."

Kade had his arms around me in a heartbeat, or as far around as he could get with my heavy pack. "We'll all be together again soon," he breathed into my hair, his voice rougher than usual. "Winnie will be back in our arms."

I couldn't break down now. There was no time to lose it, so, using my training, I pulled myself together.

"Why is there a portal to the Otherworld open in this room?" Kian's voice was deeper now, suspicion clouding it. He had clearly seen the portal still spinning behind us, and the two magic born on either side of it.

Kade and I exchanged a glance, and I gave him a nod. I trusted his brother, Shelley too. "We're going to the Otherworld to assassinate the winter queen and Dark Fae Lord," Kade said, his voice very low.

The two brothers' gazes remained locked, until Kian said, without hesitation, "I'm going with you—"

"*We're* going with you!" Shelley interrupted.

I was already shaking my head. "No, this is a stealth mission. We need to get in and out without any detection. We aren't even taking our familiars."

Shelley stepped closer, her red hair trailing across her shoulders as she moved. "There is no one better equipped than me to help you get in and out of the courts undetected. My knowledge and gift will be very useful to you."

I paused, giving myself a few moments to consider. I had forgotten that Shelley was a winter fae. A winter fae who used to work for the queen ... kind of. The queen forced her to use her gift of confusing people in repayment for her father's debt. She probably had a ton of useful information.

"If she goes, I am going," Kian added. I would not expect anything less from a bonded mate.

What do you think? I asked Kade through our bond.

Swirling copper eyes caressed my skin. *I will back whatever you decide. This is your mission. I'm just the muscle.*

I laughed, which had a few people looking my way. *I'm the muscle, buddy. You're the pretty face.*

Kade shrugged. "Nothing says I can't be the pretty muscle," he said out loud. I barely stopped myself from rolling my eyes.

I turned to the couple across from us. "Thank you, we would really appreciate your help. Do you need time to pack?"

"Do you have enough supplies for us?" Kian asked, eyeing our huge bags.

A chuckle escaped from my tense lips. "Yeah, after starving and freezing last time, we kinda overpacked. I planned on sorting it out once we saw King Samson."

Rowan piped up then. "The king will have everything you require. Now that the mecca balance has been restored, the Summer Court is filled with an abundance of food. And our weapons cache is quite impressive."

Well ... that was good to know. Rowan didn't seem too surprised to learn of my assassination plot. She was taking it all in stride.

Kade and I linked arms again. Shelley stepped up to my free side, Kian beside her. The boys had us sandwiched in between them. The four of us took a deep breath.

"Good luck," Violet and Rowan whispered together.

"We'll keep your shifters safe," Violet added at the end.

With a deep breath, we stepped into the portal. I let out a breathy sigh as my feet planted onto the soft green grasses of the fae land. My inner fae energy prickled to life the moment my body arrived in the Otherworld. New York City was now on its own.

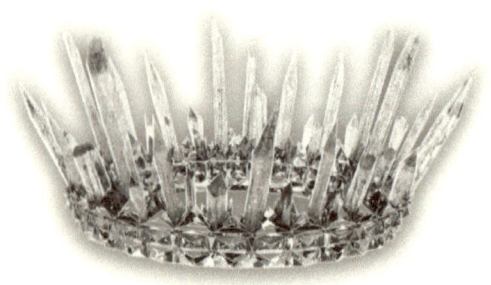

Chapter Ten

Who bears the tides of winter?

AS IF HE knew we were coming, Prince Caspien was waiting just on the other side of the portal, standing among a grove of huge trees just like those we had stepped into last time we arrived here. I hurried over to the royal, who was dressed all in black, looking like a very dazzling version of himself. His energy caressed my face like a strong brush of warm air. I could smell the summer scents, flowers, and a sweetness like honey or nectar.

"Prince Caspian, we are well met," I said, stopping before him. "How did you know we were coming?"

He bowed, rising and flashing me his dazzling smile. "Rowan needs royal permission to open a portal."

Ahh. "Well, that's perfect, because we're here to see Blaine and Bianca, and then you and your father. We didn't want to speak over the flowers, or through a mirror, because it's a … sensitive matter."

He gave a brief nod to Kian and Shelley, before his attention locked on Kade's staff. Even though it was in its protective case, it still oozed dark energy.

"Is that a dark weapon?" Caspien asked, his ageless face creasing with what looked like concern and trepidation.

I stepped closer to him and lowered my voice, unsure who was listening in these woods. "It is. And we intend to assassinate the Dark Fae Lord with it."

Prince Caspien's sharp intake of breath, followed by a tentative grin, told me everything I needed to know. He was worried, but he still approved of our plan.

"Come. We'll see my father first, because he will leave soon for the war's front. Right now he's in his private study, so the timing is perfect. You can see your friends after." With that, Caspien turned and we followed him through the forest, heading toward what looked like a shining white building in the distance, visible in between the trees.

The summer castle was spectacular. I'd likened the winter castle to a dark fairy tale. The summer castle was the opposite. It was the epitome of a five-year-old's princess castle fantasy. White stone wrapped around shining turrets; golden accents gave the entire building an ethereal glow. And then there were the masses of rose vines, climbing ivy, budding flowers, and fruits that decorated the sides of the stone walls, climbing, spreading their rich, green goodness everywhere.

Unlike the last time we were here, the plants were thick and luscious; they did not crumble under my touch. I found myself wanting to linger in the outer courtyard with its pebbled stone underfoot, and birds chirping as they fluttered about the many tall trees. But there was no time for lingering. No time to lift my face and bathe in the warm, caressing sunbeams.

I must have actually closed my eyes for a beat, because a soft stroke along my cheek had them flying open again. Kade was standing right before me. I tilted my head back to stare up into his eyes.

"Feels like home," he said.

I nodded. It must have really felt like home to him, being of the Summer Court. To me, being more than half fae, all of the Otherworld felt like home, but especially the icy lands of the Winter Court — as much as I didn't want to admit it.

"We have to win," I murmured to Kade. "I'm not ready to give any of this up. I'm not ready to give you up."

His lips were on mine before I could say another word. When he pulled away, his hand still wrapped across my chin. "We will win, love," he said with conviction. "There is no timeframe for which I would be ready to give you up. I need forever. I'm going to damn well make sure that is how long we have."

I felt the same way. My life had changed so much since becoming queen. I had found a true love, learned my parents' identities — which was not good news, but it helped me understand so much about myself, about my upbringing. It forged me into a blade that was stronger, more resilient. I was better equipped in all ways to be a mate and a queen. So now I just had to make sure it wasn't ripped away from me.

A low, smooth drawl drifted across the courtyard: "Father is ready to see us now." Prince Caspien was waiting near the twenty-foot-tall, wooden double front doors that led out into the main castle.

Kade and I pulled apart, turning to follow everyone up the stairs. Inside was as I expected: light stone work, wondrous artwork dotted across the walls, and even more greenery. There were plants, trees, and fruit growing everywhere.

"We need more plants inside back home," I said to Kade. We were both staring around, trying to take it all in.

He surprised me by cupping my face, and the way he stared down at me, it sucked all breath from my lungs. At the same time, my heart started to beat rapidly. "You're perfect," he said, his eyes whirling and alive.

Then, just as quickly, he let me go, turning to stride after the group. Shaking my head to clear it, I hurried after him, my heart still going erratically. There were dozens of floors and halls. I lost track as we followed the prince to his father's office. It ended up being at the end of a long, wide hallway. There were no guards in attendance at the doors, which I thought was odd, but maybe the king required nothing like that in his own home.

We all stepped inside. King Samson was standing behind a huge white stone-top desk. He looked the same as last time, like a golden ray of sun. The only difference was, he wore casual sort of clothes, and had ditched the cloak.

"Welcome! We are so glad to see you here safe and sound," he boomed. One by one we gave him a bow or curtsey. Before he could say anything more, I quickly launched into an explanation of what we were doing here.

He eyed the staff, but didn't comment until I was finished.

"We've been holding them at the winter woods," he said, pacing his study. "Very little movement since the last attack, when they ambushed us and killed Dalia. I haven't been able to figure out why they're only engaging in small skirmishes, not moving forward in any sort of decisive way. It's a standoff."

Kade and I exchanged a glance. "We know the winter queen has been waiting to align with the Dark Fae Lord," said Kade. "And we think he may have promised her this dark staff. Luckily, we got it first, and since we're sick of waiting for them to enact whatever they have planned..."

"We've decided to end it now," I finished.

King Samson nodded, eyeing the staff in Kade's hand for a second, before pausing at his desk and reaching out to pick up what looked like a pencil. One made of bone with symbols etched into the side of it. He twirled it in his fingers as he continued, "I have been worried about what they have been planning. It's not like Isalinda to show restraint. Usually she uses brute force for everything. But if you can thwart her in the midst of a plan, it just might work." He focused on me then, dropping the pencil back down. "You will need a guide. Last I heard, the winter queen had left her court and was elsewhere."

A guide ... I didn't want to be rude, but we had four people already. What was it about a stealth mission that no one understood?

"Your Highness, I appreciate the offer but—" A knock at the door interrupted my polite refusal.

"Enter, Dante," the king bellowed. The door opened and a huge cloak-clad fae stepped through. As he dropped the hood, bringing his face into view, I blinked a few times.

I ... knew that face. It was familiar, but in a vague way. *Where had I seen him before?*

He turned toward me, and with a slight smile tipping up his full lips he gave me a low bow. As those blue green eyes locked on mine, I recalled exactly where I'd seen this fae before.

"You got out of the Winter Court!" I exclaimed. He looked different. His hair was no longer dirty-blond, it was now a shining mass of gold pulled back at the nape of his neck. His skin was golden too, and he beamed with strength and vitality. When I'd seen him in the winter queen's dungeon, he'd been proud but hurting. I could see that.

"Thank you for your coat," I added. "It was more help than you probably know."

Dante's grin stretched. "Thanks for the keys. I planned on escaping soon anyway, but the keys made it easier for me to get the other prisoners out."

His voice was deep and rich; it filled the room. I sensed that Kade, Kian, and Shelley were all very confused by this conversation.

"Dante was in the winter queen's dungeon when I was there," I explained. "He gave me his coat, I gave him the keys so he could escape and release as many prisoners as possible." I turned back to him. "Did you save the children? The little girl who they were hurting to get to me?"

He gave me two short, sharp head nods. "Yes, Your Majesty. I got them all."

A tension I hadn't even realized I was carrying seeped out of me. *Thank the gods.*

King Samson gestured to Dante. "This man is the best assassin we have. He can track anything that walks, and kill anything that breathes."

Dante's expression did not change as he said, "Thank you, Your Grace."

Kade and I met each other's gaze. *One more man wouldn't hurt. Especially if he is as good as his king boasts*, Kade said.

I agreed. "If he's willing, knowing this is going to be a very dangerous mission, we would love his help."

Dante, who had no idea what the mission was, looked pensive. But also curious.

Kade quickly filled him in. "We intend to kill the winter queen and the Dark Fae Lord before the war can even begin. I have a weapon which can destroy the darkness."

Dante's expression morphed into one of a lethal predator. I wondered what had happened to him while he was at the queen's mercy. I could see there was no love there for Isalinda. "I can definitely help with that. Give me ten minutes to pack." There was not an ounce of hesitation in his tone, he just bowed to his king and Prince Caspien before striding from the room.

Over the next ten minutes I took the time to go through our travel bags as the king's assistants brought us more dried foods and weapons.

"Kian obviously ate fae food while he was here." I looked at the fae. "Does that mean it is safe for he and Kade to eat it now?"

Shelley cleared her throat. "The winter queen had deliveries of food from Earth, and sold some for high prices at the market. She was very partial to your food. I always made sure Kian ate only from those batches."

No doubt that was thanks to some sort of trade deal between my parents.

Caspien piped up then. "Yes, I think Shelley and Queen Arianna should be the only ones to eat our food, as we are not sure how it will affect those without fae blood."

Even though shifters had some fae blood, I understood what he meant. It might be too diluted, and it wasn't worth taking the risk.

I packed the fae food in my bag, and then Kade and Kian shared a pack with the food from Earth. I also chose a nice lightweight serrated blade and slid it into a sheath at my waist, while the others chose their weapons from the king's personal stash. Just as we were finished packing, Dante slipped back into the room, a medium-size pack on his back. His clothes were different, black, heavy material.

King Samson moved forward and clasped hands with all of us, one at a time. "Farewell, my friends. We will come if you need aid. Dante will know how to send us a message."

"Thank you," I said. It was a relief to know there was backup there if needed. But I was really hoping we would manage this without resorting to more lives lost.

I turned to Prince Caspien. He made a fist over his chest and bowed lightly. "It is a great honor to be allied with you and King Kade."

His words touched me. The entire Summer Court had been nothing but supportive and helpful since we'd started our relationship. I could barely remember the time I knew next to nothing of the Tuatha, de Danann, and the little I knew had been rife with fear and suspicion. The old me would never have believed I could ally myself with them, let alone be half one. It felt right, though. It all felt right to me now.

"We are well met, Prince Caspien," I told him.

It was time for us to leave. Just as we were striding toward the door, Caspien pulled Dante aside and whispered something in his ear. The assassin fae nodded once, before rejoining us. He led us out of the castle and into the courtyard. I wasn't sure what the plan was. We would need to discuss some things before we went any further.

Dante led us deep into the forest that surrounded the summer castle, pausing beside a large oak tree. I was just opening my mouth to ask what he was doing when Dante took to one knee, arms outstretched above his head, and began to whistle an odd tune from between his teeth.

Kade, Kian and I shared a look of confusion, but Shelley's face brightened into one of understanding.

"You're blessed with animalas affinity?" she said, prickles of awe in her voice.

Before he could respond, over two-dozen small bright yellow finches flew down from the trees and landed on his outstretched arms. I then noticed the bird seed in his outstretched palms, which all of the finches had a turn at eating.

"Animalas affinity?" I whispered to Shelley.

She was smiling, her expression soft as she watched the birds. "A very rare gift. A fae that can communicate with animals."

Interesting. Like they were all his familiars. That would be very useful for an assassin. Animals could blend in a way that people couldn't; they were often overlooked, and came in all different shapes and sizes, with different abilities.

Dante remained silent, I assumed speaking into their minds. They had stopped eating and were all looking at him, heads cocked to the side. Finally, one of them chirped and then the rest echoed their agreement, taking off from his arms and flying to the skies.

The fae assassin stood. "I've been able to speak to the minds of animals since I was a young boy. It got me through some very tough times. Animals have always been there for me, in a way that my family never was."

Just like Finn for me. "So they will track the winter queen and fae lord and report back?"

"Yes, but until then we should make our way towards the Winter Court. Isalinda is never too far from her territory. We need to get closer first, and there is no way to open a portal near their court without the queen knowing. We have to go in the old fashioned way."

"On foot?" I guessed.

He nodded. "Yes, we will make too much noise with horses. But don't you worry, I know all the shortcuts. I will have us there in no time."

"How is it that the king's top assassin found himself locked in the winter queen's basement?" Kian asked. He sounded a little suspicious, and I didn't blame him. We were putting a lot of faith and trust into someone we didn't know at all. Someone who made a living from killing people.

Dante smiled, or more like bared his teeth. "I was in there to take out one of the guards. A guard who murdered someone close to King Samson. I killed him the first day, but when I saw how many innocents were in the cells, I knew I needed to get them out. I didn't have the intel or weapons to achieve this, though."

"So you got yourself locked up on purpose?" I guessed.

Dante nodded. "Yes, I needed more time. I needed to study the inner workings of the dungeon. I would not risk leaving any of the innocents behind."

An assassin with a conscience. Who would have thought it?

"Guess I came along at the right time," I joked.

He let out a low laugh. "Yes, Your Majesty. You most certainly did."

As we started to walk, the general sounds of the summer woods slowly changed. I was starting to hear some clashing, even a few muffled yells. Enough to tell me that we were no longer alone.

I halted, and when Dante turned to me, I said, "We need to stay out of sight. It will not help having our position revealed to the queen before we get there. We don't want her preparing for this."

He nodded. "Prince Caspien said you wanted to see your people before you left, the ones who are here training with our army. They're on the edge of these woods. I was simply leading you closer."

I had almost forgotten about Blaine and Bianca. Planning to assassinate someone could do that to a girl.

"Just Bianca and Blaine at this stage." I turned to Kade. "Right? You don't need your bear guard?"

He shook his head, and I turned back to Dante.

"I will lead those two to you," he said, asking no more questions.

We hurried along this time, staying close to Dante as he led us through a veritable maze of trees and shrubbery. I couldn't keep anything straight; it all looked the same, but the noise of battle was definitely getting clearer.

"Wait here," he told us after about ten minutes of walking.

Using the trees to keep ourselves hidden, the four of us remained in a tense bundle, waiting for the fae to return. I wasn't sensing betrayal from him, but … we had to remain vigilant. Dante was not someone I knew or trusted, and I would continue to treat him with caution.

Footsteps crunching through undergrowth gave me a few seconds' notice before a figure darted out from the trees and strong arms wrapped around me, yanking me up into a hard chest.

"Princess! Why didn't you tell me you were coming?"

Blaine pulled back, his eyes raking across me, taking in my no doubt tired face and battle-ready clothing. He grew more serious. "What happened?" He crossed his arms over his chest, his expression formidable.

I marveled at how fit and healthy he looked, his skin golden, kissed by the sun of this court,

wearing fae leathers that fit his broad shoulders and slim hips to perfection. I knew Bianca was standing close behind him, but my focus remained on my old friend.

"We are here to assassinate the winter queen and Dark Fae Lord," I said in a low voice. "I wanted to let you know, because if we are not successful, you need to head back to Earth and prepare our people. There will be a war."

Blaine continued to stare down at me, his silence unnerving. I knew he was upset; he had the telltale signs, the shaking of his arms, the small flame deep in his eyes. A hand crept up across his shoulder, resting against his biceps. Bianca pressed in close to his side, and he finally tore his gaze from me to stare down at her. Something passed between them, a moment, and that flame dulled somewhat from Blaine's green eyes.

Happiness burst to life in my chest, and I found myself swallowing the sudden flurry of tears threatening to pour from me. I had loved Blaine forever, but I would never be *in love* with him. He hadn't felt the same way, and there had been a lot of rocky times between us since Kade and me. But ... there was something with him and Bianca. I saw it. And apparently so had Violet. This had to be the prophesy she spoke of. It all made sense now.

Bianca continued to comfort him; she had tamed my hotheaded friend with one look.

"What else do you need from us?" Bianca asked me, staring straight at me. I had always liked the Boston alpha. She stood by me through the Selene thing, and was strong and respected by her pack. She was a good match for my Blaine.

"Continue what you are doing now and wait for our word," I said to her, while still flicking glances at Blaine. "One way or another, you should know in the next day or so if we are successful, or if you need to head back to New York to regroup."

"Prince Caspien will let you know," Dante added. "Even if things do not go to plan for us, he will get you back to Earth."

Blaine was shaking his head now, that formidable expression still plastered across his face. "No, Ari, you cannot do this. You cannot sacrifice yourself to try and save everyone."

Kade let out a little growl of agreement. Of course. I should have expected I would have to have this same argument with the other dominant male in my life. "I am the queen of the shifters," I said, my tone filled with my annoyance. "This is the sole reason for my existence, to make sure I keep my people safe, that I take the first hit so they don't have to. A true leader stands on the front line, not behind. You know this."

"Let me go instead." Blaine's voice rippled with a growl, and Kade's bear was suddenly in our midst, his own rumbles growing in strength. Blaine, with his very annoyed wolf shining from his eyes, just lifted his head and met my mate's gaze. They had a silent conversation over my head, and must have come to some sort of agreement, because Kade backed off a little.

"You're not going," I bit out, hating to pull rank, but we didn't have time for this. My mate could protect me. I could protect myself. Blaine needed to just let it go.

Blaine's lips twitched at the corners, before finally he let out a long sigh, rubbing tiredly at his temples. "Why can't I at least come along to guard you?"

Despite my annoyance, I still wanted to comfort him. Reaching out, I placed my palm flat against his chest, right above his heart. "Because if I fail ... and I'm not planning on it, just so you know ... but if I do, I need you to lead the army."

When he exhaled in a loud huff, I knew he had accepted it. He would do as I asked. He didn't like it, but he would respect my position as queen.

"Just ... don't die, Princess," he finally said, leaning down to give me a quick hug. "Where you go, I go."

Violet, Blaine, and I had been saying that to each other since we were kids. Three musketeers. All for one and one for all.

"I'll be back, you're not getting rid of me that easily." The lighthearted tone was missing; my joke fell flat.

Before he could comment again, I turned to Bianca and she bestowed her charming smile on me, not looking at all upset at the interaction between Blaine and me. "Look after him for me. I'm really happy you two found each other."

She surprised me by reaching out and giving me a hug. "Thank you for choosing me to come to the Otherworld. Not only have we learned a lot working side by side with the fae, but I found..." Her eyes shifted to Blaine. "I found something I didn't even know I was looking for."

I thought about my first meeting with Kade. Well, second one really — the first I was way too young for a serious romance. "I know exactly what you mean."

We shared a girl moment, one I hoped I could expand on in the future.

"We have to go now," Dante warned. "The longer we linger, the greater the chance the queen hears of your plan."

Blaine gave me one last look, his eyes speaking volumes, before he spun and strode off into the trees. I knew he was still upset, but he had Bianca. He would be okay.

Kade stepped into me then, and I found myself leaning back against his strength. "You handled that very well," I murmured, as his arms came around me.

His chest shook as low rumbles of laughter left him. "I'm glad you weren't paying attention to our bond."

I tilted my head back for one last kiss, and then it was time to go. This time we walked away from the noise of training and chatter. We walked in companionable silence for over an hour, each of us preparing, in our own way, for the task that lay before us.

Eventually, Dante made a hand motion for us to stop. He got low to the ground and sniffed, looking up at two trees off to the left. They were curved into each other, making an archway.

"This way," he whispered.

Kade tightened his grasp on his staff. I readjusted my pack so that it was firm against my back, and we followed Dante to the entrance of the tree arch. He was peering into it.

"Damn," Dante whispered. Shelley broke away from Kian's side and peered through the archway as well.

"I can help," she told Dante in hushed tones.

"What is going on?" I asked.

Dante walked back a few feet and we huddled around him. "There is a magical portal here that takes us right into the Fall Court. From there we find the next portal to enter the Winter Court."

"These portals would have come in handy last time we were here," I said.

He shook his head and some of my excitement faded away. I prepared myself for the bad news. "This portal is guarded. As soon as we exit the portal, they will alert the winter queen."

"Winter? You said it was Fall Court?" Kade asked, his keen eyes tracking Dante's every movement.

Shelley was the one to answer: "The winter queen rules the Fall Court as well. Those fae are actually her guards. I recognize them. But I can confuse them with my magic and make them let us through."

A flicker of wariness crossed Dante's golden face. No doubt he wasn't used to trusting others when he was on a mission. But he simply waved a hand toward the portal.

As Shelley stepped forward, Kian reached out to wrap his hand across her shoulder. "Are you sure it's safe?"

"I'll be fine," she replied.

Kian narrowed his eyes, and I recognized that stubborn look on his face. It was Kade all over. Eventually, Kian released his mate and gave her

a nod. Shelley smoothed her coat and unsheathed her sword. "Give me sixty seconds. If I'm not back, come through fighting."

I pulled out my blade. Kian adjusted the grip on his weapon, and we all moved closer, ready to assist if she needed it.

Shelley's nerves weren't obvious as she walked to the archway, but I saw her hand shaking the slightest bit. I kept scanning our surroundings, keeping an eye on the portal. We were in the middle of an Otherworld forest, where anything could attack at any time. Surely these portals had a lot of traffic too. It would not do to be taken from behind.

Shelley was almost there by now, and I blinked a few times as the tree she was approaching started to move, just the slightest tilt toward her. A jolt of an idea slammed into me, and I could feel my pulse pick up as adrenalin surged through my body.

Kade made a noise as I started to follow Shelley's path. "I'm not going through," I said to him. "I just need to ... check something."

If Dante had an affinity for communicating with animals, then maybe there was a power associated with the way I could speak to the old fae tree in Kade's back yard. I inched closer, and when I was standing before the giant brown-barked trunk, I reached out to rest my palm on the tree.

I immediately felt an awareness there, an excitement.

Hello ... I'm Queen Arianna, I tried.

An instant reply came back: *Hello, Queen Arianna. Winter fae do not usually stop and speak with us. But ... I have heard of you from the treeling that is rooted in New York. You are different.* It sounded male, with a deep scratchy voice.

I grinned at the knowledge that all of the trees' consciousnesses must be connected. That was kind of amazing. And hugely useful. *Can you do me a favor? My friend has just walked through your arch. Can you tell me if she is okay?*

There was nothing for a moment, but then a tingling spread throughout my palm. *I can show you.*

I closed my eyes and a mini movie screen played in my mind's eye. There were four guards. Shelley was speaking with them as they surrounded her, weapons drawn.

"My friends and I wish to pass through this arch. You will not harm them. You recognize them as friends of the Winter Court. There is no need for alarm. You will simply let us pass and forget we were ever here." Shelley's voice was smooth and deep, with a trancelike quality.

Two of the men nodded, but the other two seemed to be resisting her fae-charms. Shelley stepped closer to the resistors. "You will let us through and tell no one you saw us." The close proximity must have done the trick. They both nodded, looking slack-jawed.

Shelley bowed deeply and began to back away slowly towards the tree as the projection in my mind faded.

My eyes popped open as Shelley came through the archway and motioned we all follow.

Thank you, kind friend, I said as I straightened.

That warm feeling tickled my palm again. *You always have an ally with the treefolk, Queen Arianna.*

A burst of warmth followed me as I pulled my hand away. Well ... that was interesting. Was there some way for me to use that alliance? To use the wise, ancient strength of these amazing tree-fae hybrids?

"Come, it won't last long. Two of them were hard to get through to." Shelley's voice held a note of impatience.

Dante, a small dagger clutched in his hand, was the first to go into the archway. As I walked through, pressure pushed on my skin, then there was a pop in my ears and I was on the other side. I could see the four guards standing around a fire looking at us. One nodded and another waved. I waved back and walked briskly behind Kade, trying to get away as fast as possible.

We closed ranks around Dante.

"What now?" I asked him. His posture had changed; he was tenser. It was only a subtle change, but I was trained to notice things like that, and it immediately put me more on alert.

"Now we need to be extra vigilant. We're no longer in friendly territory. Expect conflict at every turn."

All of us had our weapons out now, except Kade. His staff would not be removed from its case until we were face to face with darkness. We fanned out and walked slowly through the fall woods, which were breathtaking with their yellow and burnt orange trees, frosty snowcapped mountains just visible in the distance, and a brisk chill to the air.

Fall in the city had always been one of my favorite times, especially since I knew winter was just around the corner. Damn genetics. I suppose it wasn't winter's fault. Winter had done nothing wrong.

No one spoke a word. After about an hour, Dante paused, crouching. We all followed suit. I sat on my heels, sword held loosely before me. I sensed a disturbance; even the sound of the breeze whistling through the forest had died off.

"Down!" Dante yelled just as a flaming yellow metal disc whizzed between the trees, nearly taking my head off.

I dove to the right and pressed my face into the ground, resting on my cheek in time to see Dante pop up, two sickles in his hands.

My heart was hammering in my chest because I remembered that disc weapon. It was the same weapon the dark fae assassin had used on Staten Island to take Derek's head off.

Sure enough, as I lifted myself up slightly to see better, a black-clad fae stepped from behind the trees. His face was covered in a mask of some description, but it looked as if his skin was tinged a moss green color. "Well, well, what do we have here?" he said in a gravelly voice.

Giving no response, Dante flung his arm out, releasing a sickle. It soared through the air; the dark fae sidestepped quickly, but it nicked the outside of his arm. Blood spurted out, spraying the trees around him. Looking unperturbed, the evil fae threw another disc, lightning quick. It clipped Kian's arm, before slicing along Kade's thigh. Bear roars bellowed from both males, and rage immediately boiled within me.

"Kill him!" I said, not an ounce of remorse. Kian, already healing, took a knee and started firing arrows at the dark assassin. Dante disappeared into the woods, and I was too busy keeping an eye on the dark fae to follow his movements. These dark assassins were super fast and lethal, training and control obvious behind each of their attacks. A few more like this and they could finish us off no worries.

Not on my watch. I built up a large ball of fae magic in my hands. Kade was already at my side, preparing to help me funnel the energy if needed.

"How's your leg?" I asked him.

His chest rumbled. "It's fine, just a scratch. It's already healing."

Some of the fire in my veins dulled just a little. I was really getting sick of Kade's body having new cuts, scratches, and holes in it. Time to do something about it.

The assassin was moving again, more of the discs appearing in his hands. I let loose my ball of energy, hoping to hit him while he was on the move, but he dove to the side at the last moment. *So freaking fast.* He was up again, sprinting toward a huge tree with flaky white bark, scaling it in a second. It was almost as if he didn't even use his hands to climb. I knew from that vantage point we were going to be sitting ducks, so the four of us sprinted for a small grove of bushy weed-like plants.

"I'm going up into the trees," I whispered to Kade while dropping my pack to the ground. "Give me some cover."

I could see he wanted to protest, but he let out a sigh and nodded. "Stay safe," he warned me, turning and murmuring something to his brother.

Kian immediately lifted his arrow; Kade pulled out some small throwing knives, and the pair launched themselves up and over the bushes, creating noise and distraction.

I started scaling a nearby tree. I didn't have the same skills as that assassin, so I had to sheath my weapon first, but after that I had no trouble. I was an excellent tree climber. Sure, a few years might have passed since my last adventure, but it was like riding a bike. Right?

My foot slipped and I lost my balance for a second, almost plummeting to the ground. Only my strong grip on a nearby branch broke my fall. With a deep breath, I pulled myself up again, trying my best to ignore the shouts from below. When I made it to the first level of strong, thick branches, I let my senses roam out across the canopy. The fae was in black; he shouldn't blend in. And yet I sensed he was close, but I couldn't see him.

Two trees across, a voice whispered in my mind, and I almost fell off the branch.

Not one of ours. Otherwise we would be able to dispel him from the branches. The dark assassins avoid our kind.

Thank you, I replied to the tree that was helping me. I peered two trees to my left, and sure enough the black-clad assassin was hanging onto its uppermost branch, about twenty feet away from me.

I had a crazy idea.

Can you launch me at him? I asked my new friend. If he could sway in the wind, he could move at will, right? Broken bones took a long time to heal, and I would be of no use to this mission if I did indeed break anything, but it was also the quickest way to move. Here was hoping my tree friends kept me from going splat.

Of course. We will extend our branches to keep you from falling. There was something strong and reassuring about the ancient words of the trees.

I silently unsheathed my sword just as the assassin started throwing more discs down into the forest. *Now!* I yelled, tensing my body, while also loosening my grip on the branches I held.

The tree that held me snapped backward, dipping me low toward the ground, its trunk bowing under the weight. Then it straightened and I was airborne. Simultaneous surges of excitement and fear flushed through me as I catapulted towards the black-clad fae.

He barely had time to look up and register my approach before I came crashing down on him, my sword sliding into his abdomen. Branches from a nearby tree came up to hold me in place, and I wrenched my sword upwards, trying to inflict maximum damage.

The fae's eyes bulged, but with surprising strength he jerked his head forward, slamming into my nose. Pain exploded across my face and I dropped my hold on the sword, bringing my hands up to catch the blood gushing from my face. My eyes involuntarily watered, temporarily blinding me – pinned in close quarters with an assassin.

An assassin I had just pissed off.

I quickly blinked my eyes to clear them, the fuzzy vision disappearing in time for me to see the assassin's hand rise, a small dagger clutched in it. He struck out, aiming for my neck, ready to slice into my carotid. My breath hitched as I threw my hands forward to block the blow. Cut hands I could heal, but a sliced throat was another thing.

My first deflection worked, but the fae was already gearing up to slice into me again. Suddenly Dante's head peeked over the dark fae's shoulder, his hands wrapping around his neck, before he twisted violently, snapping his spinal cord.

A sigh of relief escaped me. The assassin was dead.

"Thank you," I said, a little breathlessly.

He nodded, his face remaining expressionless, not an ounce of evidence that he had just killed a guy showing at all.

"You okay?" he asked me.

I nodded, and then winced as the throbbing in my nose and forehead increased, not to mention the cuts on my hands. "Just a broken nose and a few scrapes. I'll heal."

I retracted my blade from the fae's belly and let his body fall through the canopy, to land with a hard thud on the ground below. Leaning over, I could see Kade was waiting at the base of my tree.

"We're okay!" I called down to him.

Dante immediately started to climb down, but I took a moment to place my hand on the tree branch that was cupping my lower back, keeping me firmly in place.

Thank you, friend.

I was surprised when a more feminine-sounding voice answered. *You are most welcome.*

Then I yelped a little as the branches began to move and configure themselves into a seat, cupping my butt, bending and lowering me to the ground. As I stepped off, I looked up to see all of my friends staring at me.

I smiled, shrugging. "Guess I have a tree affinity or something."

Dante looked the most astonished, which was a bit comical considering he spoke to and commanded animals.

After another moment of gawking, Kade gave me that slow smile I was so in love with, and I felt his warmth brush across our bond. *Glad you're okay, my little tree hugger.*

I laughed. Out loud. As usual confusing everyone who couldn't hear our inner conversation. *We need more trees in our garden.*

You got it, love.

He focused then, turning toward the woods. "You think that dark fae was sent by someone to target us specifically? Or were we just in a 'wrong place, wrong time' situation?"

Dante answered, "We're about thirty yards from the winter realm portal. His kind are a standard security measure since the war."

That made sense, and I liked that theory a lot more than the one where the winter queen knew we were here. We gathered up our packs again, walking in the direction Dante instructed. Only a few paces in, a quiet little bird's chirp sounded behind us.

Dante pursed his lips and let the air out through his teeth, creating a similar sound.

His birds had returned. A dozen finches flew down from the trees and landed on Dante's outstretched hands, all chirping and talking at the same time as Dante's face creased in concern. He sat there patiently and heard from every bird as we watched, waiting for him to translate. When they ceased their chatter, he pulled some seed from his pocket and they all had a feed.

"The winter queen and Dark Fae Lord are together. Which will help in taking both of them out at the same time," Dante said, very quietly.

Okay. That was good news. The less time we spent on this mission, the better. I had a world to rebuild back in New York.

"The bad news...?" said Kade, picking up on what Dante wasn't saying. His hand was resting on the dark staff as he stared with a hard expression at the fae.

Dante shifted his weight slightly, the only thing to betray any unease within him. "They are in the Dark Fae Lord's realm, surrounded by the vilest creatures in existence."

I didn't even have a flicker of surprise within me. I'd expected nothing less. Ever since King Samson mentioned erchos, killians, and whatever else he'd said, I'd been waiting to meet

those creatures. No way did the fae lord have such things in his army and not use them.

"Can you get us there?" I asked him, trying not to think of the oil-black ercho that had attacked me in central park.

Dante nodded. "I can."

Kade stepped forward, his hand almost crushing the handle of the case he held. "How many creatures? What types?"

The birds flew off then, in unison, and Dante stood. "I have no idea how many, but I would guess a lot. Winged beasts, water beasts, and ones that were described that I cannot even put into words."

We can do this. Kade sounded confident. I wasn't so sure, but we had come too far to back out now.

"Kade and I are still going, but I understand if any of you want to turn back," I offered. "We just need you to show us the way, Dante."

He slammed a closed fist onto his chest. "It would complete my life's work to aid in the death of the winter queen. I am all in."

Shelley stepped forward. "You can use my gift to confuse any guards on the perimeter to keep the fight small."

Tears welled in my eyes. "Thank you."

Kian placed a hand on Shelley's shoulder. "You have my sword also. Anything that will keep this war from spilling out onto the Earth and coming for our children."

His words rang true. This was for Winnie and Nathanial, and all of the innocents.

Chapter Eleven

An unexpected alliance.

IT TURNED OUT there was a secret gateway hidden between the Winter Court and the land of the Dark Fae Lord. Dante had learned this when he was imprisoned in the dungeon. He said it was guarded but that we shouldn't have too much trouble getting through.

"No one thinks twice about talking in front of prisoners," he told me when I expressed my surprise at his knowledge. "The moment you are locked up, you cease to be a living being to anyone. They have no respect for you. You become nothing more than a blight on their world. They see you as weak, powerless, and without identity. I learned much in my short time locked away."

That was interesting. I'd never stopped and thought about it, I'd never been a prisoner before my time with the winter queen, but I could imagine that once you lost your freedom, a lot of your identity disappeared with it.

"What happened to the little girl, the one they hurt to try and force me to give the queen my powers?" I asked him when we were through the second portal and heading deep into the Winter Court.

"Despite being a winter fae, she has found her place in the Summer Court." A sliver of a smile crossed his face. I hadn't seen him smile a lot; he was kind of serious. To be expected in his line of work. "She's staying in the palace under the care of those who raise our children."

Just like in the shifter world, many of our young were collectively raised.

"She deserved a chance at happiness." I had seen the fear in her eyes, but also the resignation. I had been reasonably sure that wasn't the first time she'd found herself at the mercy of the Winter Court. Probably like Shelley, repaying a debt from a member of her family.

That was no life for a child.

Kade squeezed my hand, wrapping his love around me, all of that warmth and soothing energy, which eased the ache in my chest. Kids did it to me every single time; they were a soft spot for me that I would never be able to carve out of my being. I knew it was a weakness. I'd tried to harden myself to it so that no one could use it against me, but ... I wasn't the Red Queen. Or Isalinda.

I wasn't my mother ... or my grandmother ... and I never would be.

Dante paused then, and all of us did the same. We were tuned into his actions by this stage. We were deep in a dark winter forest. This world was definitely more nature than anything else. Small villages, scattered amongst huge forests. I loved it.

My eyes flicked around; it was cold, snow thin on the ground — dirty already under our boots. I expanded my senses, used the extra sight I had as a fae and queen to try to see what had caused Dante to pause. He lifted both of his hands in front of him and started to feel across the air, almost like a mime. I stopped looking around and stared at his odd action.

What is he doing?

A sparkling navy light flashed right in front of Dante, almost hovering at his eyeline. He leaned closer, whispered something, and the light zipped away. "Come on," Dante said, still using a low whisper.

He took off, chasing after the blue sparkle of energy, or whatever it was that had appeared before him. We kept pace, even though the densely-packed forest was not well suited to sprinting. I did my best to avoid the noisier undergrowth, staying almost as stealthy and silent as Dante.

The blue spark was really zipping, leading us deeper and deeper into the darkness. After some time, the only light around us came from that little navy speck. The cold increased dramatically.

I wished Violet was here. For a multitude of reasons. I really missed her, but she'd also be able to whip us up some light and warmer clothes.

Suddenly the speck let out a little squeak and disappeared.

Like poof, gone in a blink.

Dante stopped, and we all did the same. "We mean you no harm," I heard him say.

Say what now? He was talking to the speck? The darkness hovered for a few moments, and it was so all-encompassing that I couldn't make out anything except some movement of shadows, some rustling of branches.

I prepared myself for an attack. Hand on sword.

A circle of light appeared around us. It took me a few seconds to figure out that it was formed from multiple balls of light that were being held

by ... beings ... of some kind. As more of these lights appeared, I got a very clear view of what we were facing.

They were tall, much taller than me, some of them even beating Kade, and that was a rare sight. Thin and muscled, it was difficult to tell if there were males and females or just a single androgynous sex. Humanoid in shape, they were dressed in neutral colors; leather, dark and worn, appeared to be the most common material used. It wrapped around their legs, covered their arms, across their bodies in thick armor.

Dante bowed his head. "We need your help. We need safe passage into the dark lands. You protect the entrance."

They protected the dark lands? They were going to kill us!

I think he means they protect this land from the dark creatures getting out, Kade mentally said. *I'm hoping that's what he meant.*

I was hoping that too.

The silence was uncomfortable, and then one of them, an ocher-skinned, ancient-looking ... whatever they were ... stepped forward. "Elves do not concern themselves in the battle of highborn. You know this. We have one duty — to keep the dark creatures from bleeding out into our land. Why should we help you?"

Elves! Holy shifter babies. We had found the elves! I'd thought they lived in the mountains, according to the gnome's intel from last time, but clearly some made their home in this dark forest.

Our silent stare-off continued for some time, and since they hadn't tried to kill us yet, I was going to consider them a potential ally. When the silence extended on, I realized that Dante wasn't going to speak. When I turned to him and our eyes met, he tipped his head toward Kade and then me. Okay ... this must be some kind of protocol. Maybe King Samson wouldn't allow him to make decisions where the elves were concerned. Maybe only royalty negotiated with elves.

I stepped forward and bowed my head deeply, lower than a queen of her people should, but I wanted to show them respect. We were here, in their territory, asking for help.

"I'm Queen Arianna of the wolf and bear shifters of Earth. We are well met."

A few of the statuesque creatures nodded their heads. Hopefully that meant it was okay for me to speak.

"You say your task is to keep the dark creatures from crossing into your lands. Well, we are here now to destroy the Dark Fae Lord, thereby ridding the worlds of his darkness completely." I had my fingers and toes crossed that they were on our side with this, because we did not have time to fight the elves as well.

The elves started to murmur amongst themselves, sharing looks of doubt, mixed with the slightest tinge of fear. After a minute or more of this, my breath caught as the ocher-skinned fae spoke again, his voice stronger: "The task you seek to achieve is impossible. The Dark Fae Lord and his children are born of evil and only evil can eliminate them." The ground beneath our feet trembled — only the smallest of shakes, but it was enough that my respect for their power increased.

Kade stepped forward, before he flicked the clasps of his case open, allowing the staff to become visible, its dark stone glinting softly in the elves' lights. He held it high and a swirl of energy started to brew around it.

"We are prepared," Kade announced, as each elf stared at the weapon with a mixture of awe and fear. "We will fight darkness with our own dark weapon."

I saw the way their gazes hardened on Kade, like he might now be an enemy they had not expected in their midst.

"How can you wield a dark weapon?" another elf asked, one with a slightly more feminine tone of voice. "We know of none who could touch the dark stone and not be tainted with it."

Kade's voice was strong, calm, confident. He was very good at easing the minds of others, because he seemed so very capable. He *was* capable. "I have a gift for mecca energy. More so than any other bear shifter. My gift is a complement to my bonded mate." He winked at me. "I can funnel this energy, and keep it from overloading me. It is not easy. I have fallen to the darkness before, but I am learning."

I wondered if Kade's gift — which as he said seemed to be a complement to mine — was there because of my dual heritage, being half fae and half shifter, having a tie to both sides of the mecca. Maybe without Kade, without our bond, the power would have driven me crazy, especially when my winter magic was first released within me.

The elves' faces were now masked into something more ghoulish and warrior-like. But at least it seemed they were contemplating our mission.

Finally they spoke: "We will deliberate. Put that thing away!" Then with a flash of magic they were gone.

Kade bent down and returned the staff to its case, and despite his confidence not two minutes ago, I sensed he wasn't as in control of the darkness as he believed. The longer he held on to the staff, the more it was wrapping around his energy. He didn't want to put it back in the case. I could feel that through our bond.

All of that power, it called to him.

Which was making me increasingly worried. But we were so close now. If we could just get through to the dark lands, maybe with the help of the elves, then Kade wouldn't have to wield it any longer.

I opened my mouth, but Dante moved before I could speak, wrapping his hand lightly across my face. "Speak with caution, they are still here," he murmured. "They've only cloaked themselves for privacy."

He released me, stepping back into his spot. "So we just wait?" I murmured back to our fae guide.

He nodded, leaning his pack against a tree. "We wait."

We all sat down and opened our packs, taking a moment to drink some water and to eat a few of the dried snacks. Minutes went by with nothing, and I was starting to get agitated. What were our options if they wouldn't allow us entrance into the dark lands? After an agonizing amount of time, the elves reappeared out of thin air, just like Violet always did. I had been expecting them to come back, but still, the sudden sign of them made my breath hitch. Kade and I slowly stood.

A slightly smaller — but still well over my height — dark-haired elf with pearlescent skin and a long gray cloak stepped forward. "We will grant you access to the dark lands, and I will be your host for the time you are there."

Host? Did that mean he was fighting with us, or reporting back to his people our every move? Meh, it really didn't matter. We were going in.

"Thank you," I told them as Dante came up behind me and bowed deeply to the elves.

The elf leader, who had done most of the talking, stepped forward. "If injury befalls you in the dark lands, we will not come to your aid."

At first, I thought he was speaking to us, but then I realized he was speaking to our host. The gray-cloaked elf nodded and placed a hand over his chest. "On my honor," he stated, and with that, all of the elves disappeared again.

We all stood there for a stretch of uncomfortable silence until the elf host spun around and gave us all a curt nod. His cloak fluttered in the wind and I saw an array of shiny weapons beneath. "I am Zandu, and I will bring honor to my family's name with this great quest."

Okay. Good motivation. I liked it. He had something driving him other than just our need. For creatures who normally did not involve themselves in the battles of others, I sensed this was important.

"Thank you, Zandu." I put on my most polite queen voice. "If you would lead us into the fae lands, we would be ever so grateful."

He held up a hand and gave me a half smirk. "You highborn, always rushing into everything with your swords raised and your egos engorged."

Kade gave a low rumble in his throat beside me, but I nudged his leg with my knee and he stopped. Zandu raised an eyebrow at Kade, turning back to me. "What do you know about the Dark Fae Lord's creatures?"

I squirmed under his gaze. "Not much. I've fought an ercho twice."

Zandu broke out into a full-blown grin, showcasing a mouth of slightly pointed teeth. "erchos are little pests compared to what hides in the lands beyond this gate."

I swallowed hard, suddenly feeling unprepared for this mission. It had been a rapid, ill-planned sort of journey, but there was an urgency we couldn't ignore. Every day I stayed in New York was another day for the dark ones to build their army, to initiate whatever plans they were making.

I was actually pretty good at being thrown into the deep end, learning on the job, so it had made sense ... at the time.

Kade stepped closer; he was equal height with the elf. "Queen Arianna has powerful magic, and so do I. If you have information you would like to share with us about these dark creatures, we would be grateful, but show some respect toward my mate, the same way we have shown your people respect." Kade's voice was calm, but there was no way anyone missed the deadly undertones.

I found myself holding my breath as the elf assessed him. Kian took a step closer to his brother, their broad shoulders filling a section between two trees. Something twinkled in the elf's eyes, and then he gave a half head bow.

"I've always admired how driven by love the highborn can be." His normally blunt voice held a note of wistfulness. I knew there was a story there — a story we didn't get to hear, because he was suddenly all business again. "The beasts that live in the water, the slimers, can come onto land, but they prefer to pull you into a watery grave. They cannot be killed by any normal weapon. The only enemy of a water beast is fire."

We all nodded. The five of us were slowly inching closer to Zandu, trying to absorb every piece of advice.

"Winged, or skybeasts, like ercho, harpy, and jets, can only be defeated with an arrow between their eyes."

Kian nodded, as he was our bow man on this journey. King Samson had outfitted him with a bunch of fancy silver-tipped arrows.

"Wait," I interrupted. "We have killed a harpy before, with a sword." I'd seen her chest stop moving.

The elf shook his head. "They can be disabled … their bodies mimic death, but they are able to be revived by the Dark Fae Lord if you don't kill them in the exact manner I say."

Thank the gods we found the elves. Their knowledge was going to prove invaluable, I had no doubt.

Kade intercepted my thought: *Or they found us. Maybe the divine are on our side here?*

That would be a nice change.

Zandu lowered his voice. "The killians are ground beasts and they are aplenty. It's this creature which forms the main fodder for the dark one's army. Their hide is well protected, made from something similar to metal. Completely impenetrable. Their only weakness is a soft tissue flap near their neck. Beheading them will kill them."

Dante unsheathed his sword and I knew he had just taken on the task of taking out the killians.

"There are many more smaller creatures, but they are of no real concern unless one bites or claws you. Don't get bitten or scratched by anything in the dark realm, not even a bush," Zandu warned.

With each warning my gut tightened with nerves.

Finally he looked at Kade. "The only way to kill the Dark Fae Lord is to snuff out the final sliver of humanity he has left with the dark weapon you possess, and then destroy his staff. I never believed we would end his reign, because I never believed anyone could wield a dark weapon and not succumb to its call. We will wait and see how you fare."

He might not have faith in my mate, but I did. Kade was one of the strongest beings I knew, and I would keep him from the darkness. Complementary powers went both ways. Zandu took one final glance at our small hunting party and then spun around to open a portal. I stared into the shimmery oval, seeing the land beyond.

It wasn't the stench of oil and death that had panic rising up inside of me, it was the sight of that damn lake from my dreams, and the black slithering creatures that swam within it. I welcomed the panic; it had my senses firing, my adrenalin pumping. My wolf was restless, pacing and growling in my chest, urging me forward. She was ready to end this. And so was I.

The war had begun.

Kian had his bow out. I held a long blade. Shelley had a two-pronged weapon in each hand, Dante his scary sword. Zandu appeared to be unarmed, but considering how many blades I'd seen beneath his coat, I knew he was one huge walking weapon. Our hunting party was ready.

The step through to the other side was silent and fast; the energy almost jerked me through, and I barely kept my feet on the icy ground. The cold bit into me; it felt even more all-encompassing than the winter lands. Adrenalin was keeping me warm though, my wolf prickling across my skin as she tried to force the change. It was almost unfair that I had to choose between her and my magic, because one didn't seem to work with the other. I felt her reassurance, though, that she would aid me in whatever way she could.

Taking a deep breath, knowing that things were going to get very messy soon, I decided to take a moment for a Calista-style positive affirmation. "We will defeat the Dark Fae Lord and winter queen. We will prevent war and save thousands of lives. We will not let the darkness win." My words were barely above a whisper; they were for me alone.

I felt Finn slip into my thoughts and it was a pleasant surprise that we could indeed communicate over this long distance. *You got this, Ari. I'll be waiting for you.*

My familiar was with me at all times, hearing my thoughts and hopes and dreams, my insecurities and fears. He was my other half.

"We've been spotted." Zandu's terse warning brought me back to the danger around me. Everyone was through the portal now, so we a formed a line of defense. I heard screeches in the sky, and glancing up I almost cried when I saw how many creatures were circling above us.

Zandu followed my line of sight. "I can shield us from above, for a short time, to give us a chance to make it farther into the center." He pointed across the frozen lake, the one from my dreams. "That's where the Dark Fae Lord will be."

It was a castle of sorts, thick and squat, like ice blocks dumped on top of each other. There was nothing aesthetically pleasing about it, but I could see it was solid, almost impossible to penetrate. The lake itself was mostly frozen over, with just a few patches of open water where the creatures must have broken through to the surface.

"Hopefully the Dark Fae Lord and winter queen come out to fight when they realize we are here," Kade said. "Save us some time getting through this mass to them."

"Something has definitely realized we are here," Shelley muttered.

She wasn't kidding. A horde of creatures were charging for us, the killians — I assumed — judging from the steel-like consistency to their outer layer. They looked like huge ants, with multiple round bodies, thick armor like shields on their dark brown skin, and gigantic metallic pincers on the front of their bodies. One near the front threw back its head and roared, giving me a direct visual of pink flesh. This must be the soft vulnerable part we needed to aim for.

The closer they got, the more details I was picking up. They were almost the same size as me in height, but much thicker. Their bodies were segmented, moving in ways I'd never seen before, almost like each part was disconnected from the other.

There were also a lot of them.

"Remember, hit the soft flesh in their necks," Zandu shouted, as the first line of them was almost upon us.

I braced myself, blade in attack position, zeroing in on the targets. A screech above almost knocked me off my focus, but when the harpy bounced off whatever invisible shield Zandu had erected, I was able to focus on the ant-like creatures again.

The first one slammed into me with solid strength, its weight pushing me back as I fought to stop its pinchers from carving my heart out of my chest. My wolf rose up, adding her strength to mine, and we managed to grab on to each side of the pincher, wrenching it apart. It cracked in two, and then my blade was swinging before I could think about it, slicing straight through its throat.

With a garbled grumble of a noise, the killian collapsed, melting into a pile of dark goo. Okay, then ... apparently when you killed a dark creature, it became sludge. As I stepped forward to take on the next creature, I saw Shelley slip away from our group and head for a bank of trees off to the left. At first I thought she'd gotten scared and was running away — I wouldn't blame her one bit — but then an army of white-cloaked fae stepped out. Members of the winter queen's army, complete with white fur uniform.

Shelley was doing the opposite of running in fear, she was heading right for danger, giving us time, holding off those winter soldiers. I lost sight of her as I sliced into another killian. They were strong brutes, but quite dumb and clumsy. As long as I stayed alert, I would be okay.

The killians were pushing us back towards the edge of the frozen lake. With each step, I had to look behind me to make sure I wasn't suddenly going to find myself on thin ice. Finally, Kade took down the last killian, but I saw more in the distance, hobbling our way with their wonky gait.

"I think we should cross the lake. Easiest way," I told the group.

Shelley wasn't with us, yet, but she looked safe — standing in front of the winter queen's guards. It looked like she was using her powers to influence the front line of the white-clad soldiers to start fighting with those behind. It was clever; I doubted she had enough power to influence all the soldiers in one go. This way, she just kept them fighting each other.

I glanced back at the ice again, seeing the zipping creatures below waiting for us.

"The killians are too heavy. They won't step on the ice," Zandu said, before he whipped out a weapon from under his cloak. It was a torch, which immediately burst to life, flaming with an iridescent pink fire. He handed it to me and I took it without question, assuming this was the fire we needed to kill anything that jumped out of the lake.

Then Zandu pulled a bow from his cloak — seriously, where did I get one of these magical cloaks? — and in two swift moves loosed an arrow, taking a harpy down. It fell to the ground with a thud, arrow between the eyes.

"Go!" he shouted. "I will hold off the sky creatures with your other bowman."

Kian moved in next to Zandu, both of them focused on the sky. I didn't even want to look up, didn't want to see what creatures were waiting above to pluck off our heads. Dante pulled a second sword out, so he now held a lethal blade in both hands. "I will keep the killians off you, just in case they do decide to risk the lake." He then ran straight at the approaching creatures.

I looked at Kade, who nodded. All of our friends and allies were fighting for their lives. It was up to us to finish this once and for all. Kade stepped out onto the ice first; it made a slight groan of protest but otherwise held. I followed about three feet to his right, to disperse our weight. We walked with brisk care, avoiding all ice that looked particularly thin, and the few open black pools of icy water.

We were about halfway across when I saw something dark slithering on my right.

"Kade..." I murmured.

"I saw it," he said, slowing, sword raised.

We walked a few more steps when the ice right before me cracked wide open and an oily black ercho broke the surface. It reached out with one of its claws, gashing my leg.

I cried out, swinging my torch by instinct.

Like it was doused in accelerant, the pink flames ignited its skin with ease, rushing across its back, and down the length of its bat-like wings. High-pitched screeches filled the air, and the scent of burning rubber — thick and tar-like — clogged my nostrils. The ercho flopped about as the fire burned it alive and slowly melted the ice it lay on. I peered at the hole it had broken through and saw that the lake was black and oily.

It wasn't water.

Half a dozen shadowy figures sped under the ice to answer the ercho's dying call, and I was reminded of how quickly it had caught alight.

It gave me an idea.

"Kade, how fast can you run?" I gave him a wink. He was more than fast enough. I just hoped I could keep up. I held the torch to the open oil spot.

Kade's eyes gleamed. "Do it," he said.

Needing no more encouragement, I dropped the torch into the oily water, and we both took off running.

Burn baby burn.

Today I was taking out the Dark Fae Lord and all of his evil babies.

Chapter Twelve

What hides in the darkness?

TURNED OUT THAT an oil-filled lake would burn faster and stronger than I had expected. The top layer of the ice was already starting to crack, as the flames behind us spread so fast that I could feel real heat licking my skin. This was no ordinary sort of fire. The elven flame mixed with dark magic was forming a magical fire show of epic proportions.

"Almost there, Ari," Kade shouted, but not even his soothing husky tones were going to help when the ice was breaking under my feet. At any point, I was going to plunge into the oil, and then the creatures below — or the fire — would consume me.

I kept my eyes on Kade's broad shoulders. He was not far in front of me, and I knew he was limiting his speed to stay with me. If I wasn't so busy running for my life, I would be shouting at him to move it. He was so much heavier than me; he was about to crash through. He must have realized that, because when there was about twenty feet to the shore, he dived, his muscled legs propelling him onto the snowy bank. I knew I couldn't make that distance, but I had no choice, it was jump or die. My wolf pushed further forward, assessing the situation, and in the last second she tried to force the change on me. We wouldn't make it in my human form, but I was lighter, more nimble in my wolf.

I don't have time, I told her. I could change in a minute or less, but I didn't even have a spare second.

"Jump, Ari." Kade was right on the edge of the lake, arms outstretched. He would come for me if I didn't make it, but there was no point in both of us dying.

Heat snapped behind me, ice slushed and cracked under my boots, and I launched myself forward. Using every ounce of shifter strength I could gather, I fell about three feet short of the shore, but Kade's long arms came in handy again as he snatched me out of the air and propelled us both backwards. I crashed on top of him as he hit the ground hard.

Screams and screeches filled the air, something I hadn't been paying attention to when I was running for my life. The scent of burning flesh and leather was almost overwhelming, but I fought through the nausea, forcing myself to focus. The lake was completely ablaze, flames standing ten feet or more in the air. It was probably only burning on the surface, if it required oxygen like on Earth, but the screams told me that plenty of the creatures who lived in its depths were being ignited too.

A powerful, guttural yell echoed across the lands. The fury within it boomed out, shaking the ground. Kade and I clambered to our feet.

"Guess someone found out about his precious creatures," I murmured, already scanning the darkness.

Kade stood to his full height, lifting the strap of the case holding the staff over his shoulders. Thankfully, he had not lost it in that mad dash. In a second, he had the lid open and the weapon in his hands. I fought down the urge to knock it out of his grasp, hating the eerie glint of its dark light. The cloying pressure of its energy — now that it was free from its spelled confines — swelled out and started trying to infiltrate into my power, brushing against me insidiously.

Swallowing hard, I pulled my eyes from the staff, focusing instead on the boxy castle, wanting to be prepared when the enraged Dark Fae Lord made his appearance.

I didn't have to wait long.

He flashed in with a swirl of dark smoke, his long cloak billowing behind him, his staff, the twin of Kade's, clutched tightly in his hand. Pure fury filled his face, making him look inhuman as he slammed the tip of his dark weapon into the ground. The horn Kade had sliced off was still missing, giving his face a lopsided look.

"You and I could have been great together, Arianna. Now you will join your mother, in death!" His shouts filled the air, and a giant crack split the ground where he had slammed the staff into the earth. It started small, but as it shot toward Kade and me, got wider and wider.

We sprinted away from the widening chasm in the ground, reorienting ourselves so we could approach the Dark Fae Lord from a different angle. As I ran, the ache in my leg started to increase, right where the ercho had clawed me. I pushed it from my mind. Nothing I could do about it now.

Any sign of the queen? Kade asked.

Nothing, I said, and then almost in the same instant I felt the icy shift of the wind. *Wait ... she's here.*

Her magic was familiar to me. It called to my own in a way I hated, but also accepted. I wasn't going to freak out about it anymore. I couldn't help who my family were, just who I was. *I'll go after the Dark Fae Lord*, Kade said. *The winter queen is yours. Stay safe, my love.*

I love you, King Kade. Don't you dare die.

Or turn evil.

I hid the last part from him, because I didn't want him to know of my doubts. But it was a nagging fear I couldn't erase. Kade was already focused on his target, the staff raised above his head as he ran, its dark energy seeming to increase the closer we got to the Dark Fae Lord and the other dark weapon.

Isalinda stepped out of the shadows then, gliding across the snow to stand at the side of her dark ally. The stunning white horse, which she had been riding last time I saw her, was there in the background. *Her familiar?* I'd never seen a horse as a familiar before; it was quite spectacular as it pawed the ground near the queen. I couldn't hurt a magnificent beast like that, one who had no choice in the sort of fae it was bonded with. But if I killed the queen, and fae familiar bonds were the same as shifters', the horse was going to die. *Dammit.* Why were there no easy choices in these situations? I had to save my people, but in doing so, some would be sacrificed.

The longer I was a queen, the more I was starting to understand the Red Queen and her actions. One thing was becoming very clear, the time for softness had passed. I needed to embrace my inner Red Queen if I was going to defeat Isalinda. There would be no polite conversation, no point in dragging out the inevitable. I wanted her dead and burning along with the entire lake as soon as possible.

Without a word, I gathered my magic, both fae and mecca, and sent a swirl of frosty ice right at her face. I wanted to throw her off by attacking first, but as I expected, she simply held up a hand and stopped my magic midair, using her own version of frozen magic. As our two spells collided, there was a shattering blast, and a long spiraling ice sculpture formed in that exact spot, before spreading across a ten foot radius.

The winter queen grinned, her lips still a creepy corpse-blue. "Good girl, you've been studying. This should be fun."

Before I could even pivot my weight or think of a counter-spell, she threw magic at me that traveled faster than I could see. The energy slammed into my legs, wrapping around them, bringing the chill of ice with it as it crawled up my body, immobilizing me.

She frowned, tapping one long finger nail against her chin. "That was far too easy. I take back what I said. You're actually quite pathetic. This is going to be over in a second."

I didn't struggle, sure in my ability to break her magic. But I wouldn't until she moved closer, because no doubt she thought she had won and was going to come over and gloat before she killed me. The ice had reached my pelvis now and was still rising. And sure enough, she was striding toward me. I continued feigning defeat, letting her come closer and closer.

When she was inches from me, she peered down. "Your lineage failed you, child. You're nothing but a—"

Blocking out her hatred, I reached for the energy that made me unique in this world. Fae and shifter. Dark and light. I let it surge from me in a strong, uninterrupted stream. Dark purple sparkles filled the air and the ice spell around me dissolved in an instant. I lunged forward, my wolf howling in my chest before my voice lifted and I added my own howls to the wolf's.

I wrapped my hands around her throat, the magic pouring from me so strong that it pushed us forward. The winter queen's head cracked hard against a nearby dried-out tree stump. She let out a low groan, but I didn't remove my hands from her throat. Instead I squeezed harder.

Her face was turning a shade of purple; she struggled and clawed at me. But I had shifter and fae strength. I would not be defeated again.

I felt the weakness sliding through my center, my body starting to run out of reserves of energy. Adrenalin had hidden most of my pain and injuries, the strength of my power helping me focus, but suddenly the dull ache in my leg from the ercho gash was no longer just a mild throb. The pain began stabbing at me, and my arms trembled.

Something snapped in my leg and I keeled over, losing my grip on the queen. White hot agony ripped through my leg, and I realized my shin bone had just broken ... on its own. I let out a blood-curdling scream as more pain took me over. Was this the ercho venom?

Was it actually eating my bones?

"Die!" The winter queen interrupted my anguish by unleashing a flurry of wind magic that picked me up like a tornado and whipped me into the air.

I couldn't think straight, I couldn't fight back.

I'd felt a lot of pain in my life as an heir, and then a queen, but *nothing* compared to having my bones splinter and shatter inside of me. As the wind swirled me higher into the air, I reached down and ran a hand along my shin, assessing the damage. Bile rose in my throat at the pain as I could feel at least two inches missing from my tibia bone, and that gap appeared to be growing. Just as I feared, the venom was eating my skeleton.

Finn... I couldn't think properly with the pain and nausea from being inside of a spinning, frozen tornado.

Ari!

Dark Injury. Ercho. Eating my bones. Need ... Violet. I was losing my grip on reality, seconds from unconsciousness.

The tornado stopped then, and I was falling. I used the last of my consciousness and energy to cushion my fall, landing in a thick bed of snow in a remote part of the woods. From this vantage point, flat on my back, snow and cold seeping into my clothes and body, I couldn't see Isalinda anymore.

I must have blacked out for a few seconds, only coming to when Finn's voice blasted in my head. *Ari! Violet says the mecca powder can do almost anything.*

I didn't waste energy on a reply. Gathering together every ounce of discipline and strength, I forced my hand to move, forced it to retrieve the vial. I popped the cap off just as I caught sight of the winter queen stalking towards me, ready to finish me off.

What had Rowan said? The mecca powder needed only direction and it could do anything?

Heal me, please, I begged of the small powerful glass of purple dust as my magic wrapped around the vial. I tipped my head back, taking a mouthful of the powder onto my tongue.

I had no idea if I should have made a paste of it and put it right on the wound, but from my current position I really couldn't do much except swallow it.

A low chuckle caught my attention, cold and hard, and filled with a malicious kind of enjoyment. The winter queen was looking down on me, her delight clear in her turned-up lips and shiny eyes. I chucked the empty vial to the side, hoping the stuff worked quickly. Otherwise, I could see my death on Isalinda's face, and I wasn't ready to go out yet. I still had too much to do.

A warm tingle spread out through my tongue. I let the powder sit there for a few moments, not swallowing or spitting it out for fear of something going wrong. A little energy filtered into my veins, just enough so that I could roll over to get away from the queen.

Another few moments and the sharp stabbing pains decreased enough that I could struggle to stand, using my one good leg and a shriveled tree for balance. Isalinda watched me, not attacking, enjoying my pain.

Finally she had to brag: "You really thought you could waltz in here and defeat me, Arianna?" Her voice was low, laced with all the fury one would expect of a winter storm. I could see small flurries stirring up behind her.

I searched deep for something to defend myself with, but I was still half dead, spent of energy, and fighting the ercho venom. The purple mecca was working slowly, no doubt struggling against the poison.

Arianna, friend of trees...

If I hadn't been so out of it, I would have jumped as the tree spoke in my head.

Exhaustion made it easy for me to control my reaction, keeping my eyes half lidded and calm. The powder had completely dissolved on my tongue now, and a cool tingle was working its way into my leg.

"Kill or be killed. You left me no choice," I told her, trying to keep her talking.

Can you help me? I asked the poor skeleton of a tree. I hadn't thought to use the trees here, assuming they were tainted by the darkness of this land. They all looked dead. Almost like that inverted tree on the cover of the dark book with its sliver of stone. Maybe that's what it had represented. Death. To everything living.

I was distracted by the winter queen's broad grin. It was a smile that didn't reach her eyes, her face awash in shadows.

"Oh, Arianna, can I just say that you took longer than we thought to come to us. I figured once we sent those stupid wolves to you with fae blades, you'd assume we were planning on assassinating you, and then you'd storm right over here to stop us. You were slow. I should have anticipated that, but eventually you did as we wanted. You played right into our hands."

I stared up at her in disbelief. She had been waiting for us to come across?

She kept smirking at me, and I was starting to feel like an idiot, then she tilted her head in a certain way and her familiar profile reminded me of something. The tilt of her chin. Almond shape of her eyes. They were like mine. And Luc...

"Where's your son?" The words croaked out of me as fear locked me in its grip.

This entire time we had been focused on the fae lord and the winter queen, all the while forgetting about my menace of a father. "You never planned on letting the Dark Fae Lord rule Earth, did you?"

This time her smile did reach her eyes and she stepped closer. "Of course not. I only needed him because he said he could find me the second dark staff. I almost killed him when he lost it to you *shifters*." Her lips curled in disgust. "But he assured me you would fall for the other part of our plan. You'd come and find us here, and he would be able to retrieve the staff, which is rightfully mine."

"Where is Luca?" I repeated with more force.

"In New York, marching on your people."

Everything inside of me clenched, and on instinct I reached for my bond to the thousands of wolf and bear shifters I ruled. The essence of my people so strong that I could almost scent shifter on the breeze. As their energy filled me, a power like no other strengthened my body. It was as I had always said, as I had always believed: a queen was only as strong as her people. And I would use my love for them to destroy the winter queen—a monarch who did not value the ones she should.

I lashed out with so much magic it blew both of us back a few feet.

The queen recovered quickly, throwing magic at me in one blue stream of ice. I blocked, and we traded blow for blow in a flurry of ice and wind. I had to hop to stay on my one good foot, but the power of my shifters and their bond to their queen was giving me a fighting chance. Any time I came close to a tree, I leaned against it for support. It was a comfort, like I had an ally right

at my side. Isalinda narrowed her eyes on me more than once and I knew she was trying to figure out where my sudden strength was coming from.

If she hadn't been so selfish and evil, she would have known. It was there all along for her to utilize, but as a true narcissist, she thought of no one but herself.

Neither of us gave an inch, and I was afraid we would be locked in this battle forever. Our powers were just too evenly matched, especially while I was injured.

The tree next to Isalinda moved. *What in the...?* It actually moved.

Roots ripped out of the ground, throwing dirt and bark everywhere as the queen lurched to a halt, her jaw unhinging as she stared unblinkingly at the mobile tree.

I wanted to stare too. It was probably one of the most incredible, unbelievable things I had ever seen. Animation had overtaken the tree; it had arm-like branches, leg-like roots, and it was walking.

Focus. I forced myself to look away. This was my one chance.

Building up a large ball of magic, I hopped forward, and keeping nothing inside, thrust it at the queen, directing it to encase her. This was the spell she had first used on me in her castle grounds. It felt right, poetic even, to use her own spell against her. Even though she was the winter queen, I could use the ice against her.

She froze in place, literally, too spent to break through my frost. From her toes to her neck, encased in my spell, only her head remained exposed. Kneeling down, I fashioned a sword from the ice, a long, lethal, shimmery blue number. Sometimes my winter magic was beyond incredible. I couldn't believe I'd ever been afraid of it.

Holding my weapon, I hobbled toward the queen, relieved that some strength seemed to be returning in my leg. The pain was a dull throb now. She tracked my movements, her eyes filled with a tumultuous fury. Even when vulnerable, she couldn't turn off her bitch face.

"Your reign is over," I declared. She opened her mouth, but before she got the chance to cast a spell, or speak at all, I swung my ice sword, and in one clean blow took her head off.

It was a more humane death than she deserved, considering the way she tortured people, had cut up a little girl, but I was done playing games. I wanted to prove I was not like her in any way. She would have drawn out my death, hurt me as much as she could.

Her head went one way, her body another, falling to the ground and shattering the ice, her blood gushing into the air before settling to paint the snow in a macabre artwork. Red mist settled across the white signaling the end of a monarch. A tree, the one that had walked and distracted her, shot out a branch and pierced the winter queen's abdomen, lifting her high up into the air. Another branch pierced through her skull, lifting it as well.

It then carried both to the burning lake, and flung her body out into its flaming depths.

She cared not for nature. Neglected her trees.

I realized another tree had uprooted and was standing at my side, its branch brushing my arm.

As I expected, her inability to put her land and people first had come back to bite her.

Thank you, I said. *I will always treat trees and nature with the respect they deserve. You have a friend and ally in me.*

It extended its branch arm toward me, and as I reached out to grab it, thinking it was like a handshake, a perfectly polished walking stick broke off. I smiled, sheathing my ice sword just in case I needed it again.

Placing one end of the stick on the ground, I leaned into it as I hurried forward, using my bad leg more fully than I had up to this point. My leg didn't collapse into mush, which was a great sign, but it still hurt like all hell. Pain shot up to my kneecap and I sucked in a breath.

Okay, it definitely needed more time to heal.

I eased some of my weight off it, putting more onto the stick as I headed toward Kade. Through the trees, I was catching glimpses of the darkness, and as I hobbled closer I saw that Kade had the Dark Fae Lord pinned against a tree. Now both of his antlers were hacked off — one lying in a puddle of black oil.

The back of Kade's thigh had a wide four-inch gash that didn't seem to be healing, but he was standing strong, so either it wasn't laced with dark poison or my mate had developed some sort of immunity after last time.

Just behind them was an advancing line of a half-dozen killians, no doubt trying to come to their master's aid. At this stage, they were being held off by Dante and Kian—who must have crossed the long way around the lake—the pair swinging their swords with precision, taking off heads left and right. Satisfied they were okay, I focused on the more pressing problem.

I limped closer to Kade quickly, one hand on my walking stick and the other on my sword. Whatever the ice magic had done, my weapon remained strong and cold beneath my touch. A breeze blew a wave of smoke from the lake through me, and I coughed a few times as the acridness invaded my nose and lungs.

I've killed the queen. I'm coming to help, I sent to Kade, because at the moment I couldn't see him through the blackness.

I wasn't sure what state physically or mentally he was in, I hadn't been able to focus on him during my fight. But I needed him to know that I was here now. I had his back.

Put up your shield. His response was weak and delayed. *He has more magic than we presumed. I've almost ... got him.*

I was through the smoke now, nearly at Kade's side. My focus was on him, the worry bubbling in my gut again. He had sounded so strained. I had no idea what he was doing to kill the Dark Fae Lord but ... he did seem to be in control. I slowed, erecting a shimmery bubble of magic across my skin, a technique I'd learned from Violet and Rowan. It was supposed to repel dark spells.

I had no idea if it would work against the strength of this particularly dark fae, but it was better than nothing. When I was about six feet from them, Kade lost his focus. It was no more than a split-second that his energy wavered, but it was enough for the fae lord to find strength to attack. Kade was thrown high into the air. He arced up, and then fell with a thud right at my feet.

I heard a bone snap, but as soon as Kade had fallen he was standing again. Somehow. The look on his face was beautiful and deadly. It was a Kade I didn't really know, a warrior, a killer. But, when I searched deep in our bond, I sensed my mate under his lethal intentions.

The Dark Fae Lord picked up his hacked-off antler and held it in his hands. It was freely dripping that poisonous oil. Within seconds it had transformed into a long, pointed, wickedly sharp weapon. That dark stone — his staff was in his other hand — had given him some extraordinary gifts. From the story he told me, it sounded as if he had once been just an ordinary fae. He'd wanted to be more, and he had succeeded. But at what cost?

The dark fae lifted his head and sniffed, looking over his shoulder at Kian, who was now a mere five feet from him, fighting a killian. Kian and Dante had been pushed forward to the edge of this fight.

"Your kin? He smells of you," the Dark Fae Lord murmured.

In a motion so fast I almost missed it happening, the fae dove toward Kian, antler-weapon raised. I threw my hands up, calling my magic forward.

"Kian!" Kade bellowed, sprinting toward his brother. He wasn't going to make it in time,

hampered by whatever bone his fall had broken. I shot my magic off in a quick blast, hoping to at least distract the Dark Fae Lord, but my aim was off. It hit a mere three inches from his feet, freezing the ground there.

Before Kade or I could do anything, the fae shoved his antler-weapon low into Kian's back, slowly ripping it up into his chest, inflicting maximum damage. Somewhere deep in the woods I heard Shelley scream, a haunting wail that filled the air with pain and sorrow. Tears sprang to my eyes, the pain in my heart so sharp and aching that I held a hand to my chest to try and ease it.

Kade's chest was heaving, bear roars echoing across the clearing. We both hobbled forward together — I had all but abandoned my stick now, choosing the pain for a faster gait. When I reached for Kade's mind I slammed up against a wall of darkness. It was like a thick cloud, but with much more substance.

My mate was in a bad place I could not reach. The Fae Lord spun around, staff raised, but he was too slow. In his pleasure at killing, in his bloodlust, he had forgotten there was another bear brother, one he had just enraged. Kade let out a bear roar and swiped with a partially-shifted hand claw across the dark one's face.

He was aiming to hurt, not kill. Kade was too far gone in his own pain and fury. All he wanted was revenge. A row of deep cuts sprang up across the fae lord's face, black blood oozing out of them, and that injury was enough to distract the evil bastard. As he cried out, reaching for his face, Kade swiped again. This time I thought he was going for a kill, but instead he snatched up the Dark Fae Lord's staff.

Maybe he wasn't as far gone as I had thought.

He had skipped his chance to hurt the fae lord more, going for the weapon. Because he was the only one here who could handle the dark stone. My mate staked the staff into the ground, and then with one kick snapped it in half. The fae let out a weak cry, which turned into a high-pitched screech when Kade used his mighty strength to propel the top half, with the dark crystal on it, out into the burning lake. The second it hit the fire, thunder rolled across the sky and the Dark Fae Lord fell to his knees.

Chapter Thirteen

Arianna, the great winter.

I NEVER EXPECTED fire could destroy the stone, or regular fire at least, as it did not destroy mecca, and the energy of this stone was similar. But I'd already noticed that there was something different about this dark lake of flames, this elven fire. Which hopefully meant the stone was gone. Forever. The defeated-looking fae was certainly acting like it was.

Kade, who was no longer limping, leaned down and snatched up the second dark staff, the one he had been training with. He returned with it in his grasp, face devoid of any emotion, almost as if he were a robot, and stared down at the fae still crumpled on the ground, oily blood seeping out of his face wounds.

A small, whimper-like noise escaped from me, and Kade turned in my direction. I almost screamed when I saw his eyes. Gone was that shimmery bronze that I loved, and in its place, pure darkness.

Oh shit.

When my mate turned back to his enemy, I lurched forward, halting myself. I didn't know what to do. Should I be stopping Kade from touching any more darkness? Or would the death of the Dark Fae Lord return him to me?

Before I could make a decision, Kade swung the staff around so that the stone was facing the fae. He then lifted the weapon high, shifting into his half-bear form at the same time. I had no idea why, until he slammed the staff — dark crystal side down — into the fae's chest. He must have needed the extra strength to make sure he could smash it all the way through, to make sure he killed the evil fae once and for all.

As the Dark Fae Lord fell backwards, Kade ripped the staff free, pulling out half or more of the fae's chest. Everything in the clearing stilled, it seemed as if noise ceased, and then the fae grinned, blood stained teeth on display. "Darkness has … you …now," he choked out, before coughing twice, and then with one last breath, he stilled.

The air charged with electricity, and then, in an instant, the thunder stopped and the sky shone a perfect, cloudless blue.

The Dark Fae Lord was dead.

I approached Kade slowly. "You need to throw the staff into the lake," I told him. Already I could see the fire across that expanse was dying down. The evil was dispersing from this land, and when it was gone, so too would be the fire able to remove the crystal from this world. Or at least take it somewhere that was untouchable to any more fae.

Kade snarled in my direction, spinning, and running for his brother.

I was turning to follow him when a line of tall entities stepped into view. All breath choked out of me, and I stood dumfounded for a beat.

The ... trees.

While Kade had been fighting the Dark Fae Lord, the trees had been amassing an army. There was a long line now, all of them walking over the ground; a true sense of life filled them, despite their blackened limbs. The darkness leaving had returned some of their power. I watched in awed silence as they started to toss the dark creatures into the lake—creatures who had fallen with their lord—cleaning the land.

I moved quickly toward one of them; it halted, waiting for my touch. *Can you please place the*

Dark Fae Lord's body in the fiery lake? I asked, when my hand was pressed to its middle.

With pleasure, it responded.

Thank you!

I turned then and ran, still a little awkwardly, toward Kian. As I dropped down at his side, on the opposite side to where Kade knelt, my mate lifted his face to meet my gaze. "He's dead."

Those words came out quietly, before he dropped his head back and the deepest, most grief-stricken bellow emerged from him. I heard an echoing cry, louder than before. Shelley was coming for her mate; she was going to see his lifeless body lying here.

"Kade..." I didn't know what to say. I was terrified at the darkness in his eyes, and absolutely devastated about his brother.

Kade sat there for two seconds, frozen. Then his grip on the staff tightened. "Violet," he breathed.

Violet? Violet couldn't get here in time to help, and she definitely couldn't bring people back from the dead.

"Kade..." I repeated slowly, hoping to jolt him out of whatever weird place he was in. Grief had obviously affected his mind, which was to be expected, but with so much darkness within him I was worried about his next actions.

The crystal on the end of the staff pulsed then, the black blood of the Dark Fae Lord sliding away; the veins in Kade's arm that held it turned black. I could see rivers of ink throbbing up and down his arms.

"Violet showed me the way. She foresaw this," he said in a voice I didn't recognize.

"Kade, you're scaring me. You need to let go of the staff now. It is changing you. Kade!" I moved closer, reaching for him, my energy already surging forward in preparation of siphoning the darkness from him.

"I can save him," he said as the black ink in his veins continued to expand, surging up to his throat and down in under his shirt.

"At what cost?" I shouted, losing my cool as I dove forward, ready to rip the staff away from him. Kade anticipated this move, though, and while he didn't push me away, he did angle himself so that I tumbled past him.

I crashed into the ground, and as I pushed myself up, Shelley came tearing through the woods. She was cradling Jota, Kian's lifeless familiar in her arms. We hadn't brought our familiars with us, but Kian's must have crossed over to the Otherworld somehow when he sensed his bonded one dying.

"Kian!" she shouted desperately, slipping and sliding across the melting snow as she fell at his feet.

Kade faced me warily. *I've got this, Ari. You need to trust me.*

I recoiled as his darkness brushed against my mind, and I couldn't get the fae's last words out of my head, *darkness has you.*

What the hell was I supposed to do? Charge my own mate and rip that staff from his hands, or do as he asked and trust him? In normal circumstance that wouldn't even be a question to ask. I always trusted Kade, but this was not my Kade. Not completely. The essence of him was slipping away from me, and I was afraid it might already be too late.

But what if he could save his brother?

If I stopped him, he would never forgive me. I would lose him either way. I remained frozen for a beat, taking in Shelley's sobbing figure, the dead familiar, and my mate, who was strongly resembling the Dark Fae Lord right now. I lowered my arm, knowing there was no other option.

I would just keep faith that I had saved him from the darkness once, so I could do it again.

But I still had to offer him one last thought, so he would understand how I felt. "Are you sure, Kade?" I asked him. "Will Kian return as he was?

Your brother. Or will death have taken him only to return a shadow of the shifter you knew?"

Could we truly be returned from the dead? Should anyone mess with something that was the domain of the gods?

Kade took a deep breath in, staring at me with his black eyes. "This will work, Arianna. The darkness took him and the darkness will return him. But I must hurry, there is only a short window before his soul is beyond my reach."

I nodded, stepping back, giving him space. Kade raised the staff high over his head as that black ink visibly pulsed in his veins. Then he spun the staff upside down so that the dark crystal was hovering just over Kian's chest and brought it down hard, smacking his brother in the chest quickly before pulling up again. It was the same movement he'd used on the Dark Fae Lord, only this time he didn't pierce his brother's chest.

Kian's body jerked once when the crystal hit his chest, but then he fell flat again. Shelley sat up slowly, mouth open, eyes wide.

I took a staggered step closer. "Try again!" I said.

I'd seen something when the crystal connected — a flicker of mecca had washed over Kian.

Kade obliged, slamming the staff down a bit longer this time, but not long enough to ... infect ... his brother with the darkness. I was guessing my mate was using his power to filter pure creative mecca energy through the powerful crystal, but keeping the darkness inside himself — condemning himself to save his brother.

The next time he hit, more mecca shot into Kian and his whole body jumped up.

"More!" Shelley shouted at Kade, still desperately clutching Jota.

Kade slammed the staff down, his arms shaking with the power of holding the energy.

Suddenly the crow jerked in Shelley's hands, letting out a loud caw. At the same time, Kian gasped for air. I immediately looked to Kade, and in an almost slow-motion movement, he turned his entire body in my direction, the staff clutched tightly to his chest. I swallowed my cry, trying not to burst into hysterical sobs as our gazes met. His eyes were now completely black, even the part that was supposed to be white. His veins were thick and black, and he looked ... evil.

"So ... much ... power," he rumbled, looking at the staff like it was a lover. Like it was precious. I recognized that look, I had seen it directed my way more times than I could count.

I swallowed hard, hot tears running down my face even though I was trying my best to keep it together. I couldn't fall apart yet, I had to save Kade first.

My magic swirled closer to the surface, and as much as I wanted to reach out through our bond, I knew that wasn't the right way to approach this. Not yet. I needed him to come back a little first, because I wasn't sure I could fight him.

"Kade ... babe, give me the staff." I held out my hand. *Please, please, please.* I was not above begging, hoping and praying he would just hand me the weapon.

Kade's nostrils flared but he didn't say a word, staring at me as if he was trying to remember who I was. Movement to my left drew my attention, and even though I didn't want to turn away from evil-Kade, I quickly flicked my gaze to Kian. I had temporarily forgotten him, but it was a relief to see his normal handsome face, seemingly devoid of all darkness.

Thank the gods. Only one crazy shifter to deal with.

Turning back to my mate, I reached inside my shirt, slowly, and pulled out the ring he'd given me, holding it up on the long chain for him to see. "You gave this to me. You promised me forever, and I know you're a man of your word."

I held his gaze, even though it was physically hurting me to stare into those obsidian eyes. My chest cramped tighter and tighter, making it almost impossible to breathe. But I did not break our eye contact, and I did not lower my hand holding the chain.

Kade shook his head then, startling me with the sudden movement.

"Ari ... help." His words were forced out through his clenched jaw, and it looked like he was gripping the staff tighter.

That was all I needed to hear; he was not completely gone.

I shot out with mecca — it was a controlled blast, and I was reasonably sure it wouldn't hurt him too much. Maybe just enough to give me a chance. I knew he was fighting the darkness, but without help, it would win — there was too much inside of him now. My hit knocked him off his feet, shooting him backwards. As he slammed into the ground, the staff was flung from his grip — or maybe he found the strength to drop it. Kade was the strongest man I knew, so that was definitely a possibility.

Kade and I both scrambled for the staff, but before either of us could get our hands on it, Dante came out of nowhere, scooping it up. I changed course, diving across Kade, straddling him.

"No!" Kade bellowed, his desperate eyes locked on Dante. I expected my mate to use his strength and throw me across the field, but he

didn't. He just watched as the summer fae pitched the staff straight into the last fiery embers of the lake.

The moment it touched the surface the ground shook, hard enough to throw me off Kade. Every creature left alive in this godforsaken hellhole screeched. But my eyes were on my mate. His body was frozen, tense, his hands clenched tightly on either side of him. I could see there was a war going on inside of him. A war I was going to help him win.

I crawled back to his side, reaching out and placing my fingers on each side of his temples.

Zandu's voice came from behind me. "Be careful, highborn. It could take you too."

"If he's gone, I'm gone anyway," I said, my tone dead.

I closed myself off to the world, and using our bond, fully connected with Kade. I recoiled initially, fighting the urge to run as slimy, oily, insidious energy tried to cling to me and interweave with my power.

Kade, I whispered along our bond, searching for my mate in the darkness. He had come back to me before, he had given me the chance to destroy the staff. He had to still be in there.

I grabbed hold of the dark energy, and like a sticky spider web it clung to me. I began to pull it from Kade, allowing it to travel along the mate bond and into me. When it reach my chest I shivered, cocooning it with fae magic and transforming it like I did before. But this time there was too much, too fast. The more I siphoned from Kade, the more I felt like I was drowning in sadness and disease ... in a heavy emptiness. The world was pressing in on me and I wanted to die. Anything to escape the absolute darkness of my world.

I was alone.

Useless.

Worthless.

I did not deserve to live.

Ari... Kade's whisper caressed a part of my soul through the bond, bringing with it a sliver of light. It was enough, just that tiny speck of illumination, for me to have something to cling to. It gave me the power to blast the darkness within me, a sense of purpose. And the strength I needed to get to him, to open my eyes and breathe again.

But the darkness held me tightly, unwilling to give up its victim.

In my moment of despair, it wasn't Kade that saved me — Finn's voice slammed into me, loud and firm. *Arianna, of the red house. You are capable of more than you know. You are the queen of mecca. You can control the stones, the energy, the very life force of all people. Do not forget who you are. The winter prince has come for New York and only you can save us.*

Finn's message was a slap of clarity. I sucked in as much air as I could, filling my lungs until they ached, drawing on my mecca in a way I never had before, all the way through the veil that divided the two worlds. I drew energy from the mecca stones of Earth, and for the first time ever, I also drew from the stones in the Otherworld. Together the two powers intertwined within me and eviscerated the darkness. I released it all with a scream of rage that was loud enough to shatter any remaining icicles of this world.

When I had no more breath or darkness to expel, I opened my eyes. Clumps of ash were falling from the sky.

Kade had me in his arms, holding me close to his chest.

My eyes fluttered as I pressed myself into his arms, allowing a few cleansing breaths to refill my starved lungs. I could have cried — in happiness — when my natural joy for life washed through me. The emptiness was gone.

I had never been a person who struggled with depression; it was something I was eternally grateful for. But after that moment of darkness, I understood it a little more. I understood why people couldn't just "get over it" as they were often advised. It was like I had been wearing blinders and could see nothing but darkness ahead and behind. No matter how much light existed around me, I simply couldn't see it. I couldn't escape.

I never wanted to be in that place again.

It was so clear to me now. The dark stone never brought balance. The mecca was balanced; it could be used for good or evil, depending on the person. That darkness, it was only evil. I was glad to be rid of it, glad to see it destroyed.

"Ari, baby..." Kade cradled my face in his hands, my body still draped across him.

Familiar swirling, molten bronze eyes stared down at me. I reached out with our bond to find nothing but his normal mecca powers on the other end.

I pushed deeper, unwilling to let even an ounce of darkness taint my mate.

"It's gone," he said to me. "Every last sliver. For the first time in a long time, I am free. I couldn't even see how much I was being affected."

I swallowed hard, my voice a rasp when I said, "We underestimated it. The dark energy was clever."

He nodded. "I tried to keep it from you. I knew it was bad, but I thought I could handle it. I thought I was strong enough to fight it."

I wrapped my arms tightly around him. "You were strong enough. You did fight. But … it isn't over yet. The winter prince is in New York. We need to get back now."

Kade's whole body flinched. "Our people…" he breathed.

"I know." We had to stop the prince from finishing his mother's job.

Kade stood, lifting me in his arms. He seemed unwilling to let me go, and I wasn't complaining. There hadn't been much time to realize it while trying to fight the darkness, but it was hitting me hard now.

I had almost lost him.

He started to walk, his eyes caressing my features. We only stopped staring at each other once we noticed we were now surrounded by our friends. Kian had his arms tightly wrapped around Shelley, Jota on his shoulder. Next to him was Dante and Zandu. I paused when I realized all four of them were staring at me very strangely, like I now had two heads or something.

"What?" I asked, looking between them all. They didn't look alarmed, so I wasn't panicking, but I was curious about that look.

Zandu crossed his arms, that inquisitive stare not fading. "You ate up the darkness and cleansed the land. I would have said that was an impossible thing to do, but ... there is no denying it."

It was then that I noticed the lake was no longer burning and the trees were no longer dead stumps. It didn't look like a green wonderland by any means, but ... the heavy veil of dark energy was gone. A grin ripped across my face. The trees looked healthy, tall, with a wash of red and gold leaves hanging from their branches.

And I saw now that ash was no longer falling from the sky. It was now snow. This land, which had been deprived of earth energy for so long, dying, hurt, was starting to heal.

We had done it. I almost couldn't believe it, but the evidence was clear.

"You can put me down now," I said to my mate. Kade's strong arms were like bands of steel, even though they cradled me gently.

He lowered his face to mine, and we both breathed the other in. "I'm not sure I can, actually," he murmured.

Despite those ragged words, he did set me down, his arm remaining across my body.

When I was standing, Dante gave me a low bow. "Not a dark creature lives, Your Highness. The reign of the Dark Fae Lord is over."

I nodded. Still in shock at what I had done, at what I was capable of. It wasn't over yet, though,

there was still New York city and my people to save.

I connected with Finn. *Are you all safe? What about Jen and Kevin? Did they get out okay? Where is Luca?* I was mostly worried that the poor shifters standing in for Kade and me had gotten caught in the initial scuffle.

His reply was immediate, *Jen and Kevin are fine. They got out at the last minute. Baladar got most of your people out, but Luca has taken the palace. He also captured some of your guards. A few resisted and were killed.*

My wolf and I howled internally, rage and grief combining. I sent my essence out through the alpha bonds, reassuring and thanking my shifters. Without them I would never have beaten the winter queen. A queen was only as strong as her people. I wasn't sure I had ever really understood that until becoming queen myself.

Finn joined me, our bond resonating strongly as we grieved and sent energy to our people. Eventually I let the alpha bonds go, returning to Finn. *We are on our way back. Fill me in ... how big is his army?*

Only a few hundred fae. I think he assumes you and Kade are dead.

That was good news. No mass casualties, and he thought he had won simply by having his mother eliminate the monarchy. That had been their freaking plan all along, the reason for their waiting game.

But hurry. He has some type of magical weapon. It acts as a compulsion device, making anyone under its spell do his bidding. He hasn't started using it en masse yet, but if he does, you'll be fighting your own people.

That was his smoking gun, his secret weapon. It was a pretty good one too. We had wondered how the Winter Court thought they would just get shifters to start following their lead. Shifters who mostly hated fae.

Apparently, they had a way.

Prince Caspien had said something about each court having an object of power. This must be the Winter Court's.

Get Baladar and Calista to start amassing our strongest fighters, just in case we need to battle the fae. I'm going to do everything I can to avoid that, but I will not let him take my city. See you soon.

I missed Finn so badly it was like having a constant ache in my chest, but I *would* see him, and soon. That was what I clung to.

Snuggling into Kade's side, needing the closeness, I filled the others in. "Luca has taken over Manhattan. He has access to our mecca stone there. At the moment, he only has a few hundred fae, but Finn said they are using some kind of magical weapon which forces compulsion across shifters. So we have to get back to stop him before he controls all my people."

Kade's chest was rumbling at my side, and I felt the protective king bear in him rear up.

Dante gave me a head bow. "If you head back to earth now, I will inform King Roland and he will send his army across. Is there a safe place for us to cross?"

"Wherever Rowan is should be safe," I told him.

Kade's rumbly voice filled the air as he addressed Dante: "Make sure our people are informed, and that they return with the summer fae."

I nodded. I wanted Blaine at my side, where I could keep an eye on him. Plus, we would need his skills and knowledge if this turned into a war.

A thought, which had been hovering at the back of my mind, finally made itself known to me. I had killed the winter queen, destroying a leader, which meant... "Is the Winter Court going to be okay? They just lost their leader."

I directed the question to Dante, hoping he would have some idea. The assassin fae regarded me carefully, tilting his head as his brow wrinkled. "Do you feel any sort of surge in your ice energy?" The question blindsided me, and I paused for a beat, allowing my power to swell.

Blasts of ice shot out of me, narrowly missing the group around me. *Whoops.* I tucked it back away before that could happen again.

Dante grinned. "I'll take that as a yes."

"I don't understand," I said slowly.

"In the Otherworld, the power to rule is not decided by a contest, or vote, or challenge. It is hereditary, passed down through family lines. When a monarch dies, their successor will be someone of the same blood. Unless there is no more of that bloodline left ... and then it just gets messy." No doubt it involved a lot of sacrifice and bloodletting.

"You and Luca are the last of Isalinda's line, the last able to inherit the crown. The first one to touch the mecca stone of the winter land will be the leader."

I felt my mind and body recoil at the thought. "I'm already a queen," I bit out. "I don't have time to rule another kingdom. The winter people deserve better than an absent ruler who has no time or energy for them."

Dante shrugged. "If you do not touch the stone, you will not be their queen."

But that only left Luca, and since I planned on killing him, that would leave them with no one.

"We can figure this out after we stop him." Kade's words lessened some of my worry. "I'm sure the court will be okay until then."

Dante nodded, and I was relieved. "Okay, so we just need a portal home," I said, staring around, like one would magically appear through words alone.

Zandu, who'd been quite quiet and observant until now, made a small noise in his throat. It sounded as if he was choking on a laugh.

I raised one eyebrow at him and he bestowed a rare grin on me. "You're telling me that you can funnel dark magic, restore entire lands back to harmony, kill powerful queens, *be* a queen of multiple kingdoms … but you can't create a portal?"

I didn't think that was funny or helpful right now, and I was about to say so, when Kade turned to me. "He's right. You have proven time and again that you are capable of great things, of things beyond most shifter or fae. Your magic is tied to both sides, to all sides of the mecca … the magic born fae can create portals. You most definitely can create portals, too."

I shook my head by instinct. Creating portals was way above my pay grade. "I've never done that. I mean, other than in the mecca stone room at the castle. That's the only place it works for me."

Zandu stepped forward, his humor from before fading away into a serious and contemplative expression. "You do not need the mecca stones. From what I have observed, you *are* a mecca stone. I bid you farewell. My people want a report of what happened. It was an honor to fight beside you. The elven people are in your debt."

Dante whistled low at that, as if those words were more powerful than their simple implication. I was guessing elves didn't owe debts often. A thought struck me then, the way Zandu was looking at the newly-restored land with misty eyes ... the way his people guarded the entrance...

"This was your land, wasn't it?" I asked softly. "The Dark Fae Lord drove you out, and you've been trying to keep him from taking any more land from your people."

A shadow crossed Zandu's face, giving it a drawn and haunted look. "Yes. We were never part of the four courts. We were our own people. The Dark Fae Lord came and slaughtered us, stole much of our power, and relegated us to the edges of our land. We've been waiting centuries to reclaim it. We've tried before but never succeeded. Only ever losing more of our dwindling numbers."

That made sense. Horrible and awful sense. They guarded the opening not to keep others from going in, but to keep the Dark Fae Lord's beasts from getting out.

"Well, it's yours. I mean, if you want it back … it's yours," I told him. I wasn't sure if he needed permission, but in case he did, I was giving it.

It was like a weight lifted off Zandu then. He stood taller, his eyes covered by a misty sheen, which told me everything about the emotions no doubt churning inside of him. He simply nodded. "Be well, Arianna, the great winter." Then with a blink of an eye he was gone, into thin air.

Chapter Fourteen

Queen of the mecca.

AFTER ZANDU LEFT, we all stood there silently. I took a moment to let the reality of what had transpired here seep into me. The reality and horror. Especially for the elves.

The Dark Fae Lord had almost annihilated an entire race, driven them from their lands, and together with Kade and our allies we had helped reverse some of that damage. Healing would take a long time, but the Otherworld had a chance now.

A chance is all any of us needed.

Despite my bone-deep tiredness, I straightened my shoulders, searching deep for some resolve. "Okay, I have no plan. I'm tired. I'm hungry, and we might die. But I'm going to try to open a portal into the mecca crystal room of the castle." I turned to Dante. "Are you okay to get back to the Summer Court and bring our friends and whatever army the king wants to send across?"

He nodded, gripping his sword tight. "I will move as swiftly as the summer winds. I will not let you down."

This time I was the one who lowered my head to him. "You have never let me down. I am very grateful to have met you in the prison."

A million emotions shimmered in his eyes. He opened and closed his mouth multiple times, and it was very odd to see the composed fae looking so flabbergasted. Finally he said, "We are well met. I will see you soon." He took off then, truly running as swiftly as the winds he'd mentioned before.

I turned to find Kian looking wrecked, Shelley at his side, her face wrinkled with anxiety. Kade was also eyeing his brother with a look of great concern, and I could feel his worry beating through our bond.

I sighed. "Kian, you cannot go to the castle. Shelley either. You've been through enough today already." This could turn into a war, and neither of them were up to fighting. I would not leave their son an orphan.

Relief poured through Shelley, and she finally met my eyes. "My gift could help you..." she said softly, clearly struggling with what to do.

I waved my hand. "I forbid it. That's an order."

She nodded. "I was thinking that ... maybe Kian and I could head to the Winter Court? We can help keep order there until you come back? As long as you promise to keep our son safe, and send him across whenever you can."

I didn't even hesitate. "We will do our best to protect him, don't you worry. It will be a huge relief to me to know that someone — my family — is keeping an eye on the Winter Court while it's without a leader."

The leaders were the lifeblood of the people here too, and the Winter Court would slowly die without someone funneling mecca to them. But we had a little time. So, as Kade said, I would worry about that after defeating Luca.

Kade drew me strongly into his body; a breath of air released from him as we pressed together. I wished we could stay like this forever, but we were not quite done yet. We pulled away, but kept our hands linked together.

"Let's do it." Kade took one last look at the lake. His face held a haunted expression, but he shook it off quickly enough.

Giving his hand one last squeeze, I released it, taking a deep, cleansing breath. Closing my eyes, my energy sprang forth the second I called it. It was strong and controlled. I felt no fear despite the fact I could feel the vast crisscrossing lines of mecca over this world and Earth. I no longer needed to touch a mecca stone. Now I could draw on this power at will.

I focused on the stone in the mecca room back at the castle, a power that was most familiar to me. I pulled its mecca energy forward, breathing it into me.

When Zandu told me I *was* a mecca stone, my brain couldn't quite comprehend what that meant. But right now, in this moment, I understood completely. Because I was born of two royal lines, from two sides of the mecca— from a union that would not normally produce a child—I was unique, able to control mecca in a way that no other had before. I was literally able to do things that would usually require the touch of a mecca stone.

I was the queen of the mecca.

I need a portal. I spoke directly to the stone in the Manhattan royal estate. Power flowed into me, swift and fast, and I buckled for a beat but recovered just as quickly. My capability to contain and direct the power was growing.

I opened my eyes to see a four-inch, square portal appear between my fingers, the mecca room visible within it. I pulled my hands open wider, pushing more mecca through, until the portal widened. It was hard to hold. If my thoughts strayed at all, it shimmered and wavered. All of Calista's hours of forced meditation and mantras were paying off right now. Once I'd finally gotten it big enough to let a grown man through, I kept my voice calm and low.

"Go through," I stated, unsure how much longer I could hold it.

Kade turned to Kian and they embraced quickly. "Thank you, brother," Kian said. His voice was hoarse, but he was already looking stronger.

"Stay safe," Kade said, before he turned and walked into my portal.

You better be right behind me.

His voice in my head made me smile. Once Kade was inside, I lifted the portal above my head, bringing it down over my body. There was a feeling of constriction and pressure, then a rush of warm winds, and I was inside the room. Spinning around, I lifted my arms back above my head, still holding the whirling square. Shelley and Kian were waving, smiles on their faces. With a weak smile, I nodded to them, then there was a crashing noise behind me and the portal blinked out.

The fight had already begun.

Chapter Fifteen

You can't choose your parents. But you can choose where you stash them.

THE FIGURE WHICH had popped into the room, crashing into Kade—the noise I'd heard—was almost blasted by my power. I only managed to halt my attack at the last second.

"Violet!" I whisper shouted. "What are you doing in here? I almost killed you."

She shook her head. "Not a chance. You weren't even close."

I narrowed my eyes on her and she just lifted one brow in my direction, letting out a huff. "Okay, so I might have kind of … putalittletrackingspellonyou," she said in one huge rush, slowing as she tried to reassure me. "Just an alert so I could find you at all times, no matter where you were. I sensed you the moment you stepped into Manhattan, and I followed your energy here."

I blinked at her a few times. "You and I need to have a serious talk about boundaries."

She shrugged. "You're probably right. I seem to have developed some codependency issues, but we should save that psych eval for another time."

If she was spelling me so she could have a direct line to me at all times, then codependency issues might be a small understatement. But, honestly, whatever my best friend needed to do at this point to be okay was fine with me. I could put up with it, no matter what.

"Just stay out of our bedroom," Kade said with a grin, "and there won't be a problem."

She just winked at him, but didn't give an affirmative to that.

I stepped closer, the flickering light of the mecca stone casting shadows across Violet's features. "Are you here alone? Do you have any intel which could help us?"

"I came alone, but the others will follow — now that they know you're back. We've been waiting for you both to return before we attack. Baladar and Calista will bring the shifters here. They've had a few hundred stationed in Baladar's loft." She looked over her shoulder toward the hall that led from the room, turning back to me. "We're hoping with your help we can take out his weapon. It's really hindering our ability to best him. You need to know that everyone in this building is compromised. Even if they were loyal to you before, Luca has some sort of power that can manipulate their minds. Change loyalties. Brainwash."

"We heard," I muttered. Why did the bad guys always get the best toys?

Violet eyed me. "Well, I mean, you have a weapon too, right? Something to counteract him? The dark staff?"

She looked me up and down, turning to Kade. "Right?"

I shook my head. "We don't have anything like that—"

Kade interrupted me before I could finish. "We have a very powerful weapon actually."

Violet's eyes got very wide, and she was bouncing on her feet with both hands out in the typical gimme-gimme pose. Kade reached over and pushed me gently into my friend's arms.

"Arianna is the weapon," he said.

Violet let out a low whoop, her eyes practically dancing. "I knew it, I knew it from the first day I saw you. You had so much mecca hanging around you. I kept waiting for you to do something with it, but you never did, so I assumed you just had a powerful aura..." She stepped back and looked at me with a specific sort of concentration and her mouth fell into a perfect oval shape. "I ... I didn't notice because of the energy from the mecca stone but ... you've changed. You kinda look the same as the stone now, strength-wise."

I wasn't surprised by this, I could still feel their pull, the stones' magic flowing through me, from the Otherworld and Earth. There was no way Luca could best me. I would not let him.

Arianna...

A whisper filled the room, strong and commanding, and completely unmistakable. The Red Queen. I spun around, facing the stone. Kade and Violet moved to stand on either side of me, and there was no doubting — from the look on their faces — that they had heard it too.

"I'm here!" I pushed my words across the mecca with ease. I couldn't believe how simple it was to use the power now. All those months of training, all the times the easiest of tasks felt impossible ... now that I had broken through my mental block — the block that told me there was a limit to the level of energy I could control — everything was different.

There was silence for a beat, and then, *Daughter, I need your help. Please do not leave me here for eternity. I crave an end. Living forever isn't as I thought it would be.*

The stone pulsed with the words, purple light flashing like a disco ball around the secret room. I couldn't see the Red Queen, but her presence was strong.

"She sounds so weak," Violet whispered to me.

My heart pinched; Violet was right. And the Red Queen was anything but weak. I hadn't forgotten my promise to free her, but it had been pushed into my "deal with later pile." But now that I had accepted my role as a literal queen of mecca, it should be an easy task. Right?

Focusing my inner sight, I sifted through the mecca energies, through all the lines of power, until I felt her presence, the line that tied her soul to the stone, preventing the final release. I pulled, trying to extract her from the grasp of mecca, but she slipped through my grasp like water in a sieve.

I felt her despair. *I was hoping your powers would override the spell Sabina did. Unfortunately, it looks as if there is only one out clause for me. One life for another. I cannot leave unless I am replaced.*

"Will you continue to grow weaker the longer you are in the mecca?" I said, focusing on her energy.

There was a brief pause and then: *Yes. I will eventually fade into almost nothing. But a small part of my consciousness will forever be trapped. No release. No rebirth.*

One life for another. I could not sentence another to the same fate she had ... except for *Luca.* This had all started with him — with his need for power, his greedy and evil ways. He had killed the Red Queen, betraying the love and trust she had in him. It was time I showed him what karma had in store.

"I will get you out," I told my mother. "I have an idea." I felt a sliver of her relief, before I turned to my friends. "We need to find Luca, now!" I growled.

Kade wore his warrior expression again, but there was a true twinge of pride in his eyes. He was staring at me with a look even more adoring than he had given that staff. It was nice to see that. Before I could say anything ... or maybe climb my mate and kiss the hell out of him, Violet poofed out of the room. By the time I had swung to stare at the spot she'd disappeared from, she was back, the shoulder of her dress torn.

"Good news, I found Luca in the war room. Bad news, it was really crowded in there and the guards almost got me. They know we're here."

"Good." I grinned, all focus returning to me.

Climbing will have to wait for later, mate. Kade let those words drift into my mind, and a burst of anticipation exploded in my belly. Later could not get here soon enough.

Pulling mecca power into me, I headed for the door. "Violet, please make a portal for Blaine and the Summer Court army. They will be heading to Rowan, but I need them here. Also, make sure Baladar is on his way. It's time. I am kicking these squatters out."

Kade unsheathed his sword and stepped aside. I no longer had a sword; my ice one disappeared in the Otherworld. Luckily, I didn't exactly need a weapon anymore.

I walked with purpose, fast and without care for being silent. Kade followed me out of the room just as Violet popped in right behind us.

"That was fast," I said.

My best friend grinned. "The basement is filling with soldiers as we speak."

We opened the door that led to the outer hallway. Two guards were standing there. Two of *my* guards. Shifters.

They raised their weapons at me, but I blasted them with mecca, knocking them back into the wall. My aim had been to use enough mecca to break the spell Luca had on them, but not enough to do any real damage.

I let out a relieved breath when they blinked rapidly, looking around, confused.

"Your Highness..." one mumbled as he stared at me in shock, before bowing low.

"All is well," I said swiftly. "Go to the basement and join the others," I ordered, my tone firm but not unkind.

They both nodded, clarity returning to their previously blank gazes. In a flash they were up, running toward the staircase.

I was trying not to grow overconfident, but it was a relief that the spells from Luca's *weapon* were as easy to break as everything else I'd tried. And I intended to break his weapon.

Along with his neck.

We traversed the halls quickly. I blasted guards as we went, and as more of my people came back to me, the more powerful my center of magic felt.

As we turned down the hall that led to the war room, I nearly collided with one of Luca's fae guards. Throwing out a ball of mecca, I struck the guard and he flew five feet into the air, slamming his head on the wall, and slumped to the ground.

"What is—?" Luca stepped out, and upon seeing me held up his staff, ready to emit its powers.

A staff. How original.

I didn't give him the chance, thrusting a mixture of mecca and fae magic straight at him and his little *weapon.* Kade collided with a guard behind me — Violet was blasting one on my left —both of them keeping the emerging fae from touching me while I fought their prince. The staff flew out of Luca's hand, skidding across the tiles. I was really getting sick and tired of these freaking evil staffs. I never wanted to see another one for as long as I lived.

In calm strides, I crossed to my fallen fae. Without his little weapon, he looked weak and sniveling as he stared up at me.

"You have a debt to repay to my mother," I informed him. Using great force, I slapped out with my energy, shoving Luca against the wall. His head cracked with a solid thump, and he slumped into unconsciousness.

I turned to Violet. "Can you please transport him to the mecca crystal room."

She nodded, grabbing his wrist, and in a blink they were both gone.

His guards had filed out into the hall now and were about to attack. I raised my hands, and let every ounce of mecca that was in my body flow out in a purple light show. It filled the room, and was so huge and spectacular, that it worked in halting the attack.

"The winter queen is dead!" I said, my voice was loud, strong, and brimming with fury. "As is the dark fae, and soon Luca will be also. I am the interim winter queen until I find a replacement, which means you all have a choice to make. Fight me and die ... or pledge your allegiance and I'll let you go home to live in a new, kinder winter realm."

The men and women froze, most with hardened looks, but there were more than a few who looked relieved to hear of their queen's death. I'm sure they felt it, the same way shifters did, and my confirmation was enough for them to truly believe it. Those soldiers fell to their knees, like the weight of their relief was so much they literally couldn't stand anymore. Heads fell into hands, and cries and sobs started to echo around. The winter fae still standing looked at each other, like they were trying to find a leader, like they needed someone to tell them what to do. One of the men near the front line had more decorative clothing, with large jewels inlaid along his cloak. He looked, and held himself, like a commander, or someone of great importance.

He did not hesitate. "Yield to the queen," the commander ordered. This time no one hesitated. These were a browbeaten people, used to having their will stripped from them.

I nodded. "My army is waiting in the basement for my command. If you make one move against me or my people, I won't hesitate to kill all of you."

The commander nodded, laying down his sword.

I turned to Kade. "I'm going to see if I can figure out how to trade a life for a life."

He grinned at me and straightened, arms crossed over his chest. "I will keep an eye on our people, make sure the fae don't decide they have a little more warring in them."

I stood on tiptoes, and he still had to lower his head so our lips could touch.

I love you, we both whispered through our bond at the same time.

He let me go. Turning back to the room, his body shifted into his half bear, growing larger and even more powerful. My wolf howled in my chest, as she always did when Kade stood like that. So strong. So solid.

As I walked away, I marveled at the way he let me go, barely even a sliver of worry in our bond. I loved Kade with every part of my being; he was my other heart, my soul mate, but one of the reasons I adored him so much was that he respected me as an equal. He respected my power, my position as queen. Who would have thought that a king and queen could coexist with so little ego between them? Especially for two alpha animals. Our bond was a miracle, and I needed to thank the gods for it every single day.

But first ... I needed to rid myself of one parent, and free another.

As I was striding toward the stone room, a familiar energy hit me. My throat got tight as the white wolf bounded into sight. Finn and I stopped and stared at each other for many long moments, drinking each other in. We had never been separated so much as we had since I took the crown. So many things keeping us apart. So many fights and battles. It was only as I stood there, his familiar presence before me, that I truly realized how much I needed him. How much I missed him.

I missed you too, Ari. May we never be parted again.

I ran for him as fast as I could, diving the last few feet to wrap my arms around the giant beast — a beast I loved more than life. The soul of my wolf inside rose up and collided with the soul of our familiar. Finn and I lifted our heads back and howled together, a long, happy sound. A sound of pack.

When we had sated our bond — for the moment — I rose and said to him, "I'm ready ... to free my mother ... to punish Luca. I know I can do this."

I heard a chuckle from my left. I turned to find Calista and Baladar standing there. "Nice to see my years of affirmation training has not left you."

I didn't reply, choosing instead to cross the few feet between us and throw my arms around her. "I've been looking for you," Calista said into the side of my face. "I needed to see with my own eyes that you were okay. Kade told us where you were."

Clearly our army had arrived, and I knew now that the fae would never turn on us. They were too outnumbered.

I pulled back to see her face better. "I remember everything you've taught me. I'm just going now to finish the job." Another one of her lessons: finish what you start.

She gave me a pat on the arm and then Baladar bowed his head. With a wave, the pair turned and returned the way they had come.

I turned in the opposite direction, Finn at my side. We entered the mecca stone room to see that Violet had magically confined Luca up against the mecca stone, his hands bound by purple bands of magic. It seemed to be overwhelming him.

He was awake and furious.

"I should have killed you when I had the chance," he spat at Violet.

Those words sent surges of white hot anger through me. He was one of Violet's tormenters. Something I had forgotten whilst trying to repress what my best friend had gone through.

Violet glared at him with hatred. He had been instrumental in causing her great suffering in the Winter Court. I wanted her here to bear witness.

I crouched down to meet his eyes. "Did you ever love her?"

His eyes sharpened. "Who?" I could tell he really had no idea who I was talking about, which was an answer in itself.

Me, the Red Queen's voice filtered into the room, and unlike last time, the weakness was not obvious.

Lucas's face went slack, losing all color as his body trembled a little. He looked left and right as if trying to see where she was speaking from. I was pretty sure he was muttering the word "Impossible," but I couldn't quite hear him. Leaning forward, I placed one hand on the crystal, taking care not to touch him. I focused my energy there, magnifying the Red Queen's essence until she was a transparent projection standing before him.

He gaped open-mouthed at the vision of her. *Aside from Arianna, you were the only person I ever loved*, she said to him, her face and voice devoid of all emotion.

The arrogant fae stared back at her, recovering somewhat from the shock, enough to say, "There is no room for love in our lives. We have duty, power, and responsibility. Love is for the weak."

"When I was alive, I believed the same thing," the Red Queen told him. "But I was wrong. It's only in death that I realized how much I did love you and Arianna. I missed years with her. It is my greatest regret."

The pain in my chest was almost unbearable, but I didn't crumble.

"All the years you separated us kept me alive," I told her. "You shouldn't regret that." I hated that Luca was here, witnessing these final intimate moments with my mother.

I pointed to him and wrapped mecca around his throat, tightening it to the point he could only just gasp for breath. "You should never have come to our world. This is my city. My mecca. You will now be punished how I see fit."

His eyes were bulging as I continued to constrict his air supply. Without his mother, or his staff, he was weak. Useless. Reaching down to my ankle, I pulled forth one of the fae blades I had stashed there. I was only about ten inches long, but it would be enough to do the job.

I placed the serrated tip over his heart. "May you never find the peaceful rest and rebirth of death. May you never walk in our worlds again. You are not fit for the royal blood you were borne. Goodbye, Luca."

I leaned all of my weight forward and skewered the bastard, burying my blade to the hilt. With a gasp, he took his final breath and I felt the mecca pulse. Using that pulse of magic, I pulled on the Red Queen's energy, and at the same time pushed on Luca's, pushing his soul further into the stone. Somehow the power knew what to do; knew I wanted to exchange one for another, and unlike last time when I tried to remove my mother, this time she did not slip through my grasp.

No! I heard Luca's shout echo across the room at the same time I heard my mother's voice.

Goodbye, Luca. I hope you spend eternity seeking forgiveness.

A bright light flared inside of the room before me. I saw a tunnel, and at the end was the Red Queen's familiar, the white lynx I believed I saw in Central Park after her death. Then it was gone, as if it was a mirage. I gasped. When the queen trapped herself in the mecca, her familiar must have become a spectral ghost, walking in between the two worlds. Now they were being reunited, as they should.

A blast of icy air caressed my skin, bringing with it her scent, lavender and rose.

I'm so proud of you, daughter. Thank you. I pray that you can forgive my times of cruelty. Her voice whispered in my ear and I could no longer keep my emotions inside. Tears spilled over my cheeks as a small sob escaped me. I had Calista, so I had a true mother, but it felt like I had missed so much with the Red Queen. So much we could have had together.

"Wait!" I wanted to tell her that I forgave her, that I understood everything she sacrificed for me. That I knew she did the best she could. But before I could say anything more, her scent, and the icy wind ... was gone.

Violet reached her arms around me as Finn lay his head in my lap, and they both held me tightly, mourning right along with me.

You are the strongest woman I know. You have lost a lot, but you will always have me. Kade's strong voice and energy caressed me, adding his strength to that my friends were filling me with.

I was blessed. I knew that. I would never forget it. But still, I grieved.

Thirty seconds later, Kade burst into the room, bringing with him the scent of forest and home. Finn stood and Violet released me as Kade bent over and placed one arm under my knees and one behind my back, picking me up. We both needed the closeness. I rested my head on his shoulder and breathed him in.

We've done the hard part. Now with a little more work we can have our happily ever after. Kade's words seeped into me, soothing my soul.

He set me down gingerly and placed his forehead on mine. "Are you up for dealing with the Winter Court?" he asked.

I sighed. I wanted more than anything to just abandon all responsibility and go see my little sister, but I couldn't leave the Winter Court without a leader.

"Yes," I told him, before straightening my back and smoothing out my shirt. "What about King Samson and his people? Do they know the threat is neutralized?"

Kade nodded. "Yes, they are already returning home. They will wait for word from you, but for now they give their thanks."

"Blaine and Bianca?" And whomever Kade's guard was — his name was escaping me in my dazed state.

"Home. Safe. Already ordering the shifters back to their packs and dens. Reinstating guards."

That was good. My friends and dominants would keep an eye on this world while I went to make sure the Otherworld wasn't falling apart. I really hoped Shelley and Kian were faring well there, because I didn't have it in me for another battle.

Taking a deep breath, I sought out the mecca stone in the Winter Court. Creating another portal, we stepped out into the icy lands. Well, into the room that housed the stone anyway. Violet, Finn, Kade, and I walked through the circular stone room, which had white wood floorboards, and was empty except for a purple, faceted stone. The main winter stone I was guessing. I was very careful not to touch it, remembering Dante's words about the way their leaders were chosen.

We skirted the edges, exiting through a simple wooden door. Outside of the room were two guards, lazing back against the wall, looking half asleep. The moment we stepped out, they straightened with wide eyes, drawing their weapons. My winter powers froze their feet to the spot before they could attack.

"Thank you for your service," I said. "I'm Arianna, granddaughter of the winter queen." Their eyes went even wider and I recognized the complete and total panic there. So I hurried on. "Rest assured, I am nothing like my kin. I'm only here to ensure there is a just leader left in this court. Will you continue to guard this room for me? Until there is a new leader?"

Both of them nodded and I released their feet fully from the ice magic. The two male fae dropped to their knees, white furs spilling out around them.

"It is our honor," one of them said in a thick accent.

I gave them both a wave, turning to join my family. We walked through a small stretch of woods that opened up into a courtyard of the dark stone castle. As we moved toward the moat that ran around the castle, a huge billow of smoke caught my attention.

"Kade..." I said slowly.

He followed my line of sight and then the four of us started to run. We crossed over the bridge, heading toward the main part of the town, where their markets had been held. The acrid scent of smoke was strong in the air, and it was starting to get hot. Which was more than a little noticeable in the Winter Court.

When the huge fire finally came into view, I was alarmed at the sight of papers, books, and other things stacked high in the center of the flames. Kade's hand was resting on his sword, preparing for whatever battle was next, but then we both saw Shelley and Kian at the front of the blaze. They looked fine. In fact, everyone here looked well. I would even go as far as to say there was a sense of joy in the crowd of fae tossing objects into the fire. One woman clutched a painting of the winter queen.

"Ari! Kade!" Shelley gave a shout of delight, running over to greet us, Kian right behind her.

I gave them both a quick hug. Kian and Kade bro-embraced for a few moments too, and then Shelley launched into an explanation of what was going on here. "The winter queen made it mandatory that every household have a picture of her hanging over their mantle. The majority are thrilled she's dead and are openly denouncing her rule. Only a few had to be … detained."

Whew, that was a huge weight off my shoulders. I didn't have a riot on my hands.

"There's more," Kian interrupted, bestowing an adoring look on his mate. "Shelley's been busy using her talent to interrogate the castle staff, and we finally unearthed something that might help. Apparently, the queen has a sister. She was locked away years ago because they disagreed about how to rule over the winter people."

I sucked in a deep breath, considering the wide-reaching possibilities if this was true. I didn't want to get my hopes up yet. There was so much we didn't know. But a part of me couldn't help but feel excited.

"Did you find her? Is she fit to rule?" I asked, forcing my voice to remain calm. This would be the perfect solution to all of my problems. If I could assess her and make sure she didn't inherit the evil gene, then maybe she could rule the Winter Court.

"The spells surrounding her are too strong," Shelley told me. "I wasn't able to even get to the door without being pushed back."

Well, luckily, breaking spells was my specialty. "Take me to her, please."

Shelley and Kian nodded, and with one last look at the fire-happy fae, we all moved away from the flame-filled marketplace. Shelley led us around the back side of the castle, which was quite a walk since the structure was so large. I took the time while we strolled to really observe everything. Last time I was here, there was no time to do anything but run, be captured, and fear for my life. It was nice to take in the harsh beauty of this fae court — my heritage.

I glanced across at Violet, worried that the memories of being here might be getting to her, but she looked calm. The magical essence surrounding her also seemed calm. My friend was finally healing. Piece by piece, day by day, she was finding her way back to me.

On the far side of the castle there was a barren land. Even the trees seemed to have abandoned the area; all that was left were a few spindly, dead-looking plants. And a single stone hut. It was a square, squat building of dark stone, black ivy climbing the sides.

As soon as we approached the hut, Violet put a hand up to stop us.

"This is dark magic," she said. We were about ten feet from the building. Violet took another step in, holding both of her hands up. I followed her actions, running my hands along the inky tendrils of the spell that surrounded the dwelling.

A greenish iridescent bubble appeared before us, highlighting the perimeter of the spell. My energy slapped out before I could even think about doing it, the spell popping like a balloon, dissipating into nothing.

Almost immediately a scream rang out from inside the cabin, and I focused my attention on the doorway, preparing myself for what might emerge. Violet reached out and grasped my arm before I could get any closer.

"She's been in captivity for god knows how long. Let me talk to her first." I stared into those white-blue eyes, reading between the lines of what she was saying. Violet could speak to her as someone who understood a small amount of what she had gone through.

"What if it's a trap? She could be dangerous."

Violet snorted at me. An actual snort. And I couldn't stop a chuckle from escaping. "I got this, friend. Besides, you're right outside if I need any help."

She was right, so I nodded, and then Violet was gone. Poofed into thin air. I was still worried that this woman was dangerous. She was the winter queen's sister, and she had been locked away for a reason. But ... it was Violet.

Still, as we waited and waited and waited, my worry increased. When ten minutes had passed, and I was about to go knock on the door, it opened. A tall woman with white hair and a skeletal figure stepped out with Violet. Rags hung in gray strips down her bony frame; her hair looked damp, as if she'd just tried to smooth it back and look presentable. She walked with a slight limp as she crossed the distance toward us.

There was a sheen of tears on Violet's cheeks, and I was worried that this had been too much for her. She'd only just started healing ... moving forward.

When the woman reached Kade and me, she stumbled into a small curtsy. "Your Highnesses, my name is Priscilla. Please excuse my appearance. When the spell on my home broke, it caused me some pain..."

"Of course. I'm so sorry we are meeting under this situation. I've only just learned about your existence," I told her. "My name is Arianna ... I'm the one who killed Isalinda."

Violet piped up. "I told her about the queen and prince's death, and that you are the last of

the royal line. Or that we thought you were the last."

Priscilla nodded. "I have been locked up and at the mercy of my sister for many years. When our parents died, I was supposed to touch the stone. I am the oldest. But Issie always had a plan to usurp me and take my rightful place. She dabbled in dark magic. She broke our rules."

It sounded like something the winter queen would do. Isalinda was cruel to the bone. And while it seemed Priscilla did not have the same darkness in her, I needed to make sure. I just had to figure out how to do it without destroying whatever fragile trust we had just built. I wondered ... if I could sense and filter out the darkness in Kade ... shouldn't I be able to sense it in others too?

I reached out my hand. "Well, I'm just glad to have gotten you out of there."

She reached out slowly and placed her fragile hand in mine. "We are well met," she stated, and I pushed my mecca forward a tiny bit, feeling the energy of her soul.

It took a few seconds to sift through the pieces. Her soul had been damaged, quite badly, but while there was darkness there, it seemed to only be linked to the memories of her captivity. Once I pushed through that, there was a bright light in her center, an innocence that told me exactly how Isalinda had so easily tricked her.

She's good, Kade. A good person and a great candidate to take over this realm.

She needs time to heal, but I sense great potential within her, he agreed.

Pulling my hand back, I smiled. Kade reached out his hand then and introduced himself, shaking very lightly so as not to hurt her. I decided it was best to just come out with the truth.

"Priscilla, I can't even begin to understand what you have been through. I'm sure you are feeling lost and confused right now, but you are the rightful leader of the Winter Court. Do you still want to rule over these people, with the grace and goodness they should have had years ago?"

Every tired and weary muscle in her face lifted then. The light that had been hiding in the darkness shone so brightly that I could see it without even touching her soul. "I'd be ... I'd be honored. I'd need some time to remember things and get myself together, but ... I'd be honored."

I couldn't help but smile. "I think you are exactly what this court needs. How about I keep things going here for a month or so, then you can take over when you're rested and settled in?" I didn't want to have to visit this place too often, I had my own people to worry about, but I could give her a little time.

She looked confused. "A month?"

Violet smiled. "Two fortnights? One moon cycle?"

Understanding replaced the confused expression, and she nodded a few times. "Oh, yes. I can do that. Thank you."

I looked at the woman before me, captive for who knows how long. She didn't look a day over thirty, but fae aging was akin to shifter aging — weird and unpredictable. I was sure she had thought her life was over. There was no chance of escaping while Isalinda lived. But, she could have a family now if she chose. A purpose and a future.

"Thank you for finding her," I whispered to Shelley. The fae had tears in her eyes too. She was watching Priscilla closely — no doubt reacting to the return of her rightful queen.

"Let's get you into the castle," Violet said, her tone kind and understanding. "I can shroud you so that no one sees you."

Priscilla let out a relieved breath. "Thank you. My mother always taught me that a queen needs to look put together at all times. I don't want to start on the wrong foot."

She cared about her people. About pleasing them. I was hoping she didn't take it too far, though. There was a nice middle ground between crazy Isalinda and a pushover.

I better check on her periodically. I directed my worries to Kade, and he just slung an arm around me as we started to walk.

It will be fine, Ari. She will have others to help her.

He was right, but a part of me felt like I was foisting my responsibility off onto a broken fae, one who was not ready to be a leader.

Reassess in a month, he told me.

That was a good idea. I would give her this time to rest and heal. Then we would see. I had no idea what I would do if she wasn't fit to rule, but that was another bridge I would cross when I came to it.

Inside the castle, Priscilla led us toward a wing on the east side. "These were my rooms," she said. Surprisingly, they were still there, exactly as she left them, only covered now in a thick sheen of dust.

"No doubt Issie never stepped foot in here again." She looked around, her eyes, which were a lovely lilac color, were shadowed.

I glanced around at the dusty wing, filled with ghosts of the past. "Why don't we strip the former queen's rooms," I said. "Those are your rightful quarters now. I think it would be a fresh start."

Her arms trembling, she nodded. "Yes, I think that would be a nice way to begin it all. Back in my parents' wing."

Handmaids were called in and everything happened in a hurry after that. Rooms were stripped; Priscilla was moved into the royal wing to begin her month of rest. Word was spreading fast through the castle about the return of the princess, and already flowers and gifts were arriving.

The fae were rejoicing.

By the time we all left the Winter Court, I was feeling pretty good about the way things had turned out. In one month I'd come back and make sure Priscilla was still the right person to rule the Winter Court. I had high hopes that she was. Even a short time out of the hut had seen a huge return of vitality to her. I would be present at her coronation ceremony. For now, I was going to send across some of my own shifter guards, just to keep an eye on things.

Upon returning to Manhattan, back in my mecca stone room, Shelley and I said at the same time: "Let's go get our kids."

Kade was already reaching for my hand. "Baladar and Nikoli already have a car waiting." He must have planned this before we left.

Just the thought of having Winnie back by my side, of the three of us being a family together, was enough to have joy and happiness ricocheting between us. I almost couldn't believe we had done it. We were going to be a proper family. No more absences. No more wars or fae or worry. This was finally the part where I could look back and say all of the sacrifice was worth it. We had done it, we had beaten the fae.

I started to run for the door, dragging my mate behind me. Kian and Shelley laughed as they hurried along too. We were going to get our kids. Our family.

Epilogue

Six Months Later
Happily Ever After.

"WHERE IS THE cake? It should have been here an hour ago!" I griped to Kade as he cut lemons for the water pitcher.

He chuckled. "Serves you right for ordering a four-tier cake for a six-year-old's birthday."

I pinned him with a mock glare. "Winnie had a rough year. She deserves the best." I peered past him, out into the garden of our Staten Island home.

It was just starting to warm again after the winter months, so all of the shifters were enjoying the gardens. I could see Winnie and Nathanial, both dressed as pirates, chasing each other with plastic swords.

Annette entered the kitchen. "She'll make a wonderful queen one day."

I chuckled. "I don't think I'll ever be able to get her in a dress."

I stripped off my sweater, suddenly feeling extra warm despite the end-of-winter chill still in the air.

"Cake is here!" Violet screamed from the entryway.

I bolted down the hall. "How does it look?"

I came to a halt beside my best friend, the sparkling diamond on her left finger still catching my eye. It was a massive rock. Nikoli had gone all out, knowing the way Violet loved shiny things. Their road together might have been a little rocky, but in the end he was perfect for her. I had no complaints. He'd been instrumental in her healing, and most days those shadows no longer touched her face. She was finally free.

"It looks nicer than your wedding cake," she told me, peeking in the box.

I chuckled. Kade and I had gotten married three months ago. A small affair, just as we had wanted, with only close family and friends on the rooftop terrace of our Manhattan home. The following day, we'd had a large ball for the entire shifter community, and the fae came as well. King Samson and Prince Caspien had both visited for a short time, offering their congratulations and reinforcing our alliance. So had Queen Priscilla. One month had been more than enough time for the rightful heir of the Winter Court to regain her strength and mental composure. All reports confirmed she was a fair and just queen. For the first time in a long time, the winter fae were at peace. Prosperous. Building relationships with the other courts.

The biggest surprise wedding guest had been Zandu. He'd presented both Kade and I with an elven blade, made just for us. A priceless gift.

Gently shoving Violet to the side, I peeked in the box at the rich buttercream frosting and the large golden edible pirate chest, chocolate coins spilling out onto the base of the cake. "It *is* nicer than my wedding cake," I agreed.

For once, looking at a delicious, multi-tiered cake didn't make me want to shove my face right into it and eat until I couldn't stand. The smell of all the sugar was actually making me a bit nauseous. My wolf even grumbled, and we loved cake.

Probably the six plates of fondue you had last night. Finn's voice was a husky laugh in my head. Last night had been our weekly fondue family gathering, and I had been starving. *Yep, my stomach has been off since then. Probably got a bad piece of cheese or something.*

I disconnected from my familiar when I realized Violet was staring at me with concern. "Are you okay?" she asked.

I waved her off. "I'm fine. Just feel blah today. Ate some bad cheese. Stress from party planning. I just want today to be perfect for Winnie."

She peered a little closer at me, her eyes narrowing. She gave a small cough and shook her head. "Uh … what did you get Winnie for her birthday?" she asked.

I almost squealed in excitement. Winnie was going to be so thrilled when she saw her present. "A huge rock wall. Kade had it installed in her room."

Violet raised one eyebrow. "And...?"

"And some smaller stuff like a drawing pad and a new teddy bear."

"And...?" Violet pressed.

I put one hand on my hip. "You're saying I didn't get her enough? I don't want to completely spoil her! Between Kade, Annette, Shelley, and Kian … well, she does not lack for attention or presents." The entire family had embraced us as their own, and it was the most wonderful thing I had ever known.

Violet leaned in closely. "You got her a baby sibling to play with too..." Her gaze dropped to my belly, and on cue the nausea hit me again. I let out a little shocked gasp, my hands falling to press against my flat stomach. "Are you serio—how do you know?" It wasn't like Kade and I had been trying. I mean, we weren't actively not trying, but...

Violet reached out and poked my left boob hard.

"OW!" I smacked her hand, shouting, "Take this one to the torture chamber!"

A few guards waved from their position across the yard. I glared at each of them, turning my annoyance on Violet. "I don't understand why no one will lock you up."

Violet grinned. "They know better than to mess with me. And, p.s. ... you're totally prego."

Excitement bubbled up inside of me. "Seriously?"

Violet gave me that look that said she knew everything and not to question her.

"Okay, take the cake to the party, I'll be right out." I turned tail and raced up the stairs.

Kade and I had just talked last week about wanting to try to have a baby. Calista had been the one to bring it up with her not-too-subtle way of giving me a basketful of ovulation predictor kits and pregnancy tests. She was always trying to continue to secure my position as queen, and with an heir it made me look stronger. Our line struggled to conceive and carry to term, but something told me Kade's child would be one strong little fighter.

I yanked one of the tests out of the basket and ran into the bathroom to pee on it, almost tripping over Finn as he raced in the door.

Pregnant? he asked me, his soulful yellow eyes dancing.

"I don't know! Violet says yes, so I'm going to take the test."

I'll wait out here.

I shut the bathroom door and peed on a stick — a stick, which could possibly change my entire life. I sat it on the sink, washed my hands, and opened the door to step out and stand by an anxious Finn. He had been waiting right on the other side, and I could feel his energy thrumming across our bond. We didn't talk. Neither of us could. Would the baby be a bear or wolf? Would it be healthy? I'd had a ton of chocolate last night — was that okay?

It will be fine, Ari, Finn finally said, trying to calm me down.

I forced myself to calm down, and reinforced my shield between Kade and me. With my emotional overload, I was struggling to keep him out of my head, but I didn't want to get his hopes up.

He should be here, though.

Waiting with me.

We were a team. We celebrated and comforted each other, no matter what the results.

I had just decided to run and get him — this was not something I should see without my mate — when the second hand on the clock ticked over to two minutes.

I froze to the spot.

Do you want me to look? Finn asked.

"Yes ... no ... I don't know."

He gave me a second and I finally sucked up the guts to walk forward and pick up the little stick. I held my breath and lifted it up. I then looked between the box and the test three times to make sure I was reading it right.

So...?

Finn was getting impatient, so I spun around and let my absolute joy spread across my face. My cheeks were hurting I was smiling so broadly. "I'm pregnant!"

He tipped back his head and let out a long howl, strong and filled with happiness. He then butted against me, and I dropped down and wrapped my hands around him, careful not to tangle the pee stick in his fur.

We're adding to our pack. And finding out on Winnie's birthday ... another blessing in our lives.

I buried my face in his fur, letting the tears drip down my cheeks. They were happy tears, but also a few sad ones. The battle might be over, but we had lost too many. I had lost too many. Ben and Derek. My ... mother. I had made my peace with the Red Queen, which actually made it so much harder now. She was gone. But at least she wasn't trapped in the mecca. Thankfully, Luca had made no difference to the energy of the stones. I checked regularly, and he was nothing more than a ghost trapped in a purple world.

After I pulled myself together, wiped away the tears, I stood and lovingly stroked Finn. "Let's go celebrate," I said to him.

I didn't realize until I was down the stairs and halfway across the huge landscaped lawn that I was still holding the stick in my hand. I also realized something else.

I think Kade might already suspect.

Finn paused and looked up at me.

He mentioned last night that my scent was slightly different.

I chuckled. Finn tilted his huge head, leaning in closer and pressing his nose to my stomach. *It's subtle*, he said after a few beats, *but there is a change.*

"Ari!" Blaine's call distracted me and I turned to wave. He was standing near the huge white silk party tent, his long arms wrapped around Bianca. Seeing my old friend so happy, in love, settled ... it was another perfect piece in our puzzle. They had just bought a house down the road from the Staten Island estate, and the way they couldn't keep their hands off each other, my babies were soon going to have some "cousins" to add to their pack.

I hurried, needing to tell Kade and Winnie our good news. Finn remained close behind but still gave me some space. I found my loves together, wrestling in the grass. Winnie was a competitive little thing, and even though Kade let her win, he still had to keep his wits about him. She was not only competitive, but hugely sneaky.

"Hey there, birthday girl," I sang as I closed in on them.

She let out a little shriek and jumped up to throw herself into my arms. "This is the best birthday ever. Thank you! Thank you!"

I hugged her so tightly I was afraid her little ribs would crack, but I couldn't help myself. Kade also jumped to his feet. A dozen feet away, Kian was play-wrestling with his son, while Shelley looked on at her two boys with a combination of love and exasperation.

Keeping Winnie in my arms, I tried to find where the test went. It had been knocked out of my hands when I caught the little wolf. Kade noticed what I was doing, and before I could say anything, reached down and snagged the white stick up.

He looked at it for a second, a very long second, and then those swirling bronze eyes lifted to stare at me. The intensity of that look, it knocked all air from me. "Is this ... are we...?" He seemed unable to finish a sentence, so I took pity on him.

"We're pregnant." My words were low, soft, meant only for Winnie and Kade's ears. This was a private moment. Our moment.

Before I could suck in another breath, his hands were on my cheeks, his lips crashing into mine. All rational thought disappeared, and I forgot everything in the world except the taste and scent of my mate.

"I'm going to be a big sister?" Those whispered words finally broke through my Kade haze.

Winnie sounded so happy, her excitement spilling over in one rushed sentence. I was still holding her. Kade wrapped his arms around us both, and we turned to her. "Yes, sweetheart, you're going to be a big sister." I kissed her cheek, and she sobbed a few times, even though she had the hugest smile I'd ever seen on her face.

"I'm so happy." She sobbed some more.

Kade let out a chuckle, and even his eyes looked a little shiny. "I love you both so much," he said with a fierce intensity. "I promise I will protect and love you three until the end of my days."

Gods he was perfect. I hadn't been completely sure what his reaction would be to this news, but the absolute love and happiness he was exuding told me everything. He was already an amazing father, and he would be for every single child we added to our family.

"Let's go celebrate," I whispered to them both. "Let's keep the baby a secret for a little longer," I added to Winnie. "Today is your birthday. This is all for you, my little one."

She kissed me on the cheek, wiggling down. "I'm going to get some cake." She was already moving toward the party food. Violet had the huge cake set up at center stage.

As soon as she was gone, Kade swept me up in his arms and he was kissing me again. As he pulled away, I said, "You have to stop carrying me around, love."

"Better get used to it." His voice was husky. "For the next nine months, I am not letting you lift a finger." There were slivers of worry creeping into his words, and I understood. Shifter pregnancies were dangerous. The fetus could shift, and that could cause massive blood loss. It was hard to carry a shifter pup to term, but I wasn't too worried. I had all of my magic to help with that.

I patted Kade on the shoulder and he reluctantly let me down. "I'm fine, mate. You don't need to stress over anything. Maybe when I'm huge and waddling I'll let you do some of the heavy lifting. Until then, I am perfectly capable."

He dropped his forehead onto mine. "Thank you for making me the luckiest bear in the world. Thank you for my life."

"I love you, Kade." I didn't even have the words to really express how much he meant to me.

I feel the same way. We have eternity to find those words.

He was right, and I planned on telling and showing him every single day.

An argument had broken out near the cake, so we had to cut our moment short. Violet needed backup. She was debating with a six-year-old about why she had to wait to cut her cake.

As we walked, I took another long look around — stopped to smell the roses, as they say — which in this garden was a literal statement. In truth, my life was as close to perfect as I could have ever hoped for. It was everything I ever dreamed of.

When those bells rang all that time ago, signaling the end of the Red Queen's rule, my life had changed. Her death was painful, but it had brought me to this moment. To Kade. To learning of my fae heritage and the dual powers flowing strongly inside of me.

I was queen of the shifters.

I was queen of the mecca.

I had achieved everything I set out to do in my life. But my greatest achievement, the one that brought me the most joy, was the family and love I now had in my life.

In that way, I was queen of all.

THE END

Acknowledgements from Jaymin: The end of another series. I almost can't believe it. As always the largest portion of my thanks goes to Trav, Lola, and Silvie. They put up with a lot from me when I am in author mode, and I am forever grateful to have them in my lives. Always and forever, my loves. Always and forever. #love

Second thanks to Heather Renee, PA extraordinaire, and wonderful friend. I appreciate you so much, you have no idea. Thanks for always having my back. #loyalty

Next for my review team. THANK YOU SO MUCH. Those words needed shouty caps because you all rock! Thanks for sharing and reviewing and helping with final errors. #grateful

Lastly for Leia Stone. Girl ... this is where it gets mushy. Thank you for the years of friendship, and for being there through so many of life's struggles. I couldn't have chosen a better person to share my writing world with, and I am forever grateful that fate threw us together. #BAFF4eva

Acknowledgements from Leia: As always a big thanks to my bestie Jaymin Eve for being such an amazing creative writing partner and amazing friend. I cherish our GIF conversations and ramblings about life. I have loved writing all of these books with you and I think we are both a little sad to say goodbye to Kade and Ari. Thanks to my wonderful hubby and family for helping out around the house so I can write. Without your support I couldn't do what I do! Lastly to my release team and betas for all of your support. I am so grateful for my readers who love what I write. This series has been so fun. ❤

Thank you from both of us, to Lee our editor, Jaye Cox our formatter and Tamara our cover designer. Without you these books just wouldn't come together like they do.

Books from Leia Stone

<u>Matefinder Trilogy (Optioned for film)</u>
Matefinder: Book 1
Devi: Book 2
Balance: Book 3

<u>Matefinder Next Generation</u>
Keeper: Book 1
Walker: Book 2

<u>Hive Trilogy</u>
Ash: Book 1
Anarchy: Book 2
Annihilate: Book 3

<u>NYC Mecca Series: Urban Fantasy</u>
Queen Heir
Queen Alpha
Queen Fae
Queen Mecca

<u>The Night War Saga</u>
Protector
Defender
Redeemer
Stay in touch with Leia:
www.facebook.com/leia.stone/
Mailing list: http://goo.gl/0EX98P

Books from Jaymin Eve

A Walker Saga - YA Paranormal Romance series
(complete) Ages 13+
First World - #1
Spurn - #2
Crais - #3
Regali - #4
Nephilius - #5
Dronish - #6
Earth - #7

Supernatural Prison Trilogy - NA Urban Fantasy
series (complete) Ages 17+
Dragon Marked - #1
Dragon Mystics - #2
Dragon Mated - #3

Supernatural Prison Stories
Broken Compass - #1

Sinclair Stories Ages 18+ Contemporary Sports
Romance
Songbird - Standalone Contemporary Romance

Hive Trilogy Urban Fantasy
(Vampires)(Complete) Ages 15+
Ash - #1
Anarchy - #2
Annihilate: #3

NYC Mecca Series Urban Fantasy Ages 15+
Queen Heir
Queen Alpha
Queen Fae
Queen Mecca

Curse of the Gods Series High Fantasy Reverse
Harem Series Ages 15-17+
Trickery
Persuasion
Seduction

Stay in touch with Jaymin:
www.facebook.com/JayminEve.Author
Mailing list: www.jaymineve.com
jaymineve@gmail.com

www.ingramcontent.com/pod-product-compliance
Lightning Source LLC
Chambersburg PA
CBHW020653110726
47901CB00001B/173